FINDING FAITH

Finding Faith

Deborah D Rhoades

ISBN: 979-8-9869836-0-8; 979-8-9869836-1-5; 979-8-9869836-2-2

To my beautiful family who made this all possible.
Thank you for your love, patience, and support.

A Dark Legacy

On an evening in May 1825, a buck wagon rolled down Broad Street in Richmond, Virginia. The city was engulfed in a heavy fog, so heavy it was difficult to see even five feet ahead. The sound of crickets chirping sounded as if a muffler had been placed over their tiny legs. The two men in the buck board were silent as they drove through the streets that evening. Little did they know that there was a secret passenger in the back of that buck board; a stow-a-way who had stolen aboard in hopes of glimpsing the grown-up activities of the evening.

Rumors of secret meetings of townsmen had been circulating around Richmond for a few years. Talk of political wrangling and backroom business dealings were the talk of the town. But there were more sinister rumors as well. Talk of deviant rituals, secret oaths, and violence were whispered about in the corners of the shops and taverns, in town and sometimes, the backyard of the church on Sunday mornings. People in town knew of the lynching of runaway and "disobedient" slaves but were not willing to discuss the matter in public. The passenger in the back of the buckboard that evening had heard these rumors, and he wanted to see for himself just what was going on when his father and grandfather went out together in the evenings once or twice a month. This young man greatly admired the two men driving into town this night, for one was his father, John Montgomery, and the other, his grandfather Thomas Campbell, his mother's father. Both were admired by the town as successful businessmen and honored as virtuous fathers of respectable families. Both men were a part of the original families of Virginia. The two men became quite close after John's father died.

After driving for about fifteen minutes, the buckboard came to a stop, and the two men disembarked the wagon. "Come now, John. We need to get inside and get everything set up for the meeting tonight. People will start arriving soon and we need to be ready."

"Yes, sir," responded John. The two men went inside the building. As soon as the boy felt safe, he got up from his hiding place to look around to see where he was and if anyone could see him. He could see that he was in an area a few miles outside of Richmond near a farm owned by a friend of his father. This farm had a large barn, and that was where his father and grandfather had gone. He jumped down from the wagon and quietly moved around to the back of the barn where he could not be seen by anyone else who might be coming to the meeting. There was a window on the back of the barn, so he moved as close as he could to see what was going on inside. A layer of dirty film coated the window, so he could not see everything inside clearly without squinting and rubbing some of the dirt away.

Over the next half hour about thirty men arrived at the barn. One by one, they entered the barn. Voices could be heard inside, but the boy could not make out what was being said. He could see the men walking about the barn in strange looking clothing and they were building something out of wood.

A few moments later another buckboard drove up and a man got out of the wagon carrying what appeared to be a large, wrapped package. From where the boy was sitting, this package appeared to move. It seemed so odd. The man walked into the barn and over to the front where he saw his father and grandfather standing in front of everyone. Soon after all the men stood up, the man, who he had seen carrying the package, removed the covering. The boy then saw that it was a negro woman! She stood barely clothed in front of the group of men. What happened next was disturbing, but even so, the boy could not look away.

The men wore white robes and weird hats with funny drawings on them. In a few moments, they came out of the barn to a wide-open space in front of the barn. The boy moved behind a bush to watch. The men put up three wooden crosses. They then put something on the wood and lit them on fire. The negro woman was brought out of the barn and walked over to a tree. The boy watched as the woman was hung from the tree. He could see her legs thrashing about for several minutes until they stopped. The men in the robes cheered and chanted. After seeing this, he fell back to the ground, exhausted by what he saw. He was confused and horrified. Tears began to run down his cheeks. He knew that he could never tell anyone about what he had seen that night. He ran, jumped back onto the buckboard, and covered himself up before his father and grandfather returned for the drive home.

The two men returned to the wagon in what seemed like an hour and began driving home. "Well, John, I'd say that ought to teach these folks a lesson. Why can't they just do what they're told? We have too much work to get done for these people to try and run off. That damn woman knew better than to try that. She had a nice position working in the kitchen. Far better than the ones working in the field."

"Yes, Pa," said John.

"Hey, do you think that daughter of mine has any cobbler for dessert? I sure could use some. Do you think Peter and Eli are still awake? I'd like to see those grandsons of mine before I go home tonight."

"I bet she has, and you know those boys love to stay up and wait for you. It's the only time they get to stay up late. Come on in." Peter quickly jumped out of the wagon, wiping away sweat and tears from his face, he ran to the outhouse. Just as the two men were coming into the house, Peter came in through the back door from the outhouse. The two men never knew of Peter's deception that night, and Peter would never be the same.

"Peter Montgomery! Where have you been, boy? I called for you to come help me with the firewood." Peter's mother, Hannah, yelled toward the opening door. Peter's heart felt as though it stopped. He thought he might even throw up.

"Oh, uh, Maw, that dinner didn't set right on my stomach tonight. I been in the outhouse not feeling so good. Hi, Pap!" Peter managed to think quick on his feet but hoped his mother wouldn't force him to take any Cod Liver Oil for his stomach, but he'd do it to save himself. Peter left out the backdoor again to gather wood for the fireplace.

Part One

CHAPTER 1

Cecily Montgomery

As the carriage came into the city, Miss Monroe's mind wandered back to the first time she walked up those courthouse steps. She stepped from the carriage onto the street. "Watch your step, Miss Monroe," the driver stated as he put his hand out to help her. "Oh, thank you, Eddie," she responded nervously, grasping tightly to his hand as she stepped from the carriage. Elizabeth Monroe, "Lizzie" to her friends, was now thirty-seven years old. She lived in Blacksburg, Virginia, about eighty miles from her hometown of Independence. Having never married, Lizzie moved to Blacksburg to become a teacher when she was just nineteen-years old. The life she had chosen seemed simple and quiet compared to that of her dear friend, Cecily Montgomery.

As she entered the courtroom yet again, having to answer questions about her friend, her mind went back to that first time, and it seemed like it all came rushing back in full color. That day was one of the most dreadful days she had ever experienced, having to give testimony about the woman who had been her best friend in the world.

"Miss Monroe, now place your right hand upon the Bible and raise your left hand. Do you swear that the testimony you are about to give is the whole truth and nothing but the truth so help you God?" said Bailiff Harris to Ms. Elizabeth Monroe in the court of law of Independence, Virginia on the Fourth day of May 1875.

"Why, of course I do," said Lizzie emphatically. Just then rising from his seat was attorney Patrick Bennett for the plaintiff, Carl Anderson. "Now

Miss Monroe, how long have you known the defendant Cecily Montgomery, excuse me, Mrs. Anderson?"

"I've known Mrs. Anderson since I was a little girl, about six years old", said Monroe.

"And how did you first meet her?"

"My family moved to Independence from Bristol when I was six years old, and I met Cissy at my first day of school".

"Would it be safe to say that you were fast friends?"

"Why yes, Cissy and I took to each other right off. We loved each other like sisters. I don't have any siblings and she has so many brothers and sisters. I think she liked coming to my house for some peace and quiet, and I loved going to her house to enjoy all the noise and excitement of having a house full of children."

"And did the two of you share secrets, hopes and dreams together?"

"Oh, of course, we did. Girls just do that kind of thing."

"Did you two court together, too?"

"Once or twice, but both of our Papas were strict, and we were just not allowed to court."

"Were you there when she married my client, Mr. Anderson?"

"Of course, I was in their wedding, Mr. Bennett, and I believe you were there also."

"Yes, of course." Mr. Bennett laughed slightly as not to raise too much concern with the Court.

"Did Mrs. Anderson ever confide in you about any problems in her marriage?"

"Well now, no, not exactly…no," Lizzie hesitated.

"What do you mean, not exactly," asked Mr. Bennett.

"Well, I could tell that something was not quite right with Cissy, I mean, Mrs. Anderson, and I did inquire on a few occasions, but she never would answer the question. I told her that she could trust me, but she just pulled away and asked me to leave her alone and that she was okay. So, I left it alone."

"Did you ever happen to see her in the company of Mr. Anderson's brother, Mr. Nels Anderson?"

"No, sir. I have not," answered Mrs. Monroe.

"Now, remember you are under oath Mrs. Monroe. I will ask you if you were aware that Ms. Anderson was engaged in a relationship with Mr. Nels Anderson prior to and, or during her marriage to Mr. Carl Anderson?"

"No, sir, I did not," answered Ms. Monroe quite surprised by the question.

"Did you ever see Mr. Nels Anderson talking to Ms. Montgomery prior to her marriage to my client?"

"Let me think. Maybe. I guess it is possible. I mean towns folk talk to each other. Is there something improper about that?" retorted Ms. Monroe.

"I don't suppose so unless there was something inappropriate going on between them?"

"Well, sir, if there was, I did not know about it." Ms. Monroe leaned back in her chair as if to project that she was quite finished answering any more questions of that sort.

"Your Honor, that is all I have for this witness at this time; however, I reserve the right to recall Mrs. Monroe at a later time, if necessary," said Mr. Bennett to Judge Melvin Baxter, Superior Court Judge of Grayson County, Virginia.

"Alright, Mrs. Monroe, you are dismissed for now, but you are to stay in the courthouse so that you may again appear should the court need you for further testimony. Do you understand?"

"I do, Your Honor." As Lizzie stepped down from the stand, she couldn't help but wonder why she had been asked those questions. Where was Mr. Bennett going asking such questions? What didn't she know about her friend? She thought that she knew everything, but did she? What had Cissy not told her? Suddenly she felt faint. She grabbed at the nearest thing as her body collapsed. The next thing she knew, Mr. Bennett was helping her up.

"Are you alright, Ms. Monroe?"

"Oh, my goodness. Yes, I do believe I am. I guess I just need some water. I will be fine. I am so sorry, sir. Do forgive me," and Lizzie walked into the hallway just outside the courtroom.

"Of course. Well, if everyone else is alright, Mr. Bennett, you may call your next witness."

"Your Honor, I call my client, Mr. Carl Anderson, to the stand." Just then Carl struggled to stand from the plaintiff's table as the parties in the courtroom looked on with great interest. It appeared as though Mr. Anderson had injured his left leg which looked to be causing him some difficulties. Mrs. Anderson and her attorney did not turn to look at him as he made his way to the witness stand. Carl was tall and slender, and an exceptionally handsome man of about thirty years; ten years older than Cecily. He was known in Independence as a benevolent and generous man, given to deeds of great kindness and generosity. It was known that Cecily Montgomery's father, Eli, saw the marriage between his daughter, Cecily, and Carl Anderson as just one step toward the creation of a Montgomery dynasty in southwestern Virginia. Eli Montgomery came from deep Virginia roots and his goal was to marry his daughters, of which he had five, to the wealthiest gentlemen in Southwestern Virginia to create a strong hold in the mercantile business. Many of the men he sought had made their money in manufacturing or farming. He believed that these marriages would help him gain an advantage in the goods he wanted to sell in his store. Thus far, he had been correct.

Mr. Anderson made his way to the witness stand and was sworn in by the bailiff. As his attorney began to speak, his eyes glanced towards the Defendant's table, towards his wife, Cecily. Her eyes caught his and immediately, she lowered her head and he turned to look at Mr. Bennett. "Now, Mr. Anderson, how did you come to know the Defendant, Cecily Montgomery"?

"The first time I ever saw her was at church back in August 1873. Her family was sitting just a few pews in front of where I saw sitting with my brother Nels. About a week later, I met her father, Eli, in his store, when I was purchasing some supplies for my farm. In talking, he told me about his children, and it wasn't too far into the conversation when the Defendant came into the store with her friend, Miss Elizabeth Monroe."

"And how long after that meeting did you and she start courting?"

"It was about a month, I'd say."

"How long did you court her before you proposed marriage?"

"Call me old fashioned, but it was a year, sir. I am older. I had waited this long to find a wife; I could wait a bit longer, you know? I asked her father for permission to marry her almost exactly one year from the time we met. We married six months later."

"And after you all married, did everything seem ok?"

"It did, at first."

"Explain to the Court what you mean by 'at first'?"

"Well, we took a month to travel for our honeymoon and we had a grand time, but when we returned, it seemed that she was almost immediately unhappy. She became cranky and nothing seemed to make her happy. I encouraged her to spend time with Lizzie, and to find a hobby, but nothing seemed to help."

"And were the two of you happy intimately?"

"No, we were not. She always had a reason not to be. I was extremely frustrated, but I tried to be understanding with her. She started taking walks during the evening and she would be gone for long periods of time. I did not think much of it at first. When I asked where she had been, she would usually say that she had just walked around the corn field, but one night my curiosity got the best of me."

"And what happened that night?"

"Well, I let her walk just a ways, and then I set out behind her where she couldn't see me following her. I let her keep a distance a head of me and then I kept her just within my view and I hid behind something where I could see her. I couldn't believe what I saw."

"What did you see, Mr. Anderson."

"I saw her with my brother, Nels."

"When you say you saw her with your brother, what do you mean?"

"I mean, she was having relations with my brother in the corn field!"

"What did you do when you saw this going on?"

"I ran out there and pulled my brother off her. Then, I hit him. I told her to go back to the house, get her things and get out of my house. I told her I never wanted to see her again. I told my brother that I never wanted to see him again either. He was dead to me. I couldn't believe that he could do this to me. Of course, I didn't really mean that, but I was upset at the moment, and I was talking out of my head."

"Your Honor, that is all I have for Mr. Anderson. I would now like to call Mr. Nels Anderson to the stand."

Mr. Nels Anderson was an even more handsome man than his older brother, who was eight years older than he, but Nels was known to be a rebel and for being rough and unfettered at times. He was blonde haired and light eyed. While Carl ran the business side of the farm, Nels was the farmer. He was rugged and robust. He could be loud and obnoxious. His reputation in town was not one of generosity and kindness per se, though he could be if lead in that direction. When he entered the courtroom, all eyes went to the back of the room and followed him each step of the way. His head turned immediately toward the Defendant's table, though the Defendant did not move. It was as if she were a statue. You couldn't even see her breathe. He stepped up on the stand, turned to be sworn in, and then sat in the chair.

"Mr. Anderson, of course, you know both parties here today and you know why we are here."

"Yep, I sure do," he replied.

"Will you explain to us how you came to be involved with the Defendant, Cecily Montgomery Anderson, please?"

At that moment Nels glanced over at Cissy as if he were looking at her for acknowledgment of something, but her head only hung lower, and her eyes did not move. Her attorney made no movement. She swallowed and then she lifted her head to look at the witness in a dazed stare. Nels moved his eyes back toward Mr. Bennett and began to speak, "Well, Mr. Bennett, Mrs. Anderson and I have been involved since about October 1872." There was a gasp throughout the courtroom. Lizzie turned her head toward the Defendant's table and then back toward Nels. A look of misunderstanding was written across her face. The judge struck the gavel upon the bench, "Order, order, order in the courtroom. Ladies and gentlemen let's keep our decorum about us. We'll have no more of that, or I will clear this courtroom."

"Thank you, Your Honor. Do I understand you to say that you and the Defendant have been involved in a relationship of an intimate nature since *before* the marriage of your brother and the Defendant, is that correct?"

"It is," said Nels.

"You have not told anyone this before today, have you?" asked Mr. Bennett.

"I have not."

"Why is that?" asked Mr. Bennett.

"I did not want to hurt my brother any more than I already had, and I didn't want to hurt Cissy either."

"So why did you decide to share that with us right now?"

"I mistakenly believed, like a fool, that the Defendant was going to choose me when this was all over, but now I know that isn't the case. She was just using me too. Now that she has gotten what she wanted, she is going to throw me away, just like my brother."

"When you say she has gotten what she wanted, what do you mean?" inquired Mr. Bennett

"Cecily Montgomery is not what she seems. She is a con artist, sir. She uses her womanly ways to bilk men. Well, at least she has me and my brother. We were both stupid to get involved with her. You see, she worked us to get things, expensive things that her father could not or would not give her—expensive dresses, perfumes, shoes, hats, things women like and want; those kinds of things. We both showered her with things. She has so many things that neither of us was aware that the other had bought for her. She would show these things off to her friends but hide them from us."

"Did you get anything in return for the things that you bought for the Defendant? Your brother testified that the Defendant refused to be intimate with him."

"We were intimate, quite often actually. That little lady over there, sir, is quite a seductress. I knew that she did not want to intimate with my brother. She told me that he was boring, and he didn't interest her."

"So, she preferred you to your brother, at least that is what she told you, is that correct?"

"Yes, sir, that is what she said."

"Did she tell you that she loved you?"

"She sure did. Many times, and I fell for it."

"When you say that she was a "seductress', what do you mean by this? I apologize to the ladies in the gallery for any scandalous words, but we need to know who Cecily Anderson truly is."

"Well, sir, she wanted to have sex with me all the time and anywhere, even when I was not in the mood or didn't have time to give to her, she would throw a fit until I gave in. She would, then, talk all sweet and tell me how we were going to be together forever one day. I was completely blinded by her."

"Have you had any contact with the Defendant since the night in question?"

"No, I have not. I do not care to have any further contact with the Defendant, Mr. Bennett."

"Mr. Adams, do you have any questions for this witness today?" asked Judge Baxter.

"No, Your Honor, I think we've heard enough," replied Mr. Adams.

"That is all, Your Honor. The Plaintiff rests his case." Nels Anderson walked to the back of the courtroom and sat down just behind his brother to watch the rest of the proceeding.

"That is noted, Mr. Bennett. Mr. Adams, you are up. Call your first witness."

"I call Cecily Montgomery to the stand, Your Honor." The Defendant rose from her chair slowly and cautiously and then turned to walk to the witness stand. She held her head down as she sat in the chair. Cissy was dressed in an inexpensive dress with no jewelry. Her hair, which was usually worn in an attractive up-do, was worn down in a messy sort of braid. It was a highly unusual appearance for anyone who knew her. Perhaps, this was her attempt to appear modest, in contrast to how she was being portrayed by Plaintiff's counsel.

"Hello, Mrs. Anderson. I know that this is a very difficult time for you, so I am just going to ask you a few questions."

"Yes, sir", Cecily replied in a soft voice.

"Now, you are going to need to speak louder so that everyone in the courtroom can hear you. Tell me about your relationship with your husband."

"Well, sir, we met through my father. Mr. Anderson was a good customer of his. I knew that my father had plans for me and Mr. Anderson to court.

He arranged all the marriages of my sisters, so it was to be the same for me. I had seen him, Mr. Anderson, in the store and he seemed to be quite nice, and he is quite handsome, too. We courted for about a year, and then he proposed to me, and I said yes. I wanted to make my father and everyone happy, sir."

"Tell the Court what your marriage to Mr. Anderson was like."

"Well, I would not describe it in the manner Mr. Anderson described it. We began to disagree about things almost immediately after our marriage. I wanted a large family, and he did not. I had grown up in a large family and I wanted the same thing—a big house with a big family, but Carl did not. In fact, he told me that he wanted no children. This was devastating to me. When we disagreed, Mr. Anderson would become quite upset. He would yell and grab me by the arms, sometimes squeezing so tight that he would leave bruises on my arms. I was frightened by his temper."

"Did Mr. Anderson explain to you why he did not wish to have children?"

"No, sir, not directly. I suppose, looking back at it now, that it was because he and Nels had a difficult upbringing. They were raised by their older brother, Hans, because their parents had been killed in an accident of some kind."

"I see. Now, did Mr. Anderson ever strike you?"

"No, but he would become so enraged, that the look he would give me was as if he could kill me."

"Did anyone else ever see this behavior?"

"Well, his brother would have. They were not close really. Their relationship was very much business like. They also argued, and my husband would behave in a like manner towards his brother, threatening him but not actually doing anything. It was a nightmare wondering if one day he might actually do what he threatened."

"Now you heard Nels Anderson testify that the two of you had been involved in an intimate relationship since about October 1872. To your recollection, is this a true statement?"

"Yes, it is true. You see, I met Nels first, before I knew about my father's plans for me and Carl. My father did not know about our relationship. I wasn't allowed to court, but I liked Nels, so we kept everything secret. I tried to break it off with him when Carl and I started courting because I knew my father intended for me to marry Carl. Nels knew that my father would never agree to my relationship with him. Nels has a reputation, you see. But Nels didn't want to let me go. He was angry that I would not stand up to my father and tell him the truth. When my marriage turned bad, I turned to him for compassion. He can be a kind and gentle man when he wants to be."

"Just to be clear, explain to the Court what it was that made Carl Anderson the better choice for you."

"Money, sir. My father is a traditional man. His family came from aristocracy in Scotland, and he was raised to believe that fathers must secure good marriages for their daughters. My father has many daughters, and he has married us all off to leaders in business and government in Virginia. He never wanted his daughters to have to worry about taking care of themselves or their children. He saw that in Carl Anderson. Carl has a good business mind, and I think Poppa saw an interest in Carl to possibly take over his business if one of my brothers did not want it."

"I suppose that is what most fathers want for their daughters. Now, when Carl became angry with you and the two of you would get into these rather intense arguments, what did you typically do when the argument was over?"

"I went to Nels."

Was there a specific time when you sought Nels out for help?"

"Yes, Carl and I had just had a terrible fight and Carl had bruised my arms. I was frightened because this time was far worse than before. I didn't understand why he had become so angry, and I thought he was going to kill me. I ran to the barn for help from Nels."

"Did Nels help you?"

"He talked to his brother and told him that he had better not touch me like that again. He tried to talk sense into him and to quit letting his temper take control."

"What happened next?"

"Carl left to calm down, he said he was going into town for supplies, and that left me at home alone. About five minutes after he left, Nels came to my door. He stepped in and grabbed me to hug me. I was so distraught that I gave into my fears and anguish, and I began to sob. Nels suggested that we take a walk to help me to settle down. We walked out to the corn field, and then one thing led to another. I had no idea how long we had been in the corn field, but it seemed like just minutes had passed when all the sudden Carl came out of nowhere yelling at the top of his lungs."

"What happened next?"

"I jumped up and ran to the house. If he hadn't killed me before, he surely would now, and I wanted to get away. He and Nels fought for a few minutes and then Nels ran to his house. Carl followed me into the house and told me to leave and to never come back."

"You also heard Nels here today testify that you were not interested in having relations with your husband, that he was boring. Is that an accurate statement?"

"Somewhat. After Carl told me that he did not want children, I admit that I became despondent. I wanted children so badly and I wanted them soon. It hurt me. I just couldn't get my mind to understand why he would marry anyone if he wanted no children. And after we had our fights, Carl would want to make love and I couldn't after he had frightened me so."

"You also heard Mr. Nels Anderson testify that you used both men for material things. That both men showered you with things that you wanted and couldn't get from your father. What do you make of this allegation?"

"I don't know really. Yes, they both bought me things. Did they buy me too many things? Maybe, but I don't think I am spoiled. My father had five girls and I don't think he spoiled any of us. As I said earlier, he wanted to make certain all of us were well taken care of us, and I don't think that is a crime, sir. I was not smart like Lizzie. I was never going to be a teacher and have my own money. I had to marry." Cissy lowered her head and was wringing her gloves.

Lizzie's mind suddenly came back to the present as the sounds of others beginning to enter the courthouse broke her attention. "Hello, Lizzie," came a soft voice. It was Cissy. Lizzie stood up smiling and the two embraced tightly.

"Oh, Cissy, I am so sorry you are going through this. Are you okay?"

"I will be once this is over. So much has happened." Holding on to her hand was a young man of about thirteen.

"Is this our young Jacob? Oh, my goodness, how you have grown up. You are a handsome young man." Lizzie put her hand up under his chin and looked directly into his eyes.

Jacob managed a smile, but he was shy. Jacob was Cecily's only child, born of her second marriage to a Jewish peddler named Isaac Kramer. Cissy married Isaac eighteen months after her divorce from Carl Anderson. Their marriage seemed to be a happy one from what Lizzie had been told by family and mutual friends. Isaac came to Independence from New York selling goods to merchantiles. He fell in love with the mountains and Cecily Montgomery and decided to stay. He also farmed a small plot of land given to them by Cissy's father to help supplement their income. They were excited when Jacob Isaac Kramer Jr. was born the following year. Tragically, three years after their marriage Isaac went on a trip to Charlottesville and never returned. It was rumored that he was caught up in a robbery at a store he was calling on and was murdered. However, his body was never recovered. Cissy was devastated by her loss. She raised Jacob by herself for five years before she met and married Donald Stewart.

"You have to help my mother, Ms. Monroe. Mr. Stewart is out to get her real bad."

"What do you mean, Jacob?"

"He tried to kill her with a pickax, you know. I caught him. He ran after her with it. He was crazy drunk. He is crazy in the head," said Jacob.

"Why would he try to kill your mother, Jacob? What did she do? Has he hurt her before?"

As Lizzie was trying to make sense of what Jacob was saying to her, Mr. Turner walked up. "Ms. Monroe?"

"Yes, Mr. Turner?" Lizzie did not know quite what to make of what Jacob said to her. She had been out of touch with Cissy for so long. What she was hearing did not make sense, but Cissy had not kept touch with her, only writing her about once a year or so and even then, her letters were superficial at best.

"Yes, ma'am, I am Mrs. Stewart's attorney. I wanted to talk to you, if I could for a few minutes."

"Certainly, but I don't know what help I can be. Cissy and I have not had much contact in the last few years other than writing letters and she has not confided in me."

"I know that you have been called as a witness by Mr. Stewart's attorney, Mr. Smith. I wanted to ask you if you had any idea what they might be asking you to testify to."

"I haven't met with them yet, so I really couldn't say. I suppose it is about my friendship with Cissy." Just then Mr. Smith interrupted the conversation. "Ms. Monroe, if you would please come with me."

"Yes, sir, Mr. Turner, please excuse me." Lizzie and Mr. Smith walked to a nearby table with two chairs and sat down. Mr. Smith was a younger man, appearing to be in his early to mid-thirties. He was quite handsome with light hair and green eyes. He wore glasses and had curly hair, which appeared difficult to control, as he had attempted, unsuccessfully, to control with some sort of cream which made it appear to be wet. He spoke softly as if not to let anyone else hear what he was going to say. There were many other people in the courthouse working that day, coming and going about their normal work duties.

"I am Douglas Smith, the attorney for Donald Stewart. He is currently married to Cecily Montgomery, who I understand you have been friends with since childhood. Is that right?"

"Yes, sir, it is, but I really don't see how I can help here, sir. I have not been in contact with Cissy that much in the past several years."

"That isn't why we've asked you here today. I want to ask you about your past relationship and knowledge of Mrs. Stewart."

"Ok, but I still don't see…."

"Do you recall a time when you and she were about thirteen years old, and Ms. Cecily went missing at a party at her home one evening?"

"I am not sure what you are talking about."

"Ok, let me give you some more detail. Ms. Cecily left the party and went outside and was gone for a long period of time. You missed her and when you went to look for her, you found her partially clothed, bleeding and beaten in the barn. Do you remember now, Ms. Monroe?"

"How do you know about this? Who?" Lizzie was confused.

"You and Ms. Cecily thought that you were the only ones in the world, other than the perpetrator, who knew about this incident, didn't you?"

"Yes, well…" Lizzie slipped back in her chair feeling sick and her mind racing to remember who else may have known or discovered their secret.

"Well, you were wrong. Now, I expect you to go in that courtroom and tell the court the truth of what happened that night, Ms. Monroe, or I will have the court hold you in contempt. Do you understand that?"

Panic rushed over Lizzie as the ramifications of what was about to happen filled her mind. This was a secret she and Cissy had held onto and promised never to discuss since that night. Lizzie never knew who had hurt Cissy that night. Cissy made her promise not to ask. All she knew was that her best friend was never the same after that night. She wondered if the guilty party was to be in court that day, or if there was another witness that night that they had not seen. Lizzie could not have predicted how this courtroom battle was about to play out and how devastating it would be for everyone involved.

CHAPTER 2

The Jezebel

The courtroom quickly filled with sounds of whispers and footsteps as people entered and sat down for the day's proceedings. "All rise, the case of Cecily Jane Stewart versus Alexander Donald Stewart is hereby called to order with the Honorable Thomas Cooper, presiding."

"Please be seated. Gentlemen, as I understand it this is a divorce case involving a marriage of approximately six years in which there are no biological children involved, is that correct?"

"That is correct, Your Honor," responded Mr. Turner.

"How many witnesses will we have on each side today, so we can estimate time?"

"I will have three witnesses," said Mr. Turner.

"I will have two witnesses," said Mr. Smith.

"Ok, the witnesses are asked to leave the courtroom at this time. Witnesses, you will remain in the witness room until you are called to testify. You may only leave that room to go to the bathroom or to testify. Mr. Turner, do you wish to make your opening statement first or do you wish to defer to Mr. Smith?"

"I will defer, Your Honor. I will also defer to the Defense to present their case first."

"Okay, Mr. Smith, you may proceed with your opening statements."

"Thank you, Your Honor. We are here today in the case of Stewart vs. Stewart, again a marriage of six years. Mr. Donald Stewart came to Virginia with his brother, Angus, around 1865 after being discharged from the Union Army in Tennessee. They bought a small farm and began to make their living. After a year, my client's brother decided to move further south into Georgia. Mr. Stewart met Ms. Kramer at a church picnic, and they began dating soon after. The couple dated for approximately a month before they entered into an intimate relationship. They were married six months later. Mrs. Stewart has one child, Jacob, from her previous marriage to Isaac Kramer. This is Mrs. Stewart's third marriage. Her first marriage ended in divorce after only a year due to her infidelity with her husband's brother. We will show here today that this is a pattern of behavior for Mrs. Stewart, that she has a deep hatred for men and that she seeks out men who she believes she can manipulate in order to obtain the material possessions that she wants. We will show her to be an evil, vindictive woman who will do whatever it takes to get what she wants regardless of the consequences and that she drove Mr. Stewart to the events of September 13, 1893. My client, Mr. Stewart loved his wife, and he wanted this marriage to work, but his wife had no such intentions. These are two broken people. Mr. Stewart is broken from his injuries sustained in the War of Northern Aggression, but he intended to recover from those and to be a better person. He had no intentions of hurting his wife on September 13th, Your Honor, but she drove him to those actions. We intend to show here today that her attorney, Mr. Turner, is complicit in these actions here today, Your Honor, and that he should be reprimanded, if not disbarred, for his behavior in this matter."

"Mr. Turner, your opening statement, sir," said Judge Cooper.

Mr. Turner, rising slowly from his chair, smiles toward the Defendant's chair. "My goodness that was quite dramatic, wasn't it? Boy, how. Your Honor, this is quite simply a case of a good marriage gone bad. When this couple met, they were very much in love, but this gentleman seated over here was harmed greatly by the war, as were so many of our men. He suffered from what he had seen and what he had done. These things led him to the drink, Your Honor. On the evening of September 13, 1893, this man consumed quite a bit of alcohol. He had been away from the home and when he returned home his wife was not there. He became enraged that she was not home. His stepson, Jacob Kramer, was in the barn cleaning up. He went to the barn and asked the boy where his mother was. The boy told Mr. Stewart that he did not know, but that she might be next door visiting.

At that point, he picked up a pickax and proceeded to come after Mrs. Stewart at my home which is next door. As you may know, Your Honor, I am a widower with seven children. Mrs. Stewart often comes to my house to visit with my housekeeper and children. There was nothing untoward about her actions. Jacob ran after Mr. Stewart to stop him from hurting his mother. Mr. Stewart shouted many outrageous allegations at Mrs. Stewart and attempted to hit her with the pickax; however, he did not hit her. He fell to ground. Thank God! We will show that this was simply a misunderstanding, and that Mrs. Stewart loved her husband, but that she can no longer stand the drinking, and we will ask that a divorce be granted. Thank you."

"Alright, Mr. Smith, you may call your first witness."

"I call Ms. Elizabeth Monroe, Your Honor." Whispers could be heard as her name was called and Cecily Stewart's body arched into a rigid stance as if to prepare herself for what was about to happen.

The bailiff swore Ms. Monroe in, and she sat at the left side of the judge's bench. Mr. Smith stood about three feet from the witness stand. "Ms. Monroe, thank you for being here today. I know that this was not easy for you. Now, how long have you known Ms. Stewart?"

"I have known Mrs. Stewart since we were about six years old, sir."

"And do you know my client at all?"

"No, sir, I do not."

"That's fine. I want to ask you about a time when you and Mrs. Stewart were about thirteen years old and there was a party at the Plaintiff's parent's home. Do you recall such a party?"

"I do."

"And do you recall that Mrs. Stewart went missing during that party and you went looking for her?"

"I do."

"Please tell the Court what happened."

"Well sir, I missed Cissy, Mrs. Stewart, so I went to look for her. I couldn't find her inside, so I went outside. I called her name, but I got no answer. I went to the barn. I was still calling her name, but she was still not answering, but then I heard crying. I followed the sounds and I found her in one of the stalls."

"What condition was Mrs. Stewart in when you found her?"

Lizzie looked over at the judge. "Must I, Your Honor? I really don't want to…. I mean…what has this got to do with what is going on now?"

"You must answer the question Ms. Monroe. It has everything to do with what is going on now. Your Honor, I will lay the foundation for this line of questioning, with the Court's permission."

"Yes, Ms. Monroe, you must answer the question, but Mr. Smith, this had better be relevant," responded Judge Cooper.

"She had been beaten and raped. She had a bloody lip. Her clothes were torn."

"Did she tell you who had hurt her?"

"No, she would not say. I kept asking. I told her that we needed to have the person arrested, but she wouldn't talk. She was silent. She never told me. To this day, I don't know who did it."

"What was her behavior like?"

"At first, she was sobbing. She cried for a while, and then it stopped. Suddenly she changed completely. She became rigid and her tears dried up. It was like it didn't happen. She was completely different. When I got her up, she tossed her head up and dusted her herself off, and she said that we would never speak of what had happened ever again. It would be like it never happened. After that night, it was like she was never really happy again. It was like like her joy was stolen. We went back to the house through the kitchen where no one would see her, and she changed her dress and cleaned up her face. It was strange; no one seemed to notice that she wasn't wearing the same clothes. She put on a happy face and went on with the party. I think she learned how to pretend to be happy."

"Do you know if anyone else was in the barn that night?"

"Not that I was aware of. I never saw or heard anyone else out there that night."

"By the way, did you know Mrs. Stewart's second husband, Isaac Kramer?"

"No, I did not."

"So, you wouldn't know whether or not he was actually killed like Mrs. Stewart alleges or if he simply ran away, would you?"

"No, I would not," she replied in a terse tone.

"What kind of relationship have you had with Mrs. Stewart since that time?"

"Well, shortly after that party, we finished school. I got my teaching position in Roanoke, and I left. I came back to be in her first wedding to Mr. Anderson and I was here when Jacob was born. I try to be here when I can, but most of our contact is through letters, so we really have not had a direct relationship. I love her dearly and I wish the best for her."

"That is all I have for this witness, Your Honor. I call Donald Stewart to the stand."

"Mr. Stewart, do you swear to tell the truth, whole truth, and nothing but the truth, so help you God," asked the Bailiff?

"I do," answered Mr. Stewart as he sat on the witness stand. Donald Stewart was thirty-three-year-old who was born in Boston, Massachusetts. He and his brother had served in the Union Army and were released from service due to injuries they received at the Battle of Chickamauga. They each received land for their participation in the war in Virginia. They stayed to work with hopes of one day returning home, but Donald met and fell in love Cissy. His brother, too, met and married a woman in Independence, but later moved to Georgia.

"Mr. Stewart, tell the Court how you met Mrs. Stewart."

"Well, when my brother Angus and I got out of the Army after the war, we were looking for work and we got some work at the Presbyterian Church repairing the roof. One Sunday they had a picnic and me and Angus went. That's when I met Cissy. I thought she was really pretty, and I seen her with her son, Jacob. They seemed sort of lonely. I heard what happened to her husband and all. I went over and asked if the boy wanted to play ball. We started talkin' and one thing led to another…before too long we was seein' each other. You know how that all goes."

"Now would you say Cissy was a traditional lady? I mean, did ya'll keep things platonic, or did things go further than that?"

"Oh, no sir. Cissy was a fast little filly. I was actually quite shocked that she wanted to be intimate so fast, but bein' a man with needs…I mean…I didn't stop her neither."

"So, how fast is fast?"

"Well, 'bout a month, sir."

"Well, my goodness. That was fast, wasn't it? Now, did Mrs. Stewart tell you about her other, previous relationships…marriages that is?"

"Well, yes, I guess. She told me that her first husband had died and left her the house and land that she lived on. I now know that weren't true. She cheated on him with his brother and he divorced her after a year. The house and land actually belong to her father. She told me that Jacob's father, Isaac Kramer, died. I guess that's true. I haven't heard no different on that one; and, he ain't come back."

"How did Mrs. Stewart treat you during your marriage? Was she good to you? Did she cook for you? Did she keep a clean house? Was she a good mother to Jacob?"

"No, sir. She is the most selfish woman I have ever met in my life. Everything is about her and what she wants *you* to do for her. She cannot cook anything worth eating. She did not keep the house clean. She made me get a negro woman to do it for her, even though we really could not afford it. She wanted everyone to think we was rich. She goes and charges things at her Daddy's store without me knowing. When he finds out, he would come tell me and we have to work out how to pay for it."

Nothing Jacob or I ever did was good enough for her. If I brought home a dress for her from her Daddy's shop, she would tell me the fabric weren't nice enough and to take it back. The house I built wasn't big enough. If Jacob brought home a "B" on a test, she would tell him it weren't good enough. She was always belittling him. She would tell him he was stupid and would never be anything. I tried to do what I could to make her happy, to keep her happy, but nothing ever seemed to be good enough. I am tired of trying."

"Did Mrs. Stewart ever hit you?"

"Oh, yeah. She makes it out like I am the violent one, but when we had fights, she threw things, and she would hit me and scratch me with her fingernails."

"Mr. Stewart, do you have a problem with alcohol?"

"Yes, sir, I do. I ain't proud of it, sir. I have nightmares sometimes about the war. I have tried real hard to quit. Cissy makes it hard. She yells and screams at me. She calls me names. It all fills up in my head and I just can't handle it. So, I go to the barn, and I drink."

"What happened on September 13, 1873?"

"Well, just a few weeks prior to that night I had gotten suspicious of Cissy because she had been going over to Mr. Turner's house more and more often. She thought I didn't know, but I had come home a few times, early in the day, and I seen her coming back from his house out of his back door where his private entrance to his office is. Mr. Turner's wife died a couple of years ago and he's been alone since with his seven kids. Well, I got home early on this afternoon, and yeah, I had been drinking, and I asked Jacob where his mother was. She wasn't home again. I got real mad 'cuz I wasn't thinking straight, and I grabbed my pickax and I went running over to Turner's to get my wife back. I know it was stupid. Jacob went running behind me and he stopped me from hurting anybody. I am thankful for that. But she was over there, and I know she and Turner's got something going on. She's got no reason to be over to his house. She's a married lady."

"Now, I want to ask you, you heard the testimony earlier of Mrs. Stewart's friend Ms. Monroe regarding the incident that happened when your wife was thirteen, right?"

"Yes, I did."

"Tell us how you came to know about the events of that evening since your wife and Ms. Monroe believed that they were the only two people, other than the rapist, who knew about it."

"Well, it wasn't long after I married my wife that I had a conversation with her youngest brother, Frank Montgomery. I ran into him in Richmond when I had gone to buy some hogs for the farm. Frank and Cissy have not spoken in over fifteen years. I did not know why or anything about it. Frank warned me about Cissy. He told me that she was cold, calculating and vindictive, and then he told me the story of why he thought she had become that way. He told me that he had been in the barn that night. Cissy had come out of the house during the party and was walking around, just getting some air. A few minutes later, their uncle Peter came out and walked alongside her and walked her into the barn. The next thing he knew, Peter had pushed Cissy onto the ground trying to kiss her and he was pulling her dress up. Frank heard his uncle tell Cissy that it was okay, that he loved her and that it was normal. Cissy tried to fight, but Peter started beating her and told her to shut up. He told Cissy that all she was ever going to be good for, so she might as well get used to it. When he heard Lizzie coming, he ran off. Frank was terrified. He couldn't help his sister; he was only eight at the time. He had been traumatized by what he had seen, and he felt so guilty about it. He seen the way she acted after that night. That was why he has not spoken to his sister. He felt responsible. I think the real Cissy Montgomery died that night."

"So, now when you went running over to Mr. Turner's with the pickax, did you intend to hurt or kill Cissy or Mr. Turner with the ax, Mr. Stewart?"

"No, of course, I didn't. I just wanted to get Cissy back home. I wanted Turner to leave her alone. I picked up the first thing I saw to scare Turner with. I wanted to tell her that she was worth more to me. I wanted to tell her that I knew what had happened to her and that she didn't have to be that way. I loved her, and I wanted to take care of her. I was sorry for drinking all the time. I wanted to tell her that I was going to try to stop for her and Jacob. But I didn't get a chance because Jacob called the law on me. It looked bad. I know I blew it real bad."

"Your Honor, that is all I have for this witness." Mr. Smith turned and went back to his chair.

"Alright, Mr. Turner do you wish to cross-examine at this time?" asked Judge Cooper.

"Not at this time, but I may recall him in the future, Your Honor."

"Fine, Mr. Smith, call your next witness."

"I call Frank Montgomery to the stand, Your Honor." There was a gasp in the courtroom. No one had seen Frank Montgomery in years. Once Frank became of age, he left Independence. Perhaps the events of that night in the barn had so scarred him, living in Independence was not something Frank could bare. Frank was the youngest of the Montgomery clan and he was also the smartest. He had chosen to walk in his father's footsteps and to run a mercantile store, but he chose to do so on the coast of Virginia in the town of Norfolk. Norfolk was a Navy seaport and he had been very successful.

He had married a socialite and had three children. Life had been very good to Frank Montgomery.

Frank was now seated in the witness box. He appeared nervous. His hands were clinched tightly together. Mr. Smith stepped next to the Plaintiff's table as he began to speak. "Mr. Montgomery, we thank you for being here today. You are the brother of the Defendant, is that correct?"

"Yes, I am."

"Do I understand correctly that you and she are 4 years apart in age?"

"That is correct. I am 31-years old."

"Now, let me take you back to a party some years ago when your sister was 13 and you were 9. Do you recall that party, sir?"

"I do, unfortunately. I will never forget it, sir."

"Tell the Court, sir, what happened that night as you remember it."

"My family had some friends over for cake and ice cream. Everyone was mostly inside the house. There was lots of noise inside. It got very loud. I was young and I didn't like a lot of loud noise and the crowd, so I had gone outside to play with my toy horse. I had been outside for a few minutes when my sister, Cissy, came outside. She was just walking around alone. I think she was daydreaming."

"How old was your sister, Cissy, at this time again?"

"She was 13."

"So, pretty normal for a girl of 13. What happened next, Mr. Montgomery?"

"Just a few minutes later, our Uncle Peter came out of the house, and he walked up to Cissy and started walking beside her. He was talking to her, but I couldn't hear what they were talking about. They didn't seem to notice that I was there. Cissy giggled a few times. They walked to the barn. I followed them, but they never noticed I was there."

"What happened when they got to the barn?"

"When they got to the barn, Uncle Peter picked Cissy up and put her on a bale of hay and he got right up close to her. I thought that was sort of strange. They were still talking. Everything seemed fine until, he suddenly leaned over and kissed her on her lips. I had gone into one of the stalls just across from them. He kept trying to kiss her. She was pulling away and she told him to stop. Uncle Peter told her that it was okay, and that was how girls learned about being with boys. He told her he loved her. She told him no, that it wasn't right. Then, Uncle Peter became angry, and he hit her across the face with the back of his hand. Cissy went flying off the bale of hay. She landed inside of one of the open stalls. He followed her into the stall. I couldn't really see well after that, except that I could see him leaning over her. I could hear her crying and saying "no" and "stop". I heard him hit her again. I just sat down in the stall and waited for the sounds to stop. The next thing I heard was Lizzie talking to Cissy. I sat back up and I saw Lizzie walking with Cissy out of the barn. I was so scared. I had never seen my uncle angry before. I should have tried to help Cissy, but I was young. I didn't know what to do. And, then I felt so guilty about doing nothing. I knew Cissy would hate me for doing nothing, so I never told her that I knew what had happened in the barn that night."

"How was Cissy after that night?"

"She became a completely different person. Before that night Cissy was the most loving, kind, generous person you would ever want to know, but after that night she became cold and uncaring. Everything became about her and what she could do for herself. Now, she can pretend to care about you, but when you turn your back, she'll stab you and she'll twist the knife if it means getting what she wants. She's quite an actress."

"Can you give us an example?"

"One of the things I did hear my Uncle Peter tell Cissy in the barn was that all she was ever going to good for was a roll in the hay because she was dumb as dirt. Of course, at the time, I had no idea what that meant. Well, after all of this went down, Cissy became very promiscuous. Not many people knew about this, but I did because I knew what happened and when I would see her coming out of the back side of a barn talking with a boy, I knew what they had been up to once I was old enough to know about these things. So, not long after the incident in the barn there was a barn dance coming up in town and, of course, all of my sisters wanted to go. Well, my sisters Cissy and Katie are close in age. Suddenly, they became quite competitive with each other regarding boys. They never had been that way before. Cissy never seemed to care about boys before that night, but now she cared a whole lot. She wanted a new dress, new shoes, and a new fancy comb for her hair. Momma made new dresses for both girls. Cissy thought that Katie's dress was prettier, and she was noticeably jealous.

The evening of the dance, Cissy offered to help Katie do her hair. The heated up the curling iron in the fire and Cissy started to do Katie's hair when suddenly Cissy burned a big chunk of Katie's hair off. Of course, she said it was an accident, but Katie did not believe her and none of my other sisters believed her either. Katie had to cut the rest of her hair off to fix it. She was so upset that she didn't go to the dance that night. Cissy smirked, and she skipped off to the dance with my brothers. I saw Cissy that night come out of the corn field behind the Cofield's house with a boy. I knew what she had been doing out there. Katie had a crush on the boy Cissy had been out there with."

"Out of curiosity, Frank, what ever became of your Uncle Peter?"

"Well, he never came back to Independence after that night in the barn. He died about two years later in an accident. The buckboard wagon he was driving hit a rock and he was thrown out and his head hit a rock. I heard he had been drinking."

"That is all for this witness, Your Honor."

"Mr. Turner?" Mr. Turner leaned over to his client and whispered in her ear. She whispered back into his ear.

"Now, Mr. Montgomery, when you saw your sister, Cissy, as you say coming out from behind a barn or coming out of the corn field, did you see her clothing in disarray?"

"No, sir," replied Frank Montgomery.

"So, you *don't actually know* what she had been doing, do you?"

"Well, I didn't see her doing it, no, but what other reason would she have to be out there with a boy?"

"Talking, Mr. Montgomery, they could have just been talking, now, couldn't they?"

"Well, I suppose."

"The simple matter is that you just don't know exactly what was going on because you were not there isn't that right?"

"Yes, sir."

"That is all I have at this time, Your Honor."

"Thank you, Mr. Montgomery. You are dismissed. Now, Mr. Smith do you have any other witnesses for the Court today?"

"I do not, Your Honor. The Defense rests."

"Well, then, we shall recess for today, Mr. Turner, you will commence with your portion of this case in the morning."

"Thank you, Your Honor."

"Ladies and Gentlemen, the Court shall stand adjourned for today." Just then people began to stand and walk from the courtroom to the streets of Independence, making their way to their homes, hotels, etc. Lizzie waited for Cissy and Jacob to come to rotunda. She felt ill having had to testify about what had happened all those years ago. She felt that she had betrayed her friend.

As Cissy and Jacob approached, her hand reached out, "Cissy, Jacob...." Cissy grabbed her hand, "Oh Lizzie, you did nothing wrong. You had no choice. They made you tell. Please do not feel bad."

"Lizzie fell into her arms and began to weep. Oh Cissy, I never would have told a soul. Never would I have. I would have carried it to my grave. I swear." Cissy pulled her face up and wiped her tears.

"That's enough of that. It is over and done now. What is done is done. We must move ahead now. You remember that." Lizzie looked at Cissy. It was like that night in the barn again. She was toughening up as if she were going into battle. There was little life in her eyes. At that moment, Lizzie realized for the first time that this person in front of her was not the person that she knew and loved all those years ago. This was someone quite different and strange, and she was not sure that this person was someone she would even like. Her tears dried up and she wiped her eyes.

"Thank you, Cissy. I guess I'd better catch my carriage now and get to my hotel room. I will see you tomorrow. Have a good evening, Cissy. Jacob." She smiled and turned towards the street and then walked towards the door. "Eddie, I am ready to leave now. Is my carriage ready?"

"Yes, ma'am."

That evening Lizzie went to the hotel restaurant for dinner. When she stepped into the room, she saw a familiar face. It was a dear friend, Frances

Wilson, who had also been friends with Cissy as a young girl. Lizzie went over and spoke to Frances. They embraced and smiled warmly into each other's eyes.

"Oh, it is so good to see you, Lizzie. How is life in Blacksburg?"

"It is wonderful. I love my children and my school. They make every day joyous for me. And how are you and Charles these days?"

"Oh, my, I guess you hadn't heard. Have you eaten yet? If not, let's sit down and eat together and catch up. It will be wonderful to talk for a while." The waiter took them to a table.

"What haven't I heard, Frances? What happened?"

"Oh, Charles, he's been gone a long time now, Lizzie. I guess it was about May of 1886 or June maybe, I don't exactly remember, I've tried to forget. I caught him in our barn with Cissy Montgomery."

Lizzie's heart sank as she heard Cissy's name. "How can that be? What were they doing in the barn, Frances?" Lizzie never realized the naiveté of her question; it just seemed an outrageous thought to her even after the things she had heard in court.

"You know exactly what they were doing Lizzie. This cannot really be a surprise to you, can it, Lizzie? Don't you remember all the boys whispering about Cissy in school? Don't you remember seeing her coming out of unusual places and a few minutes later this boy or that would suddenly come from the same place?" Frances looked to Lizzie to remember and to realize that the evidence was there along, but her love for her friend would not let her see it.

"Oh, my, today has been quite a day. Well, what happened to you and Charles?"

"I tried to forgive him, and he promised it wouldn't happen again. It was okay for a while, but I just had the hardest time trusting him, and I would see her looking at him in town. He left one day for the mill and never came home. I married Hal Cox two years later. He has been great to me and to Abigail. She loves him."

"I am so sorry, Frances. I wish I had known."

"Oh, what could you have done? You cannot change her, and he couldn't cope with himself. I am just glad to see you now." The pair ate dinner together and talked about fun times as children. When time came to depart, they hugged again and promised to keep in touch. Lizzie was overwhelmed with emotion and exhausted. She returned to her room for the evening.

Morning came quickly for Lizzie. She felt as though she had not slept; she tossed and turned reviewing the events of the prior day in her mind, trying to figure out what the truth was. She wanted to walk away and simply return to her quiet life, but with everything that had happened, she felt uneasy and as though she hadn't really understood her life or her dear friend. Perhaps today would bring more understanding and give her relief from the thoughts in her head.

She returned to the courthouse and waited inside for a while. As she stood just outside one of the witness rooms adjacent to the courtroom, Lizzie heard the sound of soft whispers. She turned her head slightly to listen better, as she thought she recognized one of the voices. She took one step closer to the room, but not so close to have been seen or heard.

"You know what you have to do, young man."

"But it's wrong. What happened was wrong, Poppa was wrong, but so were you, Momma. You shouldn'a dun it. You keep on a doin' it."

With her voice getting increasingly more angry but still muted, Lizzie saw Cissy grab Jacob by the arm and squeeze it tightly as she stared him in the eye and firmly said, "Jacob Isaac Kramer, you go in there and you tell that judge what I told you to say, or you'll be out on your can tonight. You hear me, boy?" Devastated at her friend's behavior, Lizzie quietly walked away and into the courtroom to find a seat.

"All rise, comes now, the case of Stewart vs. Stewart. Judge Thomas Cooper presiding." cried the Bailiff. Everyone in the courtroom arose as Judge Cooper re-entered the room.

Judge Cooper instructed everyone to be seated and for Mr. Turner to call his first witness.

"I call Jacob Isaac Kramer, Jr, Your Honor."

Jacob walked back into the courtroom appearing disheveled and worried. As he walked by where Lizzie was sitting, she could see bruises on the boy's arms. He walked forward to the witness stand and was sworn in by the bailiff. Mr. Turner stood next to Cissy as he began to speak.

"Please tell the Court your full name son."

"Jacob Isaac Kramer, Jr, sir."

"And who is this lady seated here?"

"That is my mother, Cecily Stewart, sir."

"How old are you now, Jacob?"

"I am twelve. I will be thirteen next month."

"Are you in school?

"Yes, sir, and then I work for my grandfather in the store."

"That is wonderful. Now, I know that this is an awkward situation for you, but I need to ask you some questions. Please tell me what it was like at home when your mother first met and married Mr. Stewart."

"Well, I liked him at first. He was real nice to me and my mom. Me and my momma had been all alone since my Pa died."

"Did he treat you like his own son?"

"He sure did. We went hunting together and I worked with him on the farm."

"When did all that change?"

"He and momma would argue about money and such. It seemed like things was good for a while, then he started drinking. I know my momma can be a handful. She and my Pa argued a lot too. Momma can be a real pill when she wants something. But the arguments started getting violent. Poppa, uh Mr. Stewart, would get real angry and things got thrown. He hit her, too."

"Did this happen frequently?"

"Mostly it would happen after he would find out about a bill she owed, and he knew we couldn't pay it."

"Now, Jacob, do you know my children?"

"Oh yes. Your son, Andrew, is one of my best friends."

"And you have occasion to come over to our house to visit with Andrew, don't you?"

"Yes, sir."

"And we live right next to your farm, is that right?"

"Yes, sir."

"Has your mother come with you sometimes?"

"Yes, sir. She is friends with your housekeeper, Addie."

"That's right. Have you been at the house when your mother was visiting with Addie?"

"I have."

"Have you ever seen your mother do anything inappropriate while she was visiting in my home?"

"Oh, no sir. She and Addie just sit and drink coffee and talk."

"Have I ever been there when your mother was visiting?"

"Not that I can remember, sir."

"So, I am going to ask you to speculate here, son, but do you know why Mr. Stewart would come to have the idea that your mother and I would be having an inappropriate relationship?"

"No, sir, I do not. I think he just dreamed it all up in his head when he was drinking."

"Now, there seems to be some allegation here that perhaps your father did not die. What is your understanding of what happened to your father, Jacob?"

"Well see he went on a trip for my grandpa to Charlottesville. He was going to pick up somethings that had been purchased for the store. When he didn't come back a few days later, we was worried. My grandpa sent his man Edgar up there to see about it. When Edgar got there, he was told by the store owner that my Pa never showed up. Edgar went to the Sheriff in Charlottesville to make a report and to see if he knew anything. The Sheriff told him that there had been a robbery at the hotel and some people got shot up. He thought my Pa had been there, gotten shot, and rode off for home. Maybe he died somewhere along the way home."

"What did Edgar do with that information?"

"He rode back here."

"Did anyone else go looking for him?"

"When Edgar got back and told my grandpa the story, my grandpa sent Edgar and four others back out to ride along the normal route and look again. But they still didn't find nothing."

"Ok, son, that will be all for now."

Judge Cooper looked to the Plaintiff's table, "Do you wish to cross-examine?"

"I do, Your Honor. Now, Jacob, can you please stand?"

Jacob looked at Judge Cooper and then he looked at his mother. "Do I have to?"

"Yes, son, you do," replied Judge Cooper.

Jacob stood, pushing his chair behind him. He looked frightened. Mr. Smith then asked that Jacob roll his shirt sleeves up above his elbows. Jacob moving slowly and looking down, tears began to roll down his cheeks. "Would you please show the Court your arms?"

Jacob held his arms up to Judge Cooper who looked over both arms, up and down. There was a visible frown upon his face. Judge Cooper asked Jacob, "Son, where'd you get these bruises? You've got too many bruises on these arms to just be rough housing with your buddies."

Jacob rolled his lips and swallowed hard, and said, "I don't remember, sir."

Mr. Smith continued, "Now son, this is a Judge here and this is court of law. There are stiff penalties for lying. Isn't it true, Jacob, that your mother gave you these bruises? She can be very cruel to you, isn't that true?"

"No. No, that ain't right. My Ma loves me. She takes care of me. I am just always doing things, you know. Getting into things, playing around with the fellas. Boys do that. Me and my friends are always playing around, and we get bruises, I guess. I ain't never paid them no mind. Poppa just wants to make my Momma look bad."

"That's all I have, Your Honor. He can be dismissed at this time."

"Alright then, Mr. Turner, call your next witness."

"Your Honor, I call Cecily Stewart to the stand."

Cecily Stewart rose and walked confidently to the stand, where the Bailiff swore her in. Once she was seated, Mr. Turner walked toward the lectern. "Now, Mrs. Stewart, I am going to ask you some questions about your relationship with your son first, since this issue has just arisen. Okay?"

"Certainly."

"Now, Jacob is your son with your second husband, Isaac Kramer, correct?"

"Yes, that is correct."

"So, we are not here today to argue about custody or visitation between the Plaintiff and Jacob, are we?"

"No, not at all. Jacob is my son."

"But the Plaintiff has alleged that you are an unkind mother. I believe he testified that Jacob could do nothing right, that you often yell at him; and, most recently, that you are physically abusive, having put bruises on his arms. Is any of this true, Mrs. Stewart?"

"No, of course not, I love my son. If I did anything unkind or bad to my son, my father would most assuredly know; and, believe me, he would have done something about it. He sees Jacob every day. He has never questioned my ability to care for my son. Jacob is a good boy, and he does get into things. I am always having to get his pants mended because of tears. He is just a typical boy who likes to play ball, hunt, ride horses, and all. He's a good boy. He is my world."

"Ok, so we'll move on now. What do you remember about how you and Mr. Stewart met and fell in love?"

"It was about how he described it. We met a church, and he took a liking to Jacob. We started doing things together and one thing led to another, and we got married. It was nice to have a man around the house again, especially for Jacob."

"Mr. Stewart testified that you and he entered into an intimate relationship quickly. Is that how you remember it?"

"Well, I wouldn't say it was quite that quick, but I will admit that we were quite passionate for each other. He was very kind and considerate, and he made me feel safe…at least for a little while."

"Now, when did that change?"

"I cannot give you an exact time or an exact incident, but I would say probably after the first year. Donald told me when we married that he had nightmares about the war. I understood that. It must have been horrible. My own father served in that war, and I know he was not the same when he came home either. I tried to care for him and to help him. That worked for a while, but he started drinking. I think he thought it would help him sleep, but he just kept drinking more and more."

"How bad did it get?"

"Sometimes he would drink so much that he would talk out of his head. It was like he was reliving things. I would try to talk to him, but he would misunderstand, and it would lead to an argument. I tried not to argue for a while, but it got harder and harder. I got tired. I guess after a while it seemed like we fought all the time."

"Did he get violent with you?"

"Yes, he would grab me, slap me, and throw things at me when he got angry. But, when it was over, he would apologize and promise not to do it anymore. For some time, I would forgive him, and we would go on. I just cannot do it anymore. I'm tired. I don't want that for me and Jacob anymore."

"He claims that you were more abusive to him, than he to you. Were you violent towards him?"

"When I got to my wits end and became frustrated, yes. I might throw things and scream at him. I am not proud of it, sir."

"Now let's turn to the issue that has us here today. Tell me what you remember about September 13, 1873."

"I was home alone. Jacob was out with some of his friends; so, I decided to go over and visit Addy for a bit. It hitched up the horses and rode over to the house and went in to visit with her. I don't know how long we had been talking when we heard awful screaming coming from outside. I could hear Jacob calling for me and I could Donald's voice. He sounded crazy."

"What happened next?"

"I told Addy to tell the kids to stay inside and we went outside to see what was going on and why Donald was so angry. Donald was ranting about something. I could tell that he must have been drinking for a long time that day. He was slurring his words so bad you couldn't make out what he was saying, but he was holding a pickax up over his head like a crazy person. I told Addy to get back in the house. Jacob ran in between me and Donald, and he begged Donald to put the ax down. He was shouting through his tears to put the ax down, just put the ax down, don't hurt my Momma. Donald put the ax down and fell to the ground. I guess it was around about that time when you showed up."

"What did you think Mr. Stewart was going to do with that pickax?"

"I was terrified that he was going to kill me, Jacob, or both of us, maybe even Addy. I just did not know what he was capable of in the state he was in."

"So, you were in fear for your lives, is that correct?"

"Oh, yes we were."

"Well, he didn't kill you. You are here today. What happened."

"Jacob went and got the Sheriff. By the time he got out there, Donald had gone on home, so he went to our house, and he arrested Donald. I think he spent about four days in jail before he let him out."

"So, what do you want the Judge to do here today, Mrs. Stewart?"

"I just want a divorce and I want Donald to leave me and Jacob alone."

"Your Honor, that is all I have at this time. The Defense rests."

"Alright, Mr. Smith, do you wish to cross-examine this witness?"

"No, sir. I doubt I would get a truthful answer. I do wish to call another witness, Your Honor."

"That's fine, sir. Go ahead."

"I call Mr. Turner, Your Honor." There was a collective gasp from the gallery.

"Your Honor, I object to this," declared Mr. Turner, "I certainly cannot testify against my own client."

"Mr. Turner, you might have thought about that before you took Mrs. Stewart on as a client. Proceed to the witness stand or I will hold you in contempt of this court, Mr. Turner."

Mr. Turner begrudgingly complied with the judge's demand. Once upon the stand he was sworn in and was seated. Mr. Smith searched through his notes and then looked upon his witness. "Mr. Turner, your home is directly next to this couple's, is that correct?"

"It is."

"Can you actually see your home from the Stewart's? What I mean is, can you see your residence in such a way as to know when you are home or not home?"

"I believe that you can from their front yard."

"So, on September 13, Mrs. Stewart would've been able to tell that Addy was at your residence if, perhaps there was wash out on the line drying, perhaps?"

"Yes, that would be a reasonable assumption."

"Or, if she saw your buckboard tied up just outside of the home, that would be reasonable as well?"

"Yes, perhaps. Or that could be my oldest boy, too. He takes the buckboard sometimes also."

"Do you have an occasion, sir, to work from home from time to time in your profession?"

"Yes, I do."

"How often would you say that you do this on a monthly basis?"

"Oh, maybe once a week or so."

"Were you working at home on September 13th?"

"I do not recall."

"I would remind you, sir, that you are under oath."

"I think that it would be best for me to invoke my Fifth Amendment rights at this time, Your Honor."

"I have no further questions of this witness, Your Honor. We rest our case."

"Fine. I will take a break to review my notes and I will return with my judgment before the end of the day."

"All rise," cried the bailiff.

Three hours passed before Judge Cooper returned with his judgment in favor of Donald Stewart. He had not believed that Cecily was not having an affair with Mr. Turner. He allowed her keep the house and farm, as they belonged to her father, but not much else. He encouraged Mr. Stewart to get help with his war related problems so that he could function more appropriately in society. He commended Jacob on his maturity and encouraged him to do well in school and to work hard to be a good man. Then, there was Cecily. He admonished her manipulations but gave her sympathy for the trauma in her youth but told her that circumstance had not given her justification for her ill treatment of others, specifically her son. He told her to grow up and start acting like a human being with real feelings for other people and to stop being selfish. Hard to say if his words fell into rubble or to fertile soil.

CHAPTER 3

Sins of the…Mother

Years passed and Jacob grew into a young man of seventeen. He left his mother's home to move in with his grandparents and to work full time at the O'Neal's' farm. Mr. O'Neal was a kind man who owned a dairy farm and always had work to be done. He hired Jacob to work doing odd jobs around the farm. They seemed to be a very happy family. When there was extra time, Jacob would fill in at his grandfather's store making deliveries around town. Everyone in Independence knew and liked Jacob Kramer. He looked very much like his father. He had dark, wavy hair, olive skin and beautiful dark brown eyes. He was tall and thin, but muscular from hard work. He was ruggedly handsome. The young girls would often stop and stare as he walked by.

He was also intelligent. He did well in school, particularly in math, but he never cared much for school. He left school in order to work. He wanted to be on his own and make his own money. Most people gossiped that he could not stand living with his over controlling mother, so as soon as he could he was out of her house and on his own, the better.

Jacob had many friends. He was outgoing and sociable, not at all like his mother who was now reclusive and had taken to drinking herself in the evenings when the children had all gone to bed. She had married Mr. Turner about year after the trial, but the marriage had become one more of convenience than of love. Mr. Turner needed a mother for his children and Cissy needed the security of money and a home. If it had been up to her, Jacob would never leave her side and would wait on her hand and foot, catering to her every whim. He distanced himself from her, but not completely.

He did go to see his mother, but he knew how to break away when it was time. He had learned how to break the hold she tried to have on him. He was not, however, undamaged by his childhood.

CHAPTER 4

The O'Neal Farm

Just outside Independence was a tiny village of Baywood, which was inhabited mostly by the Young, Hampton, Cox, and Kirby families, and had been since the War for Independence. The O'Neals had come to the village in 1878 after their small farm in Wytheville had been destroyed in a fire caused by a lightning strike. It had taken them some years, but they had become quite successful, becoming the primary supplier of milk and cheese for most families in the surrounding area. They started with a small home when they first settled, but after having four children, they built a larger home and used the smaller one as an office for the dairy.

In the beginning, Sean O'Neal worked the dairy alone, trying to save every penny he could to expand the dairy as quickly as he could. He put in long days. He grew his own corn to feed the cows and cut down his expenses. There were some years when the harvest was not good, and he had to buy corn on credit, but for the most part things went well and his debts were paid on time. But now, he was able to take on his first employee. He was, of course, a frequent customer of Eli Montgomery's store in Independence and he had seen Jacob Kramer in the store stocking shelves and sweeping the floors.

Mr. O'Neal asked Mr. Montgomery one day about Jacob. "Mr. Montgomery, I hope I am not talking out of turn here, sir, but I see your grandson, Jacob, here almost every day, and I wondered if you needed him all the time. You see, I am looking for some extra hands at the dairy. Jacob looks like a good worker. He's a good size young man, and I'd pay him well, give him room and board. We'd take real good care of him, sir. If that would be something he would be interested in and not putting you out, that is."

"Well, now, Mr. O'Neal, let's ask Jacob. Jacob, come over here son. We need to talk to you, son," said Mr. Montgomery in the direction of Jacob Kramer.

Jacob stood up and walked over to his grandfather as he brushed the dust off of his pants and straightened his shirt. His eyes looked in the direction of Mr. O'Neal and then toward his grandfather. "Yes, sir. Do you need me to get something for Mr. O'Neal, sir?"

"No, son. Mr. O'Neal has just made an offer of a job for you, for you to come and work at his dairy farm. He would pay you and give you room and board. Now, what do you think of that offer?"

Jacob's face lit up like a Christmas tree on Christmas morning, but he tried not to scream out in joy. He cleared his throat and said, "Uh, sure. I think that would right fine, sir. When do you want me to come out?"

"Well, Jacob, I am sure you have some things you'd like to get together and today is Friday, so how about you come on out after church on Sunday and we'll get you all set up and you can start fresh on Monday morning?"

"That sounds great, sir. Thank you, sir."

Mr. Montgomery patted Jacob on the back and said, "Ok, Jacob, you can go on back to what you were doing, and I will walk Mr. O'Neal out to his rig." Mr. O'Neal and Mr. Montgomery turned away from Jacob as he walked on back to what he was doing. As they walked to the door, Mr. Montgomery looked at Mr. O'Neal, "Now Sean, I must warn you. Jacob's mother isn't going to take to this idea. Now I love my daughter, but she has so many problems. If she comes out there to bother Jacob, you let me know and I will try my best to keep her away, but I cannot always make her do what I want her to do. She is a handful. She always has been, and that boy is her life. She is manipulative. She tries to control everything he does, and she drinks. You just let me know if she comes out there, okay?"

Jacob enjoyed working for Sean and Margaret O'Neal. After working for them for a couple of years, he became like family to them. They included him in on family outings, church gatherings, just about everything they did. Townsfolk often commented to Mr. Montgomery that they could tell just how happy Jacob was working at their farm because he was always smiling. Even their children, Brian, Joseph, Mary Frances and Sarah, seemed to adore him. When he had extra time, he could be seen playing ball with them, going on nature hikes, swimming, and doing all kinds of activities with them. It was like he had found the family he had always wanted.

But Cissy had caused problems in the time that Jacob had been with the O'Neals. She was immensely jealous of Jacob's relationship with them. She heard what the townsfolk said, and it made her heart burn with jealousy. He spent more time at the O'Neal's and less time with her. Fewer Sundays were spent in her presence for lunch and more times were spent on picnics in the meadow off Laurel Hill with the O'Neals. Her anger grew with each weekend that passed and he did not come home.

When Jacob did go home to see his mother, she hovered and smothered him. She tried to buy his love with the things she would buy for him, but she also pestered him with questions about the O'Neals. She wanted to know every detail of their life, their home, their farm. Jacob tried to ignore the incessant questions or to put her off. He did not want to talk about the family he had come to love. It felt like a betrayal.

Cissy's nagging, though, was incessant. She would nag until they would argue. It never failed that the argument would grow until he felt like her words were rumbling around in his head like a tornado and he was going to pass out if it didn't stop. All he could do to make the madness stop was to run. Cissy would always run to door apologizing and promising not to do it again if he would just return. Some days he would give in and go back in, other days he would keep going to keep from having an argument that would escalate too far.

CHAPTER 5

Accidents Happen, Or Do They?

Work on a dairy farm is tedious, but Jacob enjoyed it. The longer he worked for the O'Neals the more responsibility Sean gave Jacob, which made Jacob feel important and appreciated. Sean had even hired another hand on the farm after Jacob had been there four years to take over some of the more tedious work and he sent Jacob out to build up his accounts. Jacob enjoyed going out and meeting with businessmen to gain new accounts for the dairy. This allowed him to work in the office with Margaret O'Neal who did all the bookkeeping for the dairy.

Margaret O'Neal was an attractive woman with auburn hair, deep blue eyes and pale ivory skin. She was tall and thin and had a beautiful smile. She was, for the most part, a happy person who loved her family and her life on the farm. She was born in Ireland and came to America when she was just a little over seven years old. Her parents had settled in Lynchburg and also ran a dairy. She met Sean O'Neal when she was sixteen at a dance at the local Catholic Diocese parish. They married a year and a half later. Jacob loved to hear her talk as she had just a slight Irish accent. He often told her how beautifully she spoke after listening to her read stories to her children.

All was not perfect, however, in the O'Neal marriage. After almost twenty years of marriage, there were tensions. There had been some lean years and those led to stressors in the marriage, especially after the children were born. Sean O'Neal had a habit of attending the tavern too often which Margaret disliked intensely. He would come home late and smell of liquor.

They would argue, and, on occasion, these arguments would lead to violent outbursts by Sean. On one such occasion, Jacob was sleeping upstairs above the office when he heard Sean stumble in making a terrible racket. It sounded like he was knocking things over in the office downstairs. Then he heard Margaret come into the room and the two began to argue. "What are ya doing in here, Sean?"

"I am lookin' for the accounting records to see the balances in the accounts, Maggie."

"It is midnight, Sean. You can do that tomorrow when you've come to your senses," said Margaret in an ill-tempered tone.

"I'll be seein' them tonight!"

"You've been gambling again, haven't you? How much did you lose this time, Sean? How much do you need, huh? That's what this is all about isn't it?"

"It isn't any of your concern woman! This is my dairy and if I need money, I'll be gettin' it!" Margaret moved over to close the journal ledger and push it aside; and, as she did so, Sean pushed her back and hit her with the back of his hand across the face knocking her against the wall. The sound was loud enough to wake Jacob from his sleep in the room just above. He came running down the stairs to see Maggie slumped on the floor and Sean standing over the desk looking like a crazed monster.

"What have you done, Sean? Margaret, are you okay? Let me go get some ice for you." Jacob ran into the kitchen and took ice from the box and began to chop a piece off and place in a towel. He ran back into the office.

"This is none of your business, boy. Now, you just go back to your room and mind your business," said Sean.

"Oh, no, you don't. You aren't going to hurt her. If you hurt her, I will fix you. That's a promise." Jacob's face was red. Maggie could tell he was serious. He went over to her and gave her the ice.

"Leave it alone, Jacob. It isn't worth it. You need this job," responded Margaret.

"Ok, but only because you asked me to." He looked deep into her eyes and she into his as he placed the ice pack on her swollen cheek. She took his hand to put it down as he smiled at her, "It will be okay. I promise you that."

Jacob went back to his room, and Margaret and Sean went back to their home. Nothing was mentioned about that night again, and life at the O'Neal farm went back to its normal routine. Everything seemed to be fine for about eight months. One afternoon in the fall of 1908, Sean asked Jacob to accompany him on a trip from Independence to Wytheville to pick up a new bull he was going to purchase for the dairy. The two worked on the plan for the trip for about a week to make sure that Sean had all the money for the purchase and that the route had been properly mapped out. Margaret had insisted that Sean not go alone and that he take Jacob with him for security.

The two set out early one morning in September. Sean kissed Margaret and the children goodbye and waved as they headed out on their way. Margaret packed the men sandwiches and tea for the long trip ahead. Sean and Jacob chatted about this and that as they traveled along the way. They had been gone about two hours or so when Sean asked Jacob to change places and to take over driving the rig. Jacob gladly agreed. As they headed out again after taking a short break to relieve themselves and have a snack, the road became quite rugged and difficult. Sean commented that he hadn't remembered the road being that way before. "Jacob, are you certain that this is the right road? I would not have chosen such a road as this. It is much too hard on the team and wagon."

"Yes, sir, this is the road on the map that you have, sir." Jacob continued driving and the road became more and more treacherous. Suddenly, the wheel of the rig hit a rock and the two men were thrown violently out of the wagon. It seemed like hours, but it could have been only a few minutes when Jacob regained consciousness. His vision was blurry at first. He looked around trying to find Sean. He tried to stand but fell again. He sat for a few minutes until he could again see clearly. He looked around again and he saw Sean lying on the ground not far from the wagon. He crawled over to him. He called his name. "Sean! Sean! Can you hear me? Sean! Wake up! Sean!" Terror took over him. He grabbed Sean by the shoulders and shook him, but nothing happened. He sat back and put his head in his hands and cried.

After a few minutes, he dried his face and looked around. He knew time was short before day would turn to night, and he had to get help. There was no way to fix the wagon enough for him to drive it back home. He was going to have to walk. He picked up Sean's body and threw it over his shoulders and began to walk. Jacob walked as far as he could with Sean O'Neal's dead body on his shoulders until he could walk no more. He collapsed in exhaustion on the side of the road as darkness approached. He managed to gather enough energy to put together some sticks and to start a small fire. He knew it probably would not stay lit long, but he tried to keep it going as long as he could. All he knew to do was to wait and to keep Sean close.

When the two did not show up in Wytheville that day to pick up the bull, the livestock auctioneer knew something was wrong. Sean O'Neal had always been punctual. He sent his assistant to look for the two men. It wasn't long before the assistant came upon Jacob Kramer carrying the lifeless body of Sean O'Neal. He put them in his wagon and drove them back to Independence. Jacob met Maggie in tears and told the story of what had happened that day. The assistant confirmed the story after having seen the wreckage on the road and found the two just a few miles down the road headed back home. Maggie hugged Jacob and told him that it was not his fault and assured him that he bore no blame. Jacob held his head low and went to his room.

Days passed and the time for Sean O'Neal's funeral came. Everyone in town was there. Margaret and her children stood strong as the husband and father they knew and loved as lowered into the grave. The children left wildflowers on his grave. Jacob stayed away that day choosing to stay on the farm and work instead. When the family returned, Margaret went to find him. She found Jacob in the barn cleaning up. "I wish you had come. He would have wanted you there."

"That might be true, but there is plenty of work here to be done, Maggie."

"Yes, that is true too." She placed her hand on his shoulder. It is going to be okay, Jacob. I think we can manage with the insurance money. It was not much, but it was something; and, if the accounts stay with us and we keep our deliveries on time, I think we can manage it." Jacob quickly turned around and grabbed Maggie in a tight embrace and kissed her. At first Maggie tried to resist, but then gave in to the emotion and fatigue of all she had been through. It was a long, passionate kiss. Maggie pulled away. "Jacob, this is wrong. Not yet. I just can't."

"I know, Margaret, but it has been so long since…. I have waited so long. I couldn't wait anymore. I couldn't stand the way he treated you. I just got so angry."

"What do you mean, you got angry? When?"

"The night when he hurt you. I knew I had to do something. I just had to. I was not going to let him hurt you ever again. Just like my mother. I wasn't going to let the woman I love get hurt by a man who was supposed to love her!"

"Jacob, what did you do? Did you have something to do with Sean's death?"

Jacob came around and realized how he sounded. Of course, he couldn't let Margaret know that he had intentionally driven the rig into the rock that day and that he was driving too fast when he hit it. "No, I just mean that I was going to protect you from him no matter what and not let him do that again. That's all." He took her back into his arms and kissed her again. "I love you, Maggie O'Neal. I just want to be with you."

"I know my marriage was not a great one. Even if I have feelings for you, Jacob Kramer, it is too soon. My children have to get through all of this first, then we can be together later. Just be patient."

Margaret and Jacob went on from that day working together running the dairy together. Jacob remained in his room above the office and Margaret and her children in the main house. They went on the way they had before enjoying picnics together, church gatherings, and other social events, but as time went on their relationship became more intimate both privately and publicly. The townspeople knew that Jacob and Margaret were more than just employer and employee. At first, the gossips were wagging their tongues in a negative fashion about the widow and her children with the farmhand. Oh, how scandalous! But as time passed, they grew accustomed to it, and they could see a genuine love between the two and that the children were quite agreeable with the arrangement themselves.

Mrs. O'Neal became Mrs. Kramer on November 25, 1909, and Jacob moved into the big house at O'Neal Farm. Jacob and Margaret enjoyed what appeared to be a wonderful life. They worked hard and had a successful business for several years, but Jacob seemed to grow weary over time. Margaret was, of course, older than Jacob and she enjoyed staying at home and being with her children. Jacob was young and still wanted to go into town to see his younger friends and to socialize. Maggie tolerated his behavior for a time, but she later began to tire of it. She wanted her husband at home. They argued about it constantly. The farm also began to suffer because Jacob was not always working as much as he should. There were rumors of other women, also. It seemed that Jacob had inherited his mother's philandering ways, loving the attention he garnered from the young ladies in town.

Then one day, Jacob told Maggie that he was going on a trip to Raleigh, North Carolina, to visit the university. He told her about a symposium on new technology for dairy farms. Maggie thought it sounded wonderful and wise. She helped him pack up and kissed him as he left that morning on the train. That was the last time she ever saw him.

CHAPTER 6

The Bigamist

Margaret Kramer was heartbroken. She couldn't believe that Jacob would just leave her and the children with no word of explanation. It had never been in his character to be so cruel. She convinced herself to wait. She waited for him to write to her letting her know that he was alive. Nothing came. Occasionally, she would hear rumors that someone had heard he was in this place or that, but she didn't have the courage to act upon that knowledge, not until May 1920 when she was told by the husband of a friend that he had run into Jacob in Norfolk and that he was working for the shipyard and living with a young girl who had a baby. Margaret was so angry that she got a friend to stay with her children and she took the train to Norfolk.

When she arrived in Norfolk, she went to the address her friend had given to her as the home where Jacob was living. She was hoping to find him there, but when she got to the door and knocked only the girl was there with her child. Margaret confronted the girl, whose name was Lily. "Do you know who I am, Miss?"

In a very indignant tone, the girl responded, "No, am I supposed to?"

"Well, I think you should. The man you are living with is my husband. Do you understand that? We are married. Not divorced. Married!"

The girl looked down at her from the top of the stoop, and said, "Yeah, so what. I don't care what or who you think you are, but he is mine now. I suggest you go get a lawyer and get your divorce because he ain't comin' home to you, honey. We got this one and another one on the way." This girl was young. She had wavy strawberry blonde hair and blue eyes with a pale, freckled complexion. She was tall and thin; quite pretty, Maggie thought.

She had on bright red lipstick and a pretty skirt and blouse which seemed a bit too big for her. As angry as she was, she also felt some sympathy for this naive girl.

"You must know your marriage is not legal because he is still married to me. Your child is illegitimate. Don't you care about that? If he did this to me, he will do it to you. He will walk out on you one day," said Maggie.

"No, he won't. See I know how to hold a man. He ain't ever leavin' me 'til he's dead in the ground." She turned as the screen door slammed behind her. Marggie turned and to walk back to the train station. She stood on the road for few moments crying before she started walking to the station. She could see the girl standing in the doorway watching her. She wasn't sure whether to be more angry or more sad about it all. Her marriage was over and now she had lost two husbands. She was taken aback by the attitude of this young girl. How could this girl be so dismissive of her? Why didn't she care about another woman abandoned by this man? Didn't she care that she had been lied to, deceived? How was she going to run the dairy alone?

Lily Peterson

When Jacob left Independence for Raleigh, he had intended to go to the agricultural conference to find out about new technology for the dairy; but, when he arrived, he just didn't have his heart in it. He found himself sitting at the bar of the hotel heavily drinking; something, he had rarely done before. He was overwhelmed by the responsibility of a wife and four teenage children. The more he thought, the more stressed he became and the more he drank. Before he knew it, he woke up hung over sitting on a train headed for Norfolk. He believed that there would be plenty of work there for him. He had always been good with his hands and at fixing things. All he had to do was find a job and a small place to live. He really didn't know what it was that he wanted, but he just couldn't find it in himself to go back to Independence and back to Margaret.

When he arrived in Norfolk, he could smell the salt of the ocean in the air. It smelled wonderful to him. He had never been to the ocean before. The scent lifted his spirits. He followed it all the way to the shipyard. He wasn't certain what he could do, but he wanted to work in the shipyard. As he walked along the road, he came upon a sign that read, "WANTED MAINTENANCE WORKER". He walked inside to the office and took off his hat. There was a gentleman inside talking to a woman at a desk who was writing. They both looked up at him. The man said, "May I help you, son?" Jacob said, "The sign said you needed a maintenance man. I can do that, sir."

"Oh, you can, can you? How do I know that? What's your name, son?"

"Jacob…Jacob Stewart, sir; and well, sir, my grandpa runs a store back home, and I did all his maintenance for him, sir."

"Well, ok. Did you just get into town, boy?"

"Yes, sir. I walked here from the train station."

"My goodness, that's a long walk. So, I suspect, Mr. Jacob Stewart. That you also don't have a place to lay your head? Well, I can help you with that, too. Come on with me." The two men walk outside. "I am Mr. Brooks. I am the Foreman here. You will answer to me. You will get paid every Friday at 2:00 p.m. Work starts at 6:30 a.m. on the dot. You got that? Don't be a minute late or your pay gets docked. You will sweep and mop these floors twice a week. Once a week they will be polished. You will clean the latrines and take out the trash every day. And you'll help with any other maintenance issues that I need help with." As they walked, they came upon a small building. Mr. Brooks opened the door and led Jacob inside. Inside the building were two rooms. One room had a small kitchen, and the other was a small bedroom. "Now, you can stay in this room so long as you work for me. Your room and board will be deducted from your wages each week. If you decide to move out and live somewhere else, just let me know. You'll just need to clean it up for me. So, do we have a deal, Mr. Stewart"?

"Yes, sir. I'd be honored to work here, sir."

"Well, don't let it go to your head, kid. It ain't that great, but it is a job. I think we're going to get along just fine. Now, you get settled in here and I will see you in the morning."

Jacob started working for the shipyard and he was as happy as he ever been in his life. It was a fresh start. He made good money and he felt a sense of pride being on his own and being his own man. He made friends at work, and they enjoyed activities with each other after work. He enjoyed playing pool and cards, but it was on one of the other activities that would lead Jacob to meet the girl who would become his next wife.

One Sunday afternoon in April 1919, Jacob and his friend Daniel Davis decided to take a ride out in the country. Jacob didn't have his own car, but Daniel did. Daniel was just a bit younger than Jacob, but he came from a wealthy family in the Norfolk area. He worked as a drafter in the shipyard, so he also made more money. He and Jacob hit it off right away. Daniel was very outgoing and enjoyed having fun. One of his favorite things to do was to take long drives in his car on Sunday afternoons. On this day, they didn't know where they were or how far they had gone from Norfolk. The windows were down, and the two were enjoying the brisk, cool autumn air as they drove quickly through the country roads. Before they knew it, they were in Smithfield, Virginia, just on the other side of the James River. When they came into the center of town, they parked and got out to walk around. The two young men come upon a pool hall and decide to go in and play a game or two.

Inside the pool hall, Daniel and Jacob purchased a couple of beers and went over to a pool table to rack up the balls. They were just beginning to play when something caught Jacob's eye. He saw two young ladies walking down the sidewalk just across the street. While both were attractive, one was a tall, strawberry blonde who knocked him off his feet. He put his pool cue down and walked over to the window to see where the two women were headed.

"Hey, Jacob, where are you going?" asked Daniel.

"Come on, Daniel. Let's go." Jacob left the pool hall and crossed the street headed for where he had seen the two women go. Daniel and Jacob walked into the Blue Star Café and sat at a table just a few feet away from where the two ladies were sitting. "Wow, they're pretty. You think they'd talk to us, Dan?"

"I don't know, Jacob, with you staring at them like some sort of stalker!" Jacob grabbed his menu and held it up higher, so he wouldn't be quite so obvious. Just then giggles came from the ladies' table. The guys had been noticed.

"Why don't you just come on over here instead of staring? We won't bite, boys," said Gracie Peterson, the older of the two ladies.

"Don't mind if we do," so Daniel and Jacob walked over to the table. "Hello, I am Daniel Davis, and this goof is my friend, Jacob Stewart. We're just driving through town today and stopped to have lunch and walk around. This is a nice, little place you got here."

"Well, now, isn't that something? I am Gracie, and this is my sister, Lily. Where are you boys from?"

"Oh, we work over in Norfolk. I am originally from Richmond and Jacob, here, he is a mountain boy. He's from Grayson County."

"Oh, really. I hear it is very beautiful in the mountain country. Why on earth would you ever leave?" asked Lily.

"I got bored with it, I guess. I wanted to see what else there was in the world. There also aren't many good jobs. Norfolk has more to offer."

"Do you work in the shipyards?" Gracie asked.

"Yes, I work in maintenance and Dan is a drafter. What do you gals do around here?"

The ladies began to laugh as they sipped on their sodas. "Nothing really. Our daddy is a farmer, and he keeps us close. Our momma died when we were young, so we have to help take care of our younger brothers and sister."

"Wow, I am so sorry to hear about your mother. That must have been so hard for you to grow up without her. I don't know what I would have done without my mother. I grew up without my father." Jacob gazed into Lily's eyes as he spoke. Her eyes were the most beautiful shade of blue with little specks of amber. She had freckles across her nose and her skin was like milk. He thought she was the most beautiful creature he had ever seen. He thought Margaret was beautiful, but in a different way. He was very young when he fell in love with Margaret, and she was eleven years older than he. This feeling was something quite different than what he felt when he first met Margaret.

The couples continued to talk as they ate their lunches. When they had finished, the ladies asked if they would like to go see a movie. The men accepted the offer and so the group walked across the street to the theater to see "Miracle Man" staring Lon Chaney. After the show was over, the new group of friends decided to walk about town. Daniel and Gracie went one way and Jacob and Lily the other, deciding to meet up later back at the diner for ice cream. As they walked, Lily took Jacob's hand and began to walk quickly. She led him through a park, down a street and around the corner down a short alley way.

Jacob pushed Lily up against the wall of the building, "Lily, I like you. I would like to come back here and see you again." Lily grabbed Jacob's tie and pulled him up against her.

"I'd like that very much." Lily pulled Jacob in and kissed him lightly on the lips while running her other hand down his back.

"Lily, you shouldn't…."

"Why not, Jacob? Don't you like me?"

"Of course. I just told you that I do, but we just met." Lily continued to gaze into Jacob's eyes. Jacob kissed Lily lightly on the cheek.

Lily whispered into his ear, "Don't let that stop you."

Jacob looked into her eyes and then he looked around. There was no one around. It was quiet and secluded. He looked back at Lily, who was still staring right at him. At that very moment, she grabbed him and pulled him in closer and kissed him again, this time with more emotion. While Jacob was bit taken with her forwardness, he finally felt his heart beating again. He liked it and wanted more of it.

Jacob looked back at her. "Lily, I promise you. I will be back for you. You do not have to worry, but I cannot do this, not this way. It would be wrong for you. When we do this, we have to do it right. Okay?"

Lily pushed him away and looked relieved. "Well, you passed that test", and she pushed him away, smiling at him like a Cheshire cat. "Can you come next weekend and have dinner at my house? Gracie and I will cook. Bring Dan with you, too. That way you can meet my Daddy."

Jacob, who was breathing much easier and chuckling, said, "Sure thing. You had me going there. That really wasn't fair. Now, we'd better get back to the diner. You're crazy, you know that?" The two strolled off laughing and talking about what they would be doing for the next week. The couples enjoyed their ice cream and then said their goodbyes. The boys then drove back to Norfolk and the girls walked home.

Gracie and Lily Peterson were the two oldest daughters of George and Prudence Peterson. George Peterson was a third-generation farmer in Surry County, Virginia. His father, James, had been a successful farmer and had purchased a large tract of land in the county. He was a veteran of the Confederate States and was a founding member of the Masonic Temple in Smithfield. James had two other sons, James Jr. and Henry, who also farmed, but Henry was serving in the Virginia legislature. The sons inherited their farms from their father, and each had managed to be continue his success. They followed in their father's steps being devoted members of the Freemasons, as were their wives who were members of the Order of the Eastern Star. Tradition was very important to the Peterson family.

Life, however, for George had not been as easy as it had been for his brothers. George's wife, Prudence, died shortly after the birth of their last child, Edwin. Since that time, George had been raising his five children on his own, except for the assistance of his maid Mabel. He was a capable and strong man who took his job as father quite seriously. He kept his children close, and he knew about them and their lives. He made sure that he was in from the fields at the end of the day so that they could eat dinner together. He would ask them about their day and make certain that their studies were complete. If one of the children had a struggle in their schoolwork, he made sure someone was there to provide assistance.

The oldest girls, Gracie (19) and Lily (17), were required to assist in schoolwork and housework. George insisted that his daughters be able to take care of themselves and that they be knowledgeable in the skills needed to become good wives and mothers, so they were taught to cook, sew, clean, and care for small children. This meant that Gracie and Lily spent most of their time at home working and caring for their siblings when they were not at school or church. Mabel was not just a housekeeper to the Peterson family; she was also a tutor to the oldest girls in training them in these skills.

Most of the time the girls did not mind because they loved their family; they missed their mother dearly. They understood why their father wanted them to help and they were happy to do it, but there were many times that they missed out on activities that their friends were participating in because of their responsibilities at home. This often caused anger and resentment. The older the girls got, the more they wanted their independence and the more often they had become prone to bouts of rebellion.

Their father was also quite conservative about things like dress, hair styles, and courting. The girls were not yet allowed to court without their father's permission and approval of the young man. They were still wearing dress styles that were five years old and, though the Roaring 20s were on their way in, the girls were not allowed to cut their hair. George disapproved of the girls even reading magazines about fashion; but, as with most children, they managed to sneak the magazines they had acquired from their girlfriends into their house. They would read about current fashion, movie stars, music, and other subjects of the day. They also did odd jobs for other people in town to save money so that they could buy fabric to sew dresses that resembled those in the magazines. They knew they couldn't wear them at home, but they hid them in the attic just waiting for an opportunity to wear them. Sometimes they would sell their dresses to make money.

Lily knew she was going out on a limb inviting these boys over for dinner, but she also knew that her father was going to have to let them start courting at some point, too. She told Gracie what she had done. "Oh my, Lily. What have you done? Daddy is never going to allow this. Do you know how old those boys were? Jacob must be in his 30s. You are 17! Daddy is never going to allow that. What were you thinking? You're a child. He could be married for all you know!"

"I am not a child! Gracie, he's either going to accept it, or I am going to leave. I love Jacob and I know he's in love with me. Jacob said he is coming back for me. Daddy can't make me stay. I have had enough. You are 20 years old, Gracie. Why do you stay? Our friends have been married for two or three years already, and we cannot even court yet. It isn't right. I know Momma is gone, but he can't keep us prisoners forever," Lily pleaded with her sister.

"I get it Lily. Really, I do. But what about Emma, Johnny, and Eddie? They are still young. Are you really just going to run away from them and never look back?"

"They have Mabel, Gracie. Mabel loves us just like we're hers. She will always be there. Daddy treats her real good. Better than most people treat their negros. Heck, Daddy freed her long before he had to just because he thought it was the right thing to do, and he lets her kids live here too. I just can't take it anymore, Gracie. This is my chance. If Daddy treats Jacob badly and if he won't give us permission, then I am leaving. I promise you; I'm leaving."

"Calm down, Lily. Let's just take it one step at a time. I've got to think about this. I just don't know what to think."

The days passed and Wednesday came. Lily went down to the diner to wait for Jacob's call. At ten passed six the phone in the diner rang. It was Jacob. Janet handed the phone to Lily smiling at her, "Hello."

"Hi, Lily. Did you think I wouldn't call?" said the voice on the other end.

"Well, I hoped, but I wasn't..." Lily's voice hesitated.

"Of course, I would sweetheart. I hope you are having a good week. Do you still want Dan and I to come to dinner on Saturday? We don't want to cause you and Grace any problems. You did tell you father that you invited us, didn't you?"

"I have everything under control, Jacob. We're going to cook for you. Everyone's going to be there.

We're going to make homemade ice cream, too." Lily was excited, but nervous, too. She knew she was taking a big risk with her father. "You and Dan be here at six o'clock. We'll see you then, okay?"

"Ok, where do we come?" Lily gave Jacob directions to their home. It was a beautiful antebellum home situated on seventy-five acres in Springfield. The other Peterson brothers' farms abutted this farm. George's home was the original family home. His father left him the home because he was the eldest son.

"Sure thing, sweetie. We're looking forward to seeing you girls again. I'll be thinking of you every minute until then," said Jacob.

"Me, too, Jacob." Lily hung up the phone. A warm smile took over her face as she looked at Janet, a waitress at the diner who had known her most of her life. Lily was glowing.

"I don't think I have ever seen you look quite so happy, Lily, but have you told your father about all of this?" asked Janet. Everyone in Springfield knew about Mr. Peterson's philosophy of raising daughters.

Lily's face immediately went back to a sullen, disagreeable demeanor. "Janet, he cannot control me forever. He is going to listen to me, or he isn't going to like what happens next and that is that!" Lily picked up her handbag and walked out of the diner slamming the door behind her.

Lily and Grace spent the rest of the week preparing for their Saturday night dinner. They gathered together all the things they wanted to cook, washed clothes for their brothers and sisters to wear, and cleaned the house to a high shine. Mabel became quite curious as to what was going on that would make the girls expend so much more effort than before. "What's a goin' on with you two young'uns? I ain't never seen you a cleanin' and polishin' and cookin' like this before. You'd think tha Queen of England was a comin' to eat or somethin'. Ya'll better tell Miss Mabel what's going on right now!"

Grace and Lily looked at each other and then Grace chimed in. "Well, Mabel, you see, we have decided that it is time that Daddy accept that Lily and I are grown up and we are ready to have young men call on us. We have met two very nice young men who are coming to meet Daddy tomorrow night and ask for his permission to court us." Grace paused waiting for Mabel's reaction.

"Oh, Miss Grace and Miss Lily, I dunno about that now. You better tell him now before them men folk get here, and he goes to explodin' or somethin'. You girls can't just spring that on 'em. Oh, nah sir, nah sir, that would be a bad thing girls. You gotta do tha right thang now. You girls go on in there and you tell 'em right now, or I will!" Mabel wrung her hands in her apron nervously and shook her head back and forth. She knew no good could come from the set up these girls had planned for their father, and she had seen Mr. Peterson's temper before. He had never raised a hand to her or any of her children, who also helped around the house, but she had seen him get angry at a neighbor once who had killed a deer on his land and then tried to remove it without his permission. He became so angry that he began to shake all over and his face turned dark red. She thought for sure his heart was going to give out.

Grace and Lily looked at each other for a few minutes. "I guess Mabel is right, Lily. I mean, Daddy might really blow his head off and we wouldn't want Dan and Jacob to see that. Maybe it won't be a bad as we think?" Grace said in an inquisitive tone and an expression of doubt on her face.

"I guess that could happen. Maybe he might be willing to listen to us and give us a chance to prove that we will be okay with gentlemen callers. I guess we won't really know until we try. But now if he gets angry, I will just tell you right now, if he tells us no, I am leaving here with or without you!" Lily exclaimed.

"Ok, Lily relax. Let's go find Daddy and talk to him first before you go off halfcocked."

The girls searched through the house and found their father working at his desk in the library. It was small room with bookshelves filled with books and a small desk where their father sat each month to write out his records for the home ledger and the farm. "Hello, Daddy," Gracie said, "are you very busy now?"

"Oh, I don't guess so. What do you need my sweet girls?"

Gracie and Lily sat on a chaise just next to the desk where their father sat. George sat back in his chair and removed his glasses. "Now, you too look serious. What's going on?" It can't be that bad."

"Well, we don't think so, but you might Daddy. You see, we wanted to talk to you about courting again. We understand your feelings about it, but we are older now, as are all the children. We are older than many of our friends who are already married and have children of their own." Gracie took ahold of her father's hand and looked at him sincerely.

Lily slid to the floor just at his knees. "Daddy, we have met two very fine gentlemen who we want you to meet. We've asked them to come to dinner tomorrow night so that you can meet them (and chuckling) and give them the inquisition. Please don't say no, Daddy. Gracie and I have waited so long. All our friends make fun of us. They call us the "Spinster Petersons", because not only are we not married, but we cannot even court! It is positively humiliating, Daddy." Lily hung her head down and gazed at the floor.

George was quiet for a few minutes before he responded. "I know that I cannot keep you both at home forever, my girls. I will meet these boys and let you know, but you realize that they must meet my standards. I won't have my girls marrying just anyone. My girls deserve the best of the best! Now give your Daddy a hug and go get back to work with Mabel on dinner, I am positively famished!"

Gracie and Lily thanked their father for his change of heart, and they ran off to help Mabel finish the evening meal. They could be heard singing and laughing all through the house. The other children were surprised at the overwhelmingly happy feeling of the house that night. When they heard what their father had agreed to, the younger children were shocked but happy for their older sisters, especially Emma, who knew the outcome may be of benefit to her in the future.

CHAPTER 8

Young Hearts and New Starts

Saturday evening finally arrived, and Gracie and Lily were dressed in the prettiest new dresses they had made. Each one of their siblings had been bathed and dressed and were sworn not to get dirty before dessert! The dining room table was decorated with roses and hydrangeas from their garden. The table was as beautiful as anything they had seen in one of their magazines. They were using their mother's favorite china. The smell of roast and apple pie was circulating through the house. "My goodness girls, if those young men don't get here soon, I won't be responsible for what happens with all that yummy food in there!" declared their father.

"Oh, Daddy, they'll be here any minute," said Lily.

"Daddy, I have one other request. From now on, would you please just call me Grace? Gracie sounds so childish," implored Grace. Smiling, Lily reached over and hugged her sister.

"I think it is beautiful and so is my big sister," said Lily smiling at her father.

"Fine. I don't know how to get used to all of this growing up, but you two are so beautiful and your mother would be so proud of you both." Just then the sound of a motor came through the trees. Everyone walked outside on the front porch to watch for the vehicle to appear on the road. About three minutes later, a 1917 Dixie Flyer came up the drive toward the house.

"There they are, Daddy. There they are," exclaimed Lily.

"Kids, ya'll go on inside. We don't need ya'll getting sweaty out here. Ya'll run along inside."

In a few minutes, the men had parked the car in the drive and had walked up to the steps of the house. Dan held his hand out to shake Mr. Peterson's hand, "How do you do Mr. Peterson, I am Dan Davis? It is very nice to meet you. Thank you for the invitation to dinner tonight."

Mr. Peterson's demeanor had changed since the young men had approached the home. He was suspicious and quiet. He shook Dan's hand. "Now, which one of my daughters, young man, are you hoping to court here tonight?"

"Miss Grace, sir."

"I see. And just hold old are you, son?"

"I am 24 sir.

"Ok, that's fine." Would your father be Mr. Harvey Davis of Williamsburg?"

"Yes, sir. That is my father. My mother is June."

"Did you attend college, son?"

"Yes, sir. I attended the University of Virginia, sir."

"Well done, son. His head then turned toward Jacob. "Who exactly are you, then?"

"I am Jacob Stewart, sir. I am here at Miss Lily's invitation, sir." Jacob put his hand out to shake, but Mr. Peterson did not reciprocate. Mr. Peterson recognized the worn nature of Jacob's clothing and the noticeable age difference between the two men.

"How old are you?"

"Well, sir, I am 33, but I don't think that should…" Mr. Peterson interrupted Jacob's thought, "You have *no* authority here young man! You are entirely too old to be courting my daughter. This is unacceptable. I will not allow this happen. We will have this dinner tonight, but after tonight you will not see my daughter again, do you understand? I am only allowing this dinner to go on because my daughters have worked hard to make this special." Lily immediately stepped over to Jacob and took his hand.

"Daddy, you cannot do this. I love Jacob. I want to be with him. It doesn't matter what you say, we will be together!" Lily held on to Jacob's hand for dear life.

"Lily, you will do what I say. If you want to have this dinner, then let us go inside now, or you both can leave now. I suggest you decide now."

Mr. Peterson made his way inside toward the dining room. Grace and Dan followed behind.

"Dan, you can sit here, next to Daddy. I will sit here next to you. Please excuse me for a minute." Grace went back to talk to Lily. "Lily, come on inside and let's have our dinner. After you have eaten and had time to think about what you want to do, then you do what you want, but let's have our dinner first. Come on inside, Jacob."

The three walked inside and Grace showed Jacob where to sit. Grace and Lily went to the kitchen and returned with Mabel carrying the beautiful dinner that they had made. The dinner, for the most part was quiet. Some of the children talked to the men about the new sport of baseball and Dan's car. They asked Jacob about growing up in the mountains, since they had never been there. They wanted to know about bears and mountain lions and, most of all, snow!

Once the meal was finished, Grace and Lily helped Mabel clear the table. The children went to another room to play a game and everyone else went back to the front porch. Mr. Peterson, who liked to smoke a cigar, lit a cigar and then gazed up at the sky. "Mr. Stewart, I have nothing personal against you, sir. I want the best for my daughter, and I believe the best is not a 33-year-old man. I suspect you have story that isn't being told." He turned his head and looked at Jacob in the face again. "I do not want you to have any contact with my daughter again after tonight. She will be angry for a time, but she will forget you. Eventually, she will meet someone else closer to her age. I believe that is what is best for her. Do you understand me?" Mr. Peterson had no idea that Lily was eavesdropping from behind the front door and had heard everything. She was so angry, but tears streamed down her face.

"I do understand Mr. Peterson. I suppose if I had a daughter, I would probably feel as you do, but I would also have to wonder if I should consider the feelings of my daughter. She is almost eighteen. She will be eighteen in just a couple of months. I might have to consider whether my daughter is smart enough to make the right decision for herself, especially if she has been a good girl for her whole life."

"I want you both to leave now. Mr. Davis, you are welcome to see Grace. Mr. Stewart, good night." With that, the two men made their way to the car and drove away. Lily came out from the behind the door screaming for Jacob not to leave yet. Mr. Peterson realized that he had been overheard.

"I hate you. All you want to do is control me. Well, you cannot control me anymore. You just wait and see." Lily ran upstairs to her room slamming the door behind her.

Mr. Peterson went into this study to finish his cigar and to think. A few minutes later Grace came into the study and sat down at her father's feet. Looking up at him, "Thank you, Daddy. Thank you for allowing me to see Daniel, but I feel guilty because you won't allow Lily to see Jacob. She is going to be so angry with me."

"Well, you know it won't really be about you, darlin'; she is angry at me. She'll probably be angry with me for some time, but that is just how it has to be. I am just doing what I think is best. I didn't get a good feeling about that man. He is too old to be courting a young girl like your sister. Your sister thinks she knows the world, but she does not. You don't learn about the world in magazines. The world can be a mighty cruel place, Grace. Lily doesn't understand that. You are much more levelheaded than Lily. She is impulsive and that can get her hurt. I am just trying to protect her."

"I know you are Daddy. I love you, and she does too. She just may forget for a little while." Grace stood up and went upstairs to her room.

When Grace opened the door to her room, she found Lily packing a bag with clothes. "Where do you think you are going to go with all of that?"

"I told you that if he said no, I would leave. So, I am leaving. I am going to Norfolk to find Jacob."

"How do you think you are going to get there?"

"You and Daddy think I am stupid and that I cannot figure things out for myself, but I can. I have saved up money. It isn't that far. I have enough money to rent a room for a while. I can get a job in Norfolk. I can take care of myself. I will show him what I can do! You better not tell him either, Grace. You got what you wanted. You get Dan. Now give me this one thing, let me get away before you tell him anything. Please, Grace."

"This is a terrible idea. Daddy said he got a bad feeling about Jacob. What if he's right, Lily? I don't want anything bad to happen to you. If I help you and something bad happens, I will be responsible!"

"Nothing bad is going to happen. Jacob loves me Grace, and I love him. We are going to be together. You will see. We are going to have a great life. I will write you once I am settled and let you know how I am and where I am. Please just help me now."

"Lily, but I don't feel good about this. It scares me. Will you call Janet at the diner and let her know you are okay once you get there so that I don't have to worry?"

"Yes, okay, yes, I will call Janet. Thank you, Grace. You will see. This is going to be perfect. Jacob is perfect. I really love him, Grace."

"Well, we have to go tuck the little ones into bed now. You have to at least kiss them all good night if you aren't going to say goodbye. They won't understand you running off and not saying goodbye."

"Yes, let's go tuck them all in. Once Daddy and Mabel have gone to their rooms for the night, I will sneak out. And Grace…."

"Yes, Lily?"

"I love you, too." Lily hugged Grace as tightly as she could and kissed her on the cheek. Then the girls went to each of the other bedrooms to kiss their brothers and sister good night. They were already sound asleep. It was close to eleven o'clock by now. Lily walked back to her room to get her suitcase. She stood at the top of the stairs and looked around the house. Making a memory in her mind of what it looked like that night. She took a long, deep breath and then descended the staircase, walked out the front door, and proceeded down the road toward town. She felt free. She felt grown. She felt alive.

CHAPTER 9

Norfolk

It was a five and half mile walk into Crittenden from the Peterson farm. Lily would have to find somewhere to stay until the coach arrived at six o'clock the next morning. By the time she arrived in Crittenden, it was 3:00 a.m. and she was exhausted; her feet hurt. She decided to go to the back of St. Luke's Church and sat on the steps for a while before walking on to the coach station. As she sat on the steps, she thought about what the next few days might be like, seeing Jacob again, finding a place to live and her first job. She felt excitement and fear well up inside of her. She thought of her Momma never getting to see her leave home and become a woman. It made her sad. She was excited for the day that she might become a mother. She closed her eyes to imagine holding a baby of her own. The night was quiet except for the sound of crickets chirping. The air was cool and dry. Before she knew it, she had drifted off to sleep.

Lily was awakened by a dog licking her face. She ran toward the station hoping she had not missed it. The coach was just driving up as she arrived. She went to the ticket window, "I need a one-way ticket to Norfolk, please."

"Here you go ma'am. The coach will leave in ten minutes," reported the ticket master.

"Thank you, sir." Lily walked over and boarded the coach. Her heart was pounding with excitement. It was not a long drive from Crittenden to Norfolk. Once she arrived in Norfolk, Lily realized that she didn't know where to find Jacob other than the shipyard. Norfolk was much larger than Crittenden, and she had only been there a few times. Lily went over to the ticket master, "Do you know which way the shipyard is, sir?"

"What part of the shipyard to you want to go to, Miss? The shipyard is huge, ma'am."

"Oh, my goodness. Is there a main office?"

"Ma'am, there are many offices. It depends on what part of the shipyard you are talking about."

"Well, then, just tell me what direction I need to walk in to get to the shipyard in general. I will just have to figure it out when I get there."

"Yes, ma'am. Well, walk east down Portsmouth Road and it will take you there. You'll have to walk a good five or six miles, ma'am. Be careful, too. There can be some unseemly folks in that area. You got to watch yourself."

"Ok, I will be okay, sir. Thank you." Lily clung to her suitcase and to her dream. She struck out proudly on Portsmouth Road headed for the shipyard to find her love, Jacob Stewart. She had no idea the shipyard was so large or that there would be what seemed like thousands of people who worked there. She and her family had never done much traveling. They had gone to Richmond once to take their mother to see a doctor there before she died, and they had gone to Williamsburg to visit with their mother's sister, but other than those trips they had never been away from the farm. She was not afraid, though. She knew that she would find him and that they would be together forever.

The ticket master had been right. As Lily walked along Portsmouth Road, she came across several poor beggars in the road. Lily thought she had seen the poor in Smithfield, but they were not like these people. These people were exceptionally dirty and smelly; they were sickly and difficult for her to look at. They would jump out at her from an alley way or a doorway, which scared her. They would get into her face and beg for a piece of bread or money to buy food. Lily could smell alcohol on some of them. She told them to get away from her and to leave her alone. She could not afford to part with any of the money she had managed to save. She would need it to take care of herself if Jacob did not have enough. She wanted to be a partner to him, not just some needy wife. She had brought with her two muffins and two apples to eat along the way. Only once did she give in to one of the vagrants. There was one who had a small child, a boy who was about two years old and appeared to be malnourished. When Lily saw the boy, she felt compelled to help. So, Lily gave the boy one of her muffins and his mother an apple. She knew the boy could not survive if his mother was unwell, so she helped them both. She had less food for herself, but she felt sure that she would be fine once she found Jacob.

When Lily finally saw the shipyard in the distance, a sudden burst of energy came upon her and she ran toward the yard, but once she reached her destination much to her dismay, she found that the yard had closed early because of an accident, and no one was there. She turned around and rested against the fence. She knew that Jacob and Dan lived somewhere near the shipyard, but this area was so large, and she was exhausted. It was getting late, and she would have to find someplace for the night if she couldn't find Jacob. She started to walk down Williams Avenue to see what she could find. It wasn't long before she saw a boarding house. She went up and knocked on the door. A lady about sixty-years old came to the door, "May I help you," she said with a very pleasant smile.

"I hope so. I just got into town, and I was trying to find a friend, but I didn't find her today and I need a place to stay. Do you have a room available?" Lily tried to sound very mature; she did not want to let the lady know that she was only seventeen years old.

"Well, as it turns out I do. I just had someone check out early. I have not quite finished cleaning it up, though. The room costs five dollars a week and you get breakfast and dinner included. Is that something you can do?"

"Yes, ma'am. I hope I won't be here that long. I hope I will find my friend. How much do you need now? Oh, I can help finish cleaning up the room, if that's okay. I've been walking a long time today and I would really like to lie down."

"Well, let's start with two dollars now and we'll see how your search goes. Dinner will be ready in about thirty minutes. I will show you to your room. My name is Mrs. Cox."

"Thank you, Mrs. Cox." The two ladies went upstairs to the room. The room was larger than what Lily had expected. It had a single bed with a nightstand and a dresser, with a small bureau. There was a window, too, which looked out over a park. Lily felt at peace in knowing she had a safe place to stay while she looked for Jacob. She gave Mrs. Cox the two dollars and she excused herself. Lily threw herself across the bed and took a few minutes to let the joy of freedom sink in. She had to wonder, though, what must be going on now that everyone at home surely knew she was gone and gone forever. She prayed to God that her brothers and sisters would forgive her and that they would understand when they were older. They had Grace there to help them understand. Her Daddy was another story, though. Would he hate her for leaving? She couldn't know for sure.

Lily went down for dinner and met the other tenants of the Williams Street boarding house. There was a young man about Jacob's age who had come to Norfolk a year before to weld in the shipyard but found out that the jobs had dried up. Jimmy explained that after World War I ended, the shipyards along the East Coast were saturated merchant ships built for the war and so the country had little need for new vessels. He had gotten a job with the railroad. Jimmy told Lily that he would be glad to help her find Jacob at the shipyard after he got off work the next day.

There was also a married couple living in the house. The Brauns had moved to Norfolk about six months prior. Mr. Braun had been employed as a shoemaker at Hofheimer Shoes. Mrs. Braun worked at Hofheimer's as a bookkeeper. They seemed to be a nice couple, but quiet. Mrs. Cox's dinner was quite tasty after a long day of traveling, but Lily soon found herself tired and excused herself to her room. Lily gathered her special things together and went down the hall to the bathroom. She took her first bath as a free and independent, young woman. As happy as she felt, there was a part of her that felt scared. She was determined not to allow that feeling to take her over.

The next afternoon she waited anxiously for Jimmy to get back from work. As soon as he returned, the two headed over to the shipyard. Jimmy took Lily to the main office of the Gosport Shipyard. When they entered the office, a receptionist greeted them. "Good afternoon, may I help you?"

"I hope so, ma'am, my friend here is trying to locate a friend who she believes works here in the shipyard."

"Ok, well, is this person a friend or a spouse? We don't normally give out personal information about our employees." Responded the receptionist.

Lily moved closer to the desk, "You see, I came all this way because we've got a problem back home and I needed to let him know about it. It is very important."

"Well, this just seems a bit strange for you to come all this way to tell him something you could have told him a letter."

"Not about this. It is a sensitive matter, ma'am. I needed to see him to tell him. I came in person, but I didn't know how big the shipyard was. I guess I was a bit naive about that," said Lily smiling.

"Ok, what is your friend's name?"

"It's Jacob Stewart, ma'am."

The receptionists face immediately changed and a sort of smirk came over it. "Oh, Jacob. Jacob Stewart. Huh. Well, now, let me see. I will be back in a minute." She walked out of the room and came back a few minutes later. "Jacob has already left for the day. I spoke with my boss, Mr. Brooks, about your situation and he gave me permission to give you Jacob's address. Here is the address." Miss Richardson handed the address to Lily and gave her directions. "Good luck, Miss. I hope everything will be fine at home."

Lily and Jimmy left the office and stopped just outside of the office. "Do you want me to go with you Lily? I don't mind. That area ain't too bad. You should be safe going over there."

"Oh, you're so kind, but I think I can do it on my own. The walk will do me good. Thank you for helping me today. I will see you later." Lily began her walk toward 100 Nelson Street in excitement of seeing Jacob again. Her mind went back and forth about how she should act when she saw him again. Should she jump into his arms or play it cool like it was no big deal? She had no idea what she would do. She wished she had a mirror so that she could look to see how she looked. She took her lipstick out, put some on, and swept her hands through her hair. She ran her hands down her dress and looked it over to make sure she didn't have anything on it. She wanted to look good when she saw Jacob.

Before she knew it, she was at Nelson Street. She started walking down the street and her heart started pumping harder. The house was the third one on the right. She stopped and took a deep breath, and then she knocked on the door. Just a few seconds later the door opened, and it was Dan. "Oh my God, Lily! What are you doing here?"

"I ran away to be with Jacob. Where is he? I know he isn't at work?"

"Oh, he just went to the store, he'll be back in a few minutes. He is going to be so excited to see you. You are all he talks about. Actually, I think he was going to try to find a phone so that he could call you while he was out."

"Well, I guess he'll just be surprised when he gets home. Do you live here too, Dan?"

"Yeah, we have been living here for about a year. It isn't too bad, and it is close to work and to the market. I guess I will be looking for a new place to live soon, though. Hey, how long have you been in town? Where are you staying?"

"I got here yesterday. I got a room at a boarding house on Williams Street. I like it. The lady who owns the house is very nice. One of the men who lives there helped me find this house. He took me to the shipyard and the receptionist there gave me Jacob's address."

"Oh, Ruthie, wow, I am surprised. She usually won't tell anyone anything. She must have liked you. You said you ran away. You mean your father doesn't know where you are? He's probably out looking for you, and I bet he is angry. He probably thinks Jacob put you up to this. That cannot be good for you or for Jacob."

"No, I told him last night that if he wouldn't let me see Jacob that I was leaving. I told Grace to make him understand that he should not come after me. It would do no good."

"Grace didn't want to come with you, then?"

"Oh, Dan. No, Grace always does what she is supposed to do, but Daddy gave you permission to court her. You can go see her any time you want. I hope you will. I won't be going home." Just then the door opened, and Jacob walked in. He dropped his bags when he saw Lily sitting on the sofa. Lily jumped up and ran over to him. "Jacob! Oh, Jacob! Jacob, I thought I'd never see you."

"Oh my gosh, how did you get here? When did you get here? Oh my, I am so glad to see you. I missed you so much." Lily, Dan, and Jacob brought in the groceries, and they continued to talk. Later, Dan excused himself to his room so that Jacob and Lily could have some alone time. The couple sat on the sofa, and they talked and kissed. "I am so glad you are here. You are so brave. Your father was adamant that you not ever see me again. But I am just glad you are here and you are okay. Now, we need to figure out what we are going to do. I need some time to think about that. Is there a curfew at the boarding house?"

"Yes, unfortunately, I probably need to get going so that I can be back by dinner. When can I see you again? I know you have to work, so when can we meet?"

"Well, I happen to get off early tomorrow, so I will come to the boarding house and get you, okay? Let's go now. I will drive you back."

"Okay, that will be great." Lily was so thrilled to be with Jacob again. Jacob drove Lily back to the boarding house. Before she got out of the car, he leaned over to kiss her, "I love you, Lily. I really am so glad you came after me. I will make it all worth your bravery!"

"I love you, too, Jacob Stewart. I would go anywhere for you. See you tomorrow."

The next afternoon came quickly. Lily was so excited. She had brought one of the dresses that she and Grace made from one of the fashion magazines. She did her hair in a modern style and she made her face up. Mrs. Cox knocked on the door, "He's here to get you Lily." Lily opened the door. "Oh, my goodness, Lily, you look like a movie star. You're beautiful."

Lily walked down the stairs to the sitting room where Jacob was waiting for her. When she entered the room, his face lit up like a tree at Christmastime. Jacob stood up. He was holding a bouquet of wildflowers. "Oh, are those for me? That's so sweet, Jacob. I've never been given flowers before."

"Yes, yes, they are for you, of course. Well, I have plans for us, so we need to get going. Dan and a friend are waiting outside for us. The couple walked outside where Dan was waiting in his car along with another one of their work friends named Ted Chapman. The couple got into the backseat and Lily gazed at the beauty of the flowers. Jacob leaned up toward the driver's seat, "Ok, Dan, you know where we need to go, right?"

"Yes, sir. We are on our way."

"Where are we going Jacob?"

"Oh, no, this is a surprise. Don't you worry that gorgeous head of yours about it. You will love it. I promise." Dan drove for about five minutes before he found a place to park. Everyone got out the car and started walking.

Jacob and Lily were holding hands, and Lily was not paying attention to where they were. They went inside a building and then into a small office.

"What are we doing here? This is strange. Why won't you tell me what is going on, Jacob?"

"Because, sweetheart, it is a surprise. You will know in just a few minutes." Just then a man and woman came through a door. The man was wearing a black robe.

"Now, who here is Jacob Stewart?"

"I am, sir."

"Well, now, son, that is good. You have those papers with you?"

"I do. Here you are, sir. Everything should be as they are supposed to be."

"And who is Lily Peterson?"

Looking very puzzled, Lily said, "That's me. I am Lily Peterson."

"Very nice to meet you, ma'am. I am Judge Charles Hampton, and this is my wife, Alice. Jacob, here, has asked me to preside over your marriage today. Is that alright with you? These two gentlemen friends will serve as witnesses."

"What? Oh, my goodness, Jacob? Really, you want to marry me? Today?" She looked over at the Judge and then she looked back at Jacob. "Yes, I mean, yes, of course I will marry you today."

"Lily, I just can't wait to make you my wife and there really isn't anything to stop us now. You're here and I want you to stay with me forever. So, can we do this?"

"Oh, yes! Go ahead, Judge Hampton." So, Judge Hampton proceeded with the marriage ceremony. After the ceremony, the group went to a nearby restaurant to celebrate. Jacob and Lily ate steak and had a glass of wine, which she had never had before. "Wow, Jacob, that wine makes you feel a bit lightheaded and sleepy, doesn't it? Do you think we could go home now? I think I need a nap," asked Lily.

"Why, of course, my love." When the waitress came back by, Jacob asked her for the bill. He paid the bill, and the group went their separate ways, except for Daniel who was still living with Jacob. For the first four months of their marriage, the three would continue to live together until Daniel was able to find his own place to live.

Those first few months were both wonderful and difficult for the married couple. It was wonderful because they loved being together and difficult because money was short. The shipyard's business was still not back to full capacity and Jacob's hours had been cut back. He looked for additional work but had not yet found work. Lily offered to find a job, but Jacob did not want her to work unless it was absolutely necessary. He wanted that to be a last resort. He believed supporting the family was his responsibility.

When the couple had been married two months, Lily became concerned because she did not feel well. She had become very tired and had been sick, not being able to hold down much food. After Jacob left for work one morning, she walked back to Mrs. Cox's boarding house. Mrs. Cox had become a mother figure to her. She knocked on the door. Mrs. Cox answered the door and was pleasantly surprised to see Lily there. "Come in my girl. I am so happy to see you."

"I hope I am not bothering you this morning," Lily said, "but, I need some advice and I didn't know where to go."

"What's going on? Is everything okay with Jacob? He didn't hurt you, did he?"

"Of course, not. Why would you ask me that?"

"No reason, sometimes these shipyard boys get drunk and act crazy, that's all. What's wrong, my child?"

"I haven't been feeling well. I am tired all the time and I haven't been able to eat. I just feel sick all the time. Should I go to the doctor? Do you know one?"

Mrs. Cox smiled and laughed. "Oh, dear girl. You didn't have your mother to explain these things to you, did you?"

"No ma'am. What do you mean?"

"Honey girl, when did you have your last cycle? I am sure that you and Jacob are still on your honeymoon, dear. These things can happen rather quickly."

"What? Oh, my, you think I am…?"

"I would think so, my girl. I think we had better get you to a doctor to check you out and make sure you are healthy. When was the last time you saw a doctor?"

"I cannot remember. Daddy never took us to the doctor unless we were very sick."

"Alright then. I will call my doctor and see if we can get an appointment." Mrs. Cox walked into the next room to make the call. In a few minutes she returned. "Good news, he can see us this afternoon. I bet that husband of yours is going to very happy."

"I hope so, Mrs. Cox. It sure will be a surprise." That afternoon Mrs. Cox and Lily went to see the doctor. He confirmed that Lily was indeed pregnant and that the baby would be born seven months. He gave her some vitamins to take and told her to come back in a month for a checkup.

Lily went straight home and began to cook Jacob his favorite dinner. She planned to surprise him with the news after dinner. When he got home, she met him at the door and took his coat from him and helped him to his chair. When he sat down, she took his shoes off for him and put his slippers on his feet. "Wow, you're being very considerate today. What's going on?"

"I just know how hard you work all day, honey, and I wanted to do something nice for you today, that's all."

"Thank you, honey, that is very kind of you." He leaned over and gave Lily a kiss. "Something smells wonderful. What is it?"

"Pot roast, just the way you like it."

"Wow, I was just thinking today at work how I would love to have some roast. That is terrific."

"It won't be too much longer, and it will all be ready. I will go tell Dan." Lily went to the kitchen and gathered everything together and placed it on the table, which she had decorated with pink and blue flowers. She went to Dan's room and knocked on the door to let him know that dinner was ready. Everyone sat down and enjoyed the delicious meal. When dinner was finished Jacob and Dan cleared the table, but Lily stopped them before they started to wash the dishes. "Would ya'll come out here just a minute, please?"

"Sure," replied Dan and Jacob in unison. The two walked back out to the table where Lily had place dessert at their places on the table. It was a beautiful cake that she had iced in blue and pink icing.

"I have some news I would like to share with you both."

"Ok, are you alright? I know you've not been feeling well lately?"

"That is true; I have not been feeling to well, but…."

"Oh, okay. What is it, then?"

"Well, I am, I mean we are, having a baby." There was a silence for a few seconds.

"Really? We are? Oh, my goodness. I am going to be a dad. Oh honey, that is terrific." Jacob got up and gave Lily a tight hug and kiss. Dan jumped up from his chair and gave Lily and hug and a kiss on the cheek. He shook Jacob's hand.

"I guess I will need to find another place quick. You'll be needing that room for a nursery. I sure am happy for you both," said Dan.

"Yes, I guess so. When is the baby due, Lily?"

"Seven months. We've got six months to get ready."

Before they knew it, they were just weeks away from their baby being born. Jacob managed to find a second job so that he would have extra income to help out with the added bills. Mrs. Cox had put together a surprise baby shower for Lily with a few of her church and Eastern Star friends. Lily felt so honored and blessed to have some baby things from people she barely knew. Mrs. Cox was excited when Lily told her that her mother had been a member of the Eastern Star, so she had invited Lily to join. It gave her something to do when Jacob was at work and a way to make friends. Lily and Jacob decided to paint the nursery a pale yellow and used a green to accent since they didn't know whether they were having a boy or a girl. They had stuffed bunnies and ducks, and the crib was white. Lily thought it was beautiful.

In March 1920, Lily and Jacob welcomed Jacob Isaac Stewart III into the world. He weighed 8 pounds and 2 ounces and was 19 inches long. Mrs. Cox and Dan were there waiting to welcome him into the world. While Lily was excited, there was a part of her that was sad and a bit remorseful that her sister Grace and her father couldn't be there to share her joy, but she focused on her new family and the love she had for them.

Over the next fifteen years, Lily would have six more children: Louise, born in 1922; Lucas, born in 1923; Martin, born 1925; Jonas, born in 1926; Millicent, born in 1932; and Laura, born in 1935. The family would move from the city out to near Suffolk on a small farm in 1924. Jacob maintained a small apartment in Norfolk to live in during the week while he continued to work at the shipyard, and then he would go home to the farm on the weekends. While Lily did not necessarily care for this arrangement, it was necessary to maintain their household. Jobs were hard to come by during the Depression, so Jacob had to stay at the shipyard. The children needed to room to grow, and Lily needed land to raise food for them to eat. Mrs. Cox and the Eastern Star sisters were a good source for seeds and assistance for Lily, although she was no longer able to meet with them regularly anymore.

Life was hard for the family; they managed to keep just ahead of the bills, but they were, for the most part a happy family. However, that happiness was challenged in 1936 when Martin became ill and died. He contracted scarlet fever and died at the age of 10. Everyone in the family was devastated by the loss. Martin had been a very outgoing and affable, young boy. He loved playing baseball with his brothers and friends from school. He loved to listen to the Yankees play on the radio when his mother would let the boys have the radio in the evening. He would sit with his baseball glove and bat in hand and listen to every detail of the game. He loved everything about the game. Once he was gone, no one could bear to listen to the games for quite a while. Hearing Babe Ruth's name would bring a tear to their eyes.

It was also about this time that Jacob began to have some health problems. He began to have disabling stomach pain and, at times, would cough up blood. The doctor told him that he had ulcers. Because of their poor economic condition, Jacob would not do anything about his condition, saving the money for the family. With the family separation, Jacob had also begun to allow his eyes (and hands!) to wander. Sometimes, he would skip his weekend with his family, to go to bars and pick up women. He could often be found in the office of the shipyard flirting with the ladies in the office. There were rumors about him and other women floating around the shipyard constantly.

The rumors did make it back to Lily and she confronted her husband. They would have terrible arguments about these rumors. Lily would threaten Jacob. She would tell him that she was going to go to his supervisor and tell him that Jacob was having an affair with women at the shipyard. Jacob would call her bluff, though, because he knew she would not risk him losing his job because that would hurt the children. He knew she would never do that.

Lily would get very angry with Jacob, so angry that she would hit him with whatever she could put her hands on. Jacob tried to keep his temper at bay, but on a few occasions, he was not successful. Lily learned how to push his buttons, much like his mother had done. On one occasion, Lily had gone into Norfolk to meet Mrs. Cox. Lucinda was helping Lily with finding a job for Louise as a sitter. Louise, who was almost fifteen, loved children and wanted to become a teacher. Lily thought that a job babysitting would help her make some money to save toward her education and give her some experience. Lucinda and Lily were going to meet for lunch to talk about some families who were looking for help. As Lily was walking toward the restaurant, which was off Williams Street, she happened to see a woman come out of one of the offices by the entrance to the shipyard. The woman was dressed beautifully. She had on a suit that looked like it must have cost a hundred dollars and her hair was perfect, not a hair out of place. Lily watched to see where she was going. The woman walked just around the corner to a car that was waiting. Lily thought to herself that the car looked familiar. Then she realized when she looked closer, that it was Jacob's car. The lady got into the car and leaned over and kissed the driver, then the car drove away. Lily was infuriated.

Just a few minutes later, Lucinda met up with Lily and the two went on to lunch. Lily told Lucinda what she had witnessed. Lucinda advised Lily to talk to Jacob as soon as she could about what she had seen because she didn't need to stew on it, but Lucinda also told her to keep her head and not let her anger get the better of her. They finished their discussion of Louise's prospects for employment with Lucinda promising to give reference for Louise to two of the families. They paid their bill for lunch and parted ways. Lily then walked to Jacob's apartment.

Upon her arrival to the apartment, Lily was horrified to find Jacob coming out of the apartment with the woman she had seen him pick up. "What is this, Jacob," said Lily?

"It isn't what you think, Lily," said Jacob.

"It never is, is it Jacob," retorted Lily?

"Uh, well, I don't know what all of this is about, so I guess I will be going now. I will call you later," said the mystery woman?

"Not if you know what's good for you, you won't!" Lily walked into the apartment and went into the kitchen and got a knife out of the drawer. "I suggest you get out of the here, "pointing the knife toward the woman.

"Lily, what do you think you're doing? Have you lost your mind? Put that down!"

"You better get her out of here right now! So, what are you going to do, add wife number three? It's bad enough you got two wives. Yeah, you think I didn't know about wife number one? The one you didn't bother to divorce! Yeah, I know all about her, Jacob."

"You'd better go now. I am sorry about this."

"Yeah, you got a lot going on, Jacob. Good luck." The other woman walked away.

"Now, Lily, you give me that knife. You don't need to act like this. Let's sit down and talk." Just then a sharp pain shot through Jacob's stomach, and he doubled over on the sofa. He was breathing hard and writhing in pain.

"Jacob…Jacob…are you alright? What can I do?" Lily put the knife down and went over to see about her husband. As she sat down next to Jacob on the sofa, Jacob came up with his arm and back handed Lily across the face sending her onto the floor.

"Don't you ever threaten me again, woman, and don't you ever embarrass me in front of another person. I don't care who it is. What I do is my business. You keep your ass at the house that I bought for you and I pay for. Don't you ever come here again. Do you understand me?"

Lily did not answer. Jacob went over and pulled her head up by her hair. Her left cheek and eye were turning black and blue, and her eye was swelling shut. "Well, look at that. Aren't you the pretty one! You should not have made me do that. You keep your butt at the house, and this won't happen." Leaned down, looking her in her face. "You got that, miss priss?"

Lily looked him directly in the eye, "Yeah, I got that." As much chaos as Jacob had created, Lily was not innocent. She could be cold, brooding over her perceived injustices in her marriage. She hated Jacob for failing as a father and a husband, albeit an illegal one.

As each one of his boys became of age, they moved to Norfolk to get jobs and help out with the expenses of the household. Jacob III, Lucas, and Jonas were all living with their father by 1944. Each one of the boys got jobs wherever they could. Jake got a job working in an auto garage; Lucas worked in a barber shop; and Jonas worked in a grocery store. On pay day, the boys would go home and give their mother most of their money to help her out and keep just a little for themselves to go out and have fun.

As World War II neared each one of the boys enlisted into the military to fight for their country. Jake went into the Army while Lucas and Jonas signed up for the Navy. The day they each left for boot camp was a terrible day for their mother. Lily could hardly bare it. After they left, she went to her room and did not come out for 2 days. The rest of the children could hear her sobs through the door. Louise would cook food for her and place it on a tray and leave it outside her door.

Lucas enlisted in the Navy in 1942 and he was sent to serve in the Pacific. He served in several operations in the South Pacific before leaving active duty and returning home in 1945. He also had gotten married, which surprised everyone in the family because Lucas had always been quite shy. He had met a young woman when in training in New Jersey and had fallen in love. They got married during one of his leave sessions. Lucas couldn't wait to get back home to her. Her name was Angela. Unfortunately, Lucas was haunted by the things he had seen in war and by the things he had been called to do in war. He had terrible nightmares and flash backs. He tried to hold it in and deal with it himself, but it only got worse. It resulted in Lucas taking his own life, leaving behind a wife and small child.

By that time, too, Jacob's stomach problem had become serious. He was weak and thin, but he kept working. On the morning of July 5, 1948, Dan went by Jacob's house in Norfolk to see if he wanted to go over to the diner for breakfast and catch up. When he got to the house, he noticed all of the curtains were still drawn, something that was unusual for Jacob. He always pulled the curtains opened when he got up in the morning. Dan knocked on the door but got no answer. He knocked three times and still got no answer. He tried to see if he could see through the curtains but could not. He knew Jacob was there because his car was there. When he still got no answer, he decided to call the police.

The police arrived in about five minutes. Dan told them what he had done and that this was not typical behavior for Jacob. The police called out loudly for Jacob to open the door and they knocked very loudly on the door. There was no answer. With no response, they then broke open the door. When they entered the home, there was no one in the living room or kitchen area. They walked to Jacob's bedroom and found him on the bed dead. Dan became quite upset and had to leave the room. The police called for an ambulance.

After Dan composed himself, he drove out to Lily's house to tell her what happened. He knew that this was going to be the most difficult thing he had ever done. Lily had become like a sister to him and Jacob, a brother. When he got to the farm, he walked up to the door as Lily was coming out to get some wash off the clothesline. "Well, hi there, Dan, what brings you out my way today?" Lily said with a bright smile.

"Oh, I need to…" he began to stammer. Lily could tell something was terribly wrong and she went right over to Dan and put her arms around him.

"Dan, what is wrong?"

"It's Jacob, Lily," he said whimpering.

"What? What about Jacob, Dan? Is he out whoring around again?" She paused thinking for a minute. "Oh, no, you don't mean something has happened to Jacob. What has happened to Jacob, Dan?"

"He was. I went over to the house this morning to take him to breakfast. I knocked on the door, but he didn't answer. I had to call the police. We found him…I am sorry, Lily. I am so sorry."

"What? Oh my God! No! No!" The children could hear a commotion going on outside and they began to come out of the house.

"What's going on, Momma? Is something wrong with Daddy, Momma?" asked Jonas.

"Kids, come on out here. Come on, all of ya. Mr. Dan and I need to talk to ya." Lily said to the children. Each of the children filed out of the house and out into the yard in front of their mother and Dan Davis. "Dan went over to your Dad's house this morning and your Dad didn't answer the door, so he had to call the police. When they got in the house, they found your dad dead."

"What happened, Mr. Dan? Do you have any idea," asked Laura, who was thirteen years old.

Dan said, "Sweetheart, I don't know, but I know that in the last day or so, your daddy's stomach had been hurting him very badly. That is one reason I had gone over to take him to eat. He had not been eating very much because his stomach had been hurting."

Dan and the family went inside, and he helped Lily take care of dinner that night and getting everyone taken care of. The next day, he went with Lily to the funeral home to make arrangements for Jacob's services. They planned a small, graveside service to be held at the city cemetery. Over the next few days, Mrs. Cox, Dan, the ladies of the Evening Star made their way to the Stewart home. Friends assisted the family with food and funds for the services and even clothing for the children.

Lily was having a very difficult time having lost both a son and a husband with in just a few of months of each other and her daughter living in a children's home. She had become depressed. She found it difficult to perform her normal routine. The children were having to do more and more of the chores around the house. Finally, Louise decided to call Mrs. Cox for help. Mrs. Cox was glad to help. She came to the house and took Lily out in her car for a drive. Lily was able to open up and talk to Mrs. Cox about her feelings about the past six months and how losing her son and husband made her feel. Mrs. Cox shared with Lily that she had experienced the same thing and that she had opened her boarding house just after losing her son in World War I as a way to interact with others and provide an income for her. She suggested that Lily think about finding a job since the children were old enough to care for themselves, except for Laura who needed some help because she had contracted polio and needed some assistance with her physical limitations.

Lily thought it was a good idea and decided to look for a job the next day. When the children had all left the house for school, she set out with a list of places to look for a job. When she entered the second place on her list, she had a sense that this would be the place for her, but that her children would not approve. It was her children's school. There was an advertisement for a cook in the cafeteria. Lily loved to cook, and she couldn't imagine anything better than cooking for children. She was interviewed first by the school principal and then by the cafeteria manager. She felt very confident when she left, but she worried that there were more qualified candidates who had applied, so she was uncertain. She did not tell her children about the job possibility, so she returned home and stayed quiet.

In two days, Lily was in the kitchen baking a cake for an Eastern Star event when the telephone rang. When she answered it, it was the cafeteria manager informing her that the job was hers if she wanted it. Lily was excited and nervous. She gladly accepted the job and anxiously waited for the children to get home from school. She decided to make a big fried chicken dinner with all of their favorite side dishes and a chocolate cake for dessert. The house smelled warm and yummy.

When the children entered the house, they knew something was going on. Their mother was beaming. "Hey, Momma, what is going on?" asked Laura.

"I will tell you at dinner, honey."

"You can't just tell us now, Momma?" said Millie?

"Well, we need to wait on Louise and the others to get here. They're all coming in from Norfolk tonight to eat with us. We are all going to be together as a family tonight."

"Okay, Momma," said Millie, "That sounds nice."

Once all the children were there and sitting around the table, Lily stood at the head of the table and announced that she had accepted the job at the school. She had expected discontent from her audience, but instead she got complete acceptance and joy from her family. They were supportive of her. She was relieved.

CHAPTER 10

A New Chapter

After a few months of working, Mrs. Cox talked to Lily about doing some volunteering with her Eastern Star group at the local hospital. This was something that Lily had always wanted to do. Having a child with polio, she knew what it was like to have a child with an illness and how difficult that could be, particularly during the holidays. She, Laura, and Millie made a few batches of cookies, and she went with Mrs. Cox and a few other ladies and went to the hospital to the children's ward the day during the Thanksgiving holidays to pass out the cookies and some other gifts to the children. It was a very fulfilling time for Lily.

There were other volunteers there, too. There was a group of Odd Fellows, who were volunteering that day as well. There was one particular member who caught Lily's attention. He looked to be about 40-years old. He had dark brown hair and blue eyes. He had noticed Lily, too. Within a few minutes, the two found themselves in the same room visiting the same child. Lily found this man, Paul, to be very endearing, sweet, and kind. They both sat at the bed of the child, Abbie, a little girl who was suffering from polio. Lily talked to Abbie about her daughter Laura and how she was doing with her polio. Paul seemed to listen intently to every word Lily said.

When Lily left Abbie's room, Paul walked over to her, "that was wonderful what you said to Abbie. It seemed to make her feel better knowing that she would get better and be able to go back to school and have a good life, even if she has to have braces on her legs. You helped her. It was very nice."

"Oh, it was nothing. Just our experience. Children just need comfort in knowing their life doesn't have to be over. But you did really good with her too. Little girls need to hear from a male figure, too."

"Oh, you think so. I don't know. I have never been married or had children. I have just been around my nieces and nephews some. I like children, though. Your husband is very lucky to have such a great wife like you."

"Well, my husband is gone. He passed away a few months ago."

"Oh, my goodness, I am sorry. I shouldn't have…. I have stuck my foot in my mouth. I am always…. I am sorry really. Oh, I am Paul, Paul Clarke, by the way."

Lily smiled at him. "Paul, I am Lily Stewart. You didn't do anything wrong. Don't apologize. It's fine." The two new friends walked together out of the hospital talking about themselves and getting to know each other. Before they knew it, the two found themselves holding hands and standing in front of a motel. Standing face to face, Lily and Paul embraced and began to kiss. Passion wrapped around them like smoke in a bar room.

"Lily, do you want me to go…"

"Yes…" Paul walked over to the lobby of the motel room and got a room. For the next two hours the couple enjoyed sexual passion. Paul had never known a woman quite like Lily. Although, he was no virgin, his sexual experience was limited, and Lily was more passionate than he had experienced. He almost felt inadequate and insecure. Lily tried to assure him otherwise.

They planned to meet again for their volunteer time the following week. Before they knew it, months had passed and the two had become quite serious and Lily wanted to introduce Paul to her family. Lily and Paul were ready to take their relationship to a more permanent level, and Lily needed to let her family in on her decision.

Once again, Lily prepared a huge meal and called all the family together. Once everyone was seated around the table, Louise said, "Momma, there is an extra plate here, is Dan coming for dinner?"

"No, not tonight, but I should have him over soon. I have someone else coming that I would like you to meet."

"Who is it, Momma?" asked Millie

"Well, if you will just wait a minute, you will find out sweet girl." Just then Paul walked in the room. Lily walked over and grabbed Paul's hand. Just then, Millie looked at her mother's hand and noticed something.

"Momma, what's that on your hand? Is that a ring? Where is Daddy's ring? Momma?"

"Children, this is Paul Clarke. We met while I was volunteering at the hospital. He was there volunteering too. We've been seeing each other for a while, and now Paul has asked me to marry him." The was a dead silence in the room. The children stared at each other and then they looked at Paul and their mother. Millie burst into tears and ran from the table to go to her room. Loiuse stood up and hugged her mother.

"Momma, if this makes you happy. Then I will be happy."

"Thank you. Yes, honey, I will write to Jake and Jonas. I appreciate the support and you will see. We'll be happy."

Paul looked at the girls, "I love your Momma. All I want is the best for all of you. I promise to do my best to give you and your Momma what you need."

Louise retorted, "Well, all my Daddy did was give her a heartache, so I expect you better be keeping your word, sir, or you'll have all of us to answer to."

"Louise Anna Stewart! You should not talk about your father that way! Ever! He provided food, clothing, and a home for you and you should respect that. Don't ever talk about your father that way in my presence again."

"Mother, you think that we kids did not see how he hurt you, but we did. We knew about all of it. We hurt because you hurt. We couldn't do anything to change it and that hurt us more. Don't be so oblivious!"

Lily and Paul decided to elope rather than spend money on a wedding. They drove to nearby Williamsburg and got married by a justice of the peace and spent the night at one of the historic bed and breakfast hotels.

CHAPTER 11

Jonas

At the time of his father's death, Jonas Stewart had returned home from serving his time in the Navy. He had served in the Pacific during World War II and had been fortunate to not have suffered any physical injury. When he returned home, he had wanted to find work and settle down, but unfortunately, he had found that to be impossible. Norfolk was suffering the effects of the Great Depression and a housing shortage. Jonas spent several months searching for work before he determined it was hopeless and decided to enlist into the Army after hearing from a friend that new technology in communications was going to lead the way for the Army and that he might be able to get in on the ground of a great opportunity for training.

Jonas left for boot camp right after his father's funeral. He would be stationed at Fort Monmouth, New Jersey. Jonas fell in love with his career. He studied everything he could about communications and what new technologies were being developed. He was a good soldier and advanced quickly. He was smart and able to quickly learn what was required to do his job. Because of his abilities, his superiors often called on him to assist in training lower ranking soldiers, something that Jonas enjoyed doing.

He was also quite popular with his fellow soldiers. He was friendly and outgoing. He enjoyed telling stories, and he loved a good joke. On one their weekends off, the soldiers would go into Eatontown to go to a local club to blow off steam from their week. On one particular weekend in 1948, Jonas observed a young lady who had come in with a couple of girlfriends. She was gorgeous. She was raven haired with ivory skin and piercing blue eyes.

He had never seen such a beauty before. "Why don't you just go over and talk to her, Jonas?" said Matthew, one of Jonas' friends.

"Oh, I don't know. What would a gal like that want with a joker like me?"

"Stop it, ya big goof! You're a great catch for a gal like her. You're just what she's looking for…a paycheck!" and he started laughing like a fool. Jonas hit Matthew on the arm and took a drink of his beer, and then sat it down on the table. He walked over to where the girls were standing.

"Excuse me, ma'am. My friends and I were wondering if you gals would like to come over and join us. We're just in town for the evening and don't know anyone here. Maybe ya'll could tell us what goes on around here," said Jonas looking at the raven-haired girl.

Smiling back at him, she said, "Well, hello, that is a very nice offer, but how do we know you guys aren't crazy or something? We don't know you. We've never seen you around here before." The other girls began to giggle.

"Well, ma'am, I guess you don't really. You'll just have to trust me when I tell you. We are all Army boys. We're stationed at Fort Monmouth. The Army tries hard to weed out the crazies you know."

"Well, then, Army boys. I guess that's okay, then. Girls let's go join them. My name is Anna, and this is Madge and Sonya."

The girls joined the boys that night and the crew became a regular group for some time, meeting on weekends to dance or go to movies. As time went on, Jonas and Anna became more and more of a couple. They would separate themselves from the group to talk. Eventually, they started seeing each other at other times without the rest of the group. It wasn't long before Jonas told Anna that he was in love with her.

"Well, now, Jonas, you don't really know me that well. I mean you do, but there is something that I haven't told you about myself; and it may change the way you feel," Anna turned her back and waited for Jonas to respond. She thought he would dump her immediately just for having a secret.

"Oh, it can't be as bad as all that. What is it, honey? Are ya broke? So, am I," smiling he put his hand on her shoulder and turned her around so that he could look into her eyes.

"No, Jonas. You see, I have been married before and I have a child, a son. He's two and a half years old. The marriage didn't last, and it has been just me and Jack for a year now. I will understand if you want to walk away." She lowered her eyes expecting to hearing bad news from Jonas.

"Well, that is something, isn't it? You were mighty young to be married, so I suppose you could say it was just that you were too young to be married. I can understand that. I've seen it happen to my own friends. But Jack, he has to be considered now in everything. He has to be taken care of, and if you'll have me, I will treat him as my own. I love you, Anna, and I will love him, too." Anna melted into Jonas' arms surprised that he had not rejected her. A great sense of relief came over her.

Over the next month, Jonas, Anna, and Jack spent much time together. Go to the park and swinging was Jack's favorite thing to do. Jack seemed to take to Jonas, but then he had never really known his real father. By the end of the year Jonas and Anna were married and living in an apartment on base, close to Jonas' job. Anna still visited with her girlfriends in town, but she made friends with a few of her neighbors, too. Sometimes, Jonas and Anna would go to the NCO Club on base to drink and dance. They had many friends and loved entertaining. They seemed to settle into a good life together quickly.

In May 1949, Anna announced to Jonas that they would be expecting a baby soon. Jonas was so happy. He loved children and was looking forward to being a daddy. He doted on Anna. Cooking for her, helping with cleaning and laundry, but things weren't changing for Anna like he had hoped. She didn't seem to be settling into a family lifestyle. Even pregnant, she still socialized as much as she ever had. He often came home to find a friend watching Jack, while Anna had gone to the NCO club with another friend. She was letting the cleaning and the laundry go for many days undone. Jonas was quite concerned. This was not the behavior of a mother that he was accustomed to.

In December, at about 24 weeks of pregnancy, Anna went into labor. Jonas and Anna were terrified that they would lose their baby. He rushed Anna to the Army hospital. She was immediately taken back while Jonas was left in the waiting room to worry. About an hour and half later, the doctor emerged from behind the double doors. "Sergeant Stewart, I am Doctor Martin Jones. I have been caring for your wife. I am pleased to let you know that you have a little girl, but she is very premature, as you are aware, and she is very small and fragile. We are watching her and caring for her, but I have to tell you that the next several hours and days will be critical for your little girl. You need to pray."

"Oh, I sure will be, doctor. May I see my wife, sir?"

"Let us clean her up and a nurse will come and get you when she is presentable." Thirty minutes seemed like hours to Jonas. He couldn't wait to see Anna. He walked down the hall until he came to a large window. He turned to look in and he found himself standing at the nursery. At that time, a nurse was bringing little, tiny baby girl Stewart in. He tapped on the window to the get the nurse's attention. Her eyes lit up and she shook her head "yes". Jonas was beaming from ear to ear at the sight of his little baby girl. Just then, another nurse tapped Jonas on the shoulder. "You may see your wife now, Sergeant Stewart."

Jonas walked into Anna's room. She was sitting up and looked like she was ready to go shopping, like nothing at all had happened. As soon as she made eye contact with Jonas, though, she began to sob. "Our little girl! Jonas, she has to make it. She just has to!"

"It's okay honey. The doctors and nurses are taking real fine care of her right now, and they will keep doing it until we can take her home. Right now, we need to name her, so she has a good, strong name. Do you have any thoughts on that?"

"I have always loved the name Susan. Would that be okay for her first name?"

"I love it. Now, for her middle name…How about Cecily, after my grandmother?"

"Oh, that sounds so beautiful together…Susan Cecily Stewart. Yes, that is her name. Go, go tell the nurses so they can put it on her crib. Oh, that's wonderful, Jonas."

Little Susan spent six weeks in the hospital at Fort Monmouth before she was allowed to go home. On that day Jonas brought Jack with him to pick up the girls from the hospital. Jack was not quite sure what to make out of this little creature that looked like a doll. He was very excited to see his mother. He jumped into her lap in the wheelchair and threw his arms around her neck and said, "Mommy, I missed you so much." Jonas was smiling until he noticed that Anna removed Jack's arms and fussed at him for jumping on her tummy. She did not smile at him. She did not tell him that she loved him or missed him. Jonas was worried.

As the days and weeks followed, Jonas kept an eye out for Anna. He often found her dazing into space, not aware of what Jack was doing or if Susan was crying. She wasn't getting dressed either. She would wear her nightgown all day. He didn't know what to do.

After a month of putting up with this, Jonas went to the base doctor to talk about what was going on with Anna. He met with Dr. Jones, who told him that Anna's behavior was not that odd for new mothers, that they often see women with the "baby blues", particularly because women get so little sleep in those first few months. He told Jonas to wait it out and that it would get better. He was right.

Normalcy returned in about four months. Anna seemed to back to her old self. She was happy, charming, and back to socializing with her friends. Life went on and the couple were transferred from one Army base to another. It wouldn't be until six and half years later that they would find out that they were expecting baby number two. This time, however, the pregnancy went on without a hitch. Another precious little girl for the Stewart household was born at Aberdeen Proving Grounds, Maryland in October 1956. This little beauty was named Anna Katherine Stewart, but they decided to call her Anna Kate. Her older sister, Susan, and brother Jack were ecstatic about the new baby. Susan would sit for hours just looking at her. Jack liked to read to her between his rounds of baseball with his friends.

But all was not completely well in the Stewart household. Life had become quite stressful. Anna did not like being stuck at home all day with three children to tend to, especially Susan, who required the most help. She had not made friends at the base like she had in New Jersey. She frequently sullen and moody and took her moods out on everyone around her. Jonas tried to be patient, but Anna had learned how and when to push his buttons and there would often be shouting. Sometimes, Anna would get so upset that she would grab whatever was near and throw it at Jonas. It was during one of her tirades that she threw a bookend that swept just by the head of

Susan. This was the line Jonas could not cross. He scooped up his two girls, grabbed some clothes and told Anna that she needed to be out of the house in five days or he would be back with an MP to have her removed. He left with the children and never looked back.

CHAPTER 12

Special Needs & Special Joys

Because of Susan's premature birth, she encountered some serious developmental issues. Her IQ was well below the normal range, and she was slow to crawl, walk, and speak. Despite that, she was a very happy child with beautiful, dark-brown, curly hair and dimples. She had inherited her mother's blue eyes and ivory skin.

After leaving Anna, Jonas sued her for divorce and gained sole custody of the girls. He was transferred to Fort Gordon, Georgia. Because of his inability to keep house and his frequency of deployment to other bases, Jonas had to reconsider what was best for his girls. He felt would be best if they lived, for a little while, with his mother and Paul. Lily and Paul were more than willing to help Jonas for a little while. When Lily first set eyes on her granddaughters, she was immediately smitten. They were not rich people who could shower them with things, but they had a whole lot of love to share.

Jonas talked to his mother about Susan and how he wanted her to be treated the same as Anna Kate. He did not want Susan to be treated as inferior to her sister simply because she was slower in her learning. Lily agreed and promised her son that she would work with Susan to read and write and to do math. He took the girls to show them their room. He stayed for a few minutes and then left them there to play. He had bought each girl a special doll for their trip. Once he was out of the room, he hugged his mother and thanked her for her help. He brushed a tear from his eye and said, "Goodbye, Momma. I love you. I will be in touch soon when I get back to the base. Tell my girls I love them." Lily and Paul stood on the front porch of their small, shanty house and waved goodbye as Jonas drove away.

Although Jonas never intended to leave his girls for long, the months turned into years. He did come to visit a few times a year, but he was moving from base to base and he was moving up in ranks. He was constantly being called on to go to this base or that to install one thing, fix another, or train troops on new systems. He loved his work, but he missed his girls terribly. Jonas was successful, but lonely.

Unfortunately for Lily, though, Jonas did not share his success with his mother and children. He did not send money to her for their clothing or support during the time that the girls were with her. His mother and Paul often struggled to pay their bills. Lily sewed many of the girls' dresses, but her eyesight grew bad and sewing became more and more difficult. They wore the same clothes until they were worn completely through.

In July 1960, while stationed at Fort Gordon, Jonas was shopping in the Commissary. He was waiting in the line to check out and was reading a magazine as he waited. He finally got to the front of the line when he looked up and saw a beautiful site. She was about five foot five, one hundred pounds and auburn haired. Jonas smiled, "Excuse me, ma'am, I was a bit distracted. I didn't mean to hold you up." He quickly put his items up for her to start checking him out. He couldn't help but keep looking at her and smiling. She was a pleasant site. When she finished and he paid, she handed him his receipt rather than placing in the bag as she normally did. "Thank you, Sergeant Stewart. I hope you have a nice day."

"Thank you, ma'am. I hope you do too." Jonas left the Commissary and went to his truck. Once he got home and unloaded his groceries, he glanced at the receipt and noticed there was something written on the back of it. When he flipped it over, she had written her name and number on the receipt. Jonas' heart started pounding and he was beaming. It read, "DINAH MARTIN 555-6768"

Within a day or so, Jonas began to think about Dinah. He had written her number on his phone book in case he decided to call. Friday was coming soon, and Jonas didn't feel like sitting at home alone. He picked up the phone and called his girls first. He spoke to each girl for three or four minutes about what was going on with them, about schoolwork, and whether they had been good for their grandmother. He told them that he would see them at Christmas and that he had gotten them some special things. During his conversation with the girls, both Susan and Anna Kate asked about seeing their mother and Jack. Jonas told them that he didn't think that would be possible. He didn't have the heart to tell them that he didn't even know where they were. He had heard that Anna had gone back to live with her parents for a short time, but he had no idea how to get in touch with her. Both girls ended their conversations with their daddy in tears. Jonas was devastated.

Hoping to cheer himself up, he decided to call Dinah. When she answered the phone, Jonas' heart leaped up into his throat. He had to clear his voice a few times before he could speak without stuttering. Dinah had a very sweet-sounding voice on the phone which made him feel more at ease. They talked for quite a while before he asked her what she was doing on Friday. She told him that she had no plans. They planned to go to a movie and to dinner. Jonas was so excited.

On that Friday, Jonas drove over to the address Dinah had given him. When he arrived, her house was a small, white house with black shutters and there was a small garage in the back. He walked up to the door and rang the bell. As soon as the bell rang, he could hear the voices of children coming from inside. Dinah opened the door and invited Jonas in. He stood inside the door in a small living room. Two boys were sitting on the floor watching television. Dinah said, "Jonas, these are my two boys—Christopher who is twelve and Marcus who is nine. Ok boys, remember what I told you--bed at nine-thirty. No candy or snacks and you better behave for Mrs. Kendrick, or you'll get it when I get home. Understand?" Both boys looked and her and nodded "yes".

The couple ate dinner and then attended a showing of "Inherit the Wind" at the local movie theater. At dinner, they enjoyed getting to know each other and talking about their children. "I have never met a man who had custody of his children before. That is quite astounding. You are so brave and wonderful for taking your girls like that, Jonas."

"I just did what I knew I had to do. Their mother was never going to be a good mother to them. She just never seemed to bond with them. It wasn't normal, you know?"

"Sure, I have heard about that happening to some women."

"I am gone so much. I just wouldn't be fair to them. They are much better off with my mother."

"You're lucky to have her. She must be a wonderful mother."

"She raised seven of us on her own since my father lived primarily in Norfolk because of work. It was a hard life, but it was a good life."

As dinner was winding down, the two seemed to hang on every word. As they walked together, now holding hands, emotions began to whelm up inside of them both. Before they knew it, they were kissing. They got into the car and drove back to Dinah's house. Jonas walked to her to the door."

"Do you want to come inside?"

"Sure, just for a little while. I don't want to wake the boys."

"Oh, that is okay. They both sleep like rocks."

Dinah made them both a drink and then they sat on the couch together. The television was on, but they didn't notice. One thing led to another and before they knew it, they were in Dinah's bedroom. "I don't want to do anything wrong here. Are you sure about this?"

"Don't talk, Jonas, just come here…." A new romance had blossomed for Jonas. In every available moment, he was with Dinah. They started doing everything together. He loved spending all of his extra time her Dinah and her boys. And it wasn't too long before talk of making the relationship a permanent one also began. Jonas wanted his family back together. He loved Dinah and her boys, and he wanted his girls. If they were married, he could have his family back.

However, it was not going to be quite that simple. Dinah failed to tell Jonas that she was still legally married. One evening when the couple did not have plans to meet, Jonas decided he would surprise Dinah and the boys with a pizza dinner and a movie. He went to the PX and bought some flowers, a pizza, chips, and some drinks, and then he drove over to Dinah's home. As he arrived at the home, he saw Dinah and a man coming out of the house together and two embraced tightly before the man kissed her and left. Jonas was instantly enraged. What was going on? He did not believe her to be this type of woman who would run around with multiple men, and they had been together so much, he couldn't imagine when she would have the time. He parked his truck and rushed up to the door yelling at them. "What is going on here Dinah? Who was that man? What were you doing letting him kiss you like that? I ain't gonna be lied to, Dinah. What kind of fool do you think I am? I ain't gonna be taken advantage of by no hussy, I can tell you that!" and Jonas looked at her in the face with anger.

"Calm down, Jonas. Calm down, I can explain. It isn't what you think," said Dinah.

"Well, then, I guess you better start explaining?"

"Come inside and I will explain, but you have to calm down. I am not going to talk to you while you are yelling at me."

"Let me get somethings out of my truck and I will be right there." Jonas walked back to his truck to get the things he had bought, and then went back to the house. He went inside and took the items to the kitchen where Dinah was waiting. The two sat down at the kitchen table to talk.

"Jonas, that was my husband, David. He had come by the see the boys for a few minutes. Our divorce was final today. He's leaving town and he was just saying goodbye. That's all it was."

"You mean you've been married all this time we've been seeing each other? You didn't tell me. I just assumed that...."

"Would it have really made a difference, Jonas? David has been gone for over a year now. There was no chance of us getting back together. Was it really that wrong?"

Jonas smiled. "You're right about it not really making a difference, but I would have rather known. I told you that I was divorced. You knew about my situation with Anna. I never kept you in the dark about my life."

Dinah took his hand and looked at him closely and said, "I am very sorry, Jonas. It was not intentional. I thought it would be over before now. Forgive me?"

"I guess so. You're so darn cute. I cannot stay mad at you. Love you!"

In December 1960, Jonas, Dinah, and her sons all drove to his mother's. As they drove into the yard, he could see Susan, now 11, and Anna Kate, 6, playing in the yard. As soon as they saw the car, they dropped their jumping ropes and ran over to their daddy's car. "Daddy, daddy, daddy," Susan exclaimed, "You're here! You're here!" Anna Kate stood beside her big sister with a giant smile on her face. Both girls were terribly dirty. Their dresses were torn and covered in dirt from the yard.

"My goodness, my girls, look at you two! You are filthy. Come give your daddy a kiss!" Both girls jumped on top of their daddy to kiss him. Dinah and the boys began to giggle. Just then Susan looked over at them.

"Daddy, who's that?" asked Susan.

"Oh, oh, yes! This is Dinah and Christopher and Marcus. Let's go inside and I can tell you what is going on." Just then Lily and Paul appeared at the door.

"Jonas, you should've called and told us you were coming. I would've cooked something special. Ya'll come in now and sit down. You've been driving a long time. You must be exhausted." Everyone went inside the small, shanty like house. Dinah and her sons were not accustomed to such poverty, but they just smiled and sat down on the sofa. Susan and Anna Kate sat down beside the chair where their father sat. Susan reached over and took his hand. "Now, tell me, what brings you home out of the blue like this, Jonas."

"Well, Momma, Dinah and I are getting married. I want my family together, so I came to get the girls and take them back with us."

"Oh, I see. I never expected that. Well, we can have dinner tonight and ya'll can sleep tonight and I have the girls already to go in the morning. Will that be, okay?"

"Sure, Momma, that sounds just fine. Let me get everything in from the car so we can figure out where everyone is going to sleep." The family ate fried chicken for dinner and talked about how Jonas and Dinah met, about her boys, and their plans for the future. Susan and Anna Kate could not wait for the next day to come. As soon as the sun was up, the girls were dressed and waiting at the door with their small suitcase ready to go back to Georgia. The air was filled with hope and excitement of what was to come.

As they drove back to Fort Gordon, the children sang songs, played games and took turns sleeping. Susan and Anna Kate imagined that they were princesses on a grand adventure to a new kingdom called Gordon. It was such great fun for girls who had not been on a trip for a very long time.

Broken Hearts
& Broken Dreams

The family quickly settled into their base housing and into their schools. Jonas was very strict about rules within the home and each child was given a list of chores to be done each day around the home to help Dinah. If those chores were not done as directed, then there were clear penalties. It soon became clear, however, to Susan and Anna Kate that those penalties were much stiffer for them than they were for Christopher and Marcus, and those penalties were harsher when their father was away from home.

One of Susan's chores was to sweep the floor in the kitchen each day. One afternoon Susan had arrived home from school and had gone and gotten the broom and dustpan. She was just finishing up when Dinah appeared in the doorway. "I hope you don't think you are finished little girl!" she announced, "That floor is atrocious! You aren't going to get away with doing a half ass job. Not in my house!"

"I'm sorry Miss Dinah, Ma'am. I will do it again." Susan said to her stepmother.

"Well, I should hope so, you stupid girl. You missed a spot under that table. If you can't get it right, I will have to show you."

Susan went over to the table and started to sweep up under it. As she swept, Dinah stood tapping her foot and watching her. "You are the most pathetic, little shit I have ever seen. I don't know why they even let you come home from the hospital. What a waste!" Susan began sobbing quietly as she swept.

"What! Are you crying? Did I hurt your precious little feelings? You poor, rotten piece of shit. You can't take a little criticism. Poor thing." Dinah walked over and grabbed the broom out of Susan's hand, looked down and her and then hit her with the back of her hand across the face leaving a huge red mark across her cheek. Susan fell to the floor in tremendous pain. "You better buckle up kid or I will find a way to get rid of you. You just watch."

A few seconds later, Anna Kate came in and saw her sister on the floor.

Dinah walked away to another room. Anna Kate went to her sister and asked her if she was ok. "It's okay. Let's just finish this and go to our room."

"Ok, Sissy. I will help you." The girls worked together and finished their remaining chores and then went quietly to their room. They tried to keep their heads low and out of trouble any time their father was away, but sometimes it simply did not matter. There just wasn't any rhyme or reason to Dinah's moods, and sometimes even her own sons were not immune to her cruel treatment.

There were times, too, when even having Jonas home didn't matter. One evening, Jonas had been gone for about two weeks. Dinah had been at home working on a special dinner. She was trying a new recipe and was excited to have some time with Jonas. Everything seemed to be going well. She had music playing and had made some cocktails. Problem was, she had consumed several cocktails prior to Jonas getting home and she was already pretty well lit. She was buzzed enough that she did misinterpret the recipe and had made some critical errors. When the family sat down to eat their dinner and had taken a bite, she was beaming with joy and was awaiting a glorious announcement of how tremendously wonderful this new dish was. However, the family looked at each other in horror and spit the food out. Dinah's face immediately changed. Her demeanor went to one of anger and resentment at their attitudes. Jonas tried to soften the blow. Maybe the recipe was wrong, but she wouldn't hear of it. She had eaten it at her friend's home while he was away, and she had gone over to a party. She knew how good the dish was supposed to be. Her anger took over and would not let go. She grabbed her sons by the backs of their collars and drug them to their rooms. Screaming could be heard coming from the room. A door slam, and then silence.

Susan and Anna Kate sat at the table stiff as boards, terrified of what was going to happen next. Jonas looked at Dinah, "Now, honey, you are being unreasonable. No one is blaming you…"

"Yes, you are! They did this! (Looking over at the children). They are always causing me trouble! I don't have anything to say to right now! You hear me."

Jonas was done. He went to his room and shut the door. There sat Susan and Anna Kate alone and unprotected. Dinah staring at them. "What do you two think you're looking at? You get up and clean up this mess and there better not be one thing out of place or done wrong. You hear me?" The girls jumped up and got to work, but it didn't matter. It never did. When Dinah returned, she "found" an insignificant speck of food left on a plate and her rage exploded. She grabbed Susan by the back of her head and swung her around, down to the floor. She began to kick her over and over again, calling her names and cursing her while threatening Anna Kate if she did anything. When she stopped Susan lay still on the floor not moving. Anna Kate was next.

Dinah swung around with her arm out and hit Anna Kate on the side of her face with her hand. She fell back against a cabinet and hit the back of her head. "That will teach you to say anything about my food. Next time, you'll eat and be happy about it, won't you?" The girls knew not to make a sound or any expression of emotion, so they sat on the floor and shook their heads in agreement.

This is how life was to be with Dinah. Each day was an emotional nightmare for the children, never knowing who they were going to find at home waiting for them. There were days when Dinah could be wonderful. She could be happy and waiting for them with fresh baked, chocolate chip cookies. But there were other days when they would find her sullen and unhappy, already drinking and given to bouts of screaming and lashing out at them in fits of rage and violence. Jonas was frequently gone, and the children did not dare tell him what was happening in their home.

For Susan, there were other horrors to endure in this home, too. Despite her diminished mental abilities, her body developed ahead of most her age and she began her monthly cycle. Lily had been taken aback by that when it occurred, but she took Susan aside and talked to her in language she thought she could understand and showed her what she needed to do when she had her cycle. When Susan was under Dinah's roof, however, there was not as much care and concern given to Susan and her special needs. Dinah did not show any compassion to either of the girls, but she was harsher towards Susan and so were her sons.

In 1962, Dinah and Jonas welcomed another little girl into the Stewart household. Her name was Colleen Marie. Dinah and Jonas were so busy with Colleen that they never seemed to notice what else was going on with the other children in their home, or at least they never seemed to have the time to address their suspicions that something nefarious was going on.

Not long after baby Colleen was born, Christopher began what he called "sleep walking" at night. He claimed that he couldn't sleep because of all the crying to explain why he was often found in Susan and Anna Kate's room. When Dinah found him, she would shuffle him back to his own room. If only this were true. Christopher was sneaking into the girl's room and climbing into bed with Susan and was forcing her to let him touch her. The first time that he had ever forced her, he had caught her on their walk home from school. He pushed her down behind some bushes and forced her to kiss him and touch him. He told her that if she dared to tell anyone, he would call her a liar and then he would hurt Anna Kate. He knew that she would believe anything he told her because of her mental disability.

It wasn't long before Christopher dared his brother Marcus to go in and touch Susan too. As a result, she became withdrawn and tried to only interact with Anna Kate. As soon as she finished her chores, she went straight to her room and shut her door.

Anna Kate, being so young, really did not understand what was going on in the bed next to hers in the middle of the night. She knew that she heard strange noises sometimes, but she was far too frightened of her stepbrothers to ever look over to see what was going on; and she loved her sister too much to ask her why she was so sad all of the time. She had been the object of her stepbrothers' bullying many times. She just hugged her frequently and told her that she loved her often. That was usually the only way to get Susan to smile.

Fortunately, Christopher and Marcus' obsession with Susan was short lived. They each found girlfriends at school and moved their focus from Susan to these young women. They also spent less and less time at home. Christopher had a job at a local grocery store after school and on weekends. Marcus was mowing lawns to make spending money. This meant that the girls were left at home with Dinah to take the brunt of her behavior, but that too was soon to change.

Jonas happened to come home early from a trip. He was so excited to get home early to spend time with his family, but he never imagined what he was walking into that day. For his daughters, it was just another day in hell. As he turned the key in the door, he heard a blood curdling scream. He threw up the door and ran inside. He just knew he was interrupting a robbery. Instead, he saw his wife standing over his daughters with her hand raised above her head holding a belt. The girls were laid out on the floor bare skinned with bloody whelps all over their backs and buttocks. Jonas yelled, "Dinah, put that down right now. Don't you lay another hand on my girls!"

"Jonas! You don't know what these two put me through. You don't know what I put up with! You don't know. You are never here!"

Jonas grabbed Dinah by the arm and swung her around and looked her directly in the eye, "Let me tell you one thing, the only one here who has done wrong is YOU. You don't have any cause to lay a hand on a child like this. You get your stuff and get out of my house, and don't you ever come back here!" He leaned over and pulled Susan and Anna Kate up off the floor. He could barely speak but softly whispered, "I am sorry. I did not know." The girls just held their daddy and cried.

A few days passed and Jonas told the girls that he was going to have to take them back to their grandparents since he was going to be divorcing Dinah. Again, he promised them that it would just be a temporary solution. He told them that he only had a few more years to work for the Army and then he could get a more permanent position and they could all be a family again. While Susan and Anna Kate did not like it, they knew it was not a terrible place to be. They would not be physically hurt with their grandparents. At least that was what they thought.

The Ultimate Betrayal

When the family returned to Virginia in 1964, there was a sense of relief. The girls felt safe away from Dinah and a home filled with bad memories. Jonas felt a sense of relief from the obligation of his family, but conflict within himself for feeling that way. He knew that he loved them, but he was happiest when he was at work. He knew that was not normal and that gave great conflict.

Lily and Paul quickly settled back into their routine with Susan and Anna Kate. Susan had not been doing well in school and had to repeat eighth grade a second time. This time Lily arranged for her to be in a special education class where she would receive more intensive, one-on-one time with the teacher. On the other hand, Anna Kate, who was ten and in the fourth grade, was doing wonderfully in school. In fact, she often helped Susan with spelling and simple math. Anna Kate was a compassionate child and a supportive sister.

All was not as it had been in the Clark home, though. Anna Kate soon noticed that the noises she had heard in the night in her father's home were now being heard in her grandparents. She was confused by it all but thought maybe she was dreaming. She did not want to ask about it because she might be wrong. She kept quiet. These sounds were repeated at somewhat regular intervals for over a couple years.

Around January 1966, Susan began throwing up and she appeared ill. Lily was concerned so she took her to the doctor. The doctor ran several tests and then came back into the room. He asked Lily to step out so that he could speak to Susan for a few minutes. This perplexed Lily, but she did as she was asked.

"So, Susan, how long have you been throwing up?"

"I guess about two weeks."

"Now, Susan, I am going to ask you some questions and I need you to answer truthfully. If you don't understand the question, you tell me, and I will explain. I am going to ask my nurse, Ms. Markham, to come in so that she can assist you and hear your answers also. Is that okay with you?"

"Sure, sir, Doctor Harris," replied Susan. Dr. Harris opened the door and asked his nurse to come in.

"Susan, do you know what sex is?"

"Yes, sir, I do." Susan replied with much confidence when she answered.

"Ok, do you have a boyfriend?"

"No, sir. Ain't nobody gonna date me, sir. I am too stupid." Susan lowered her head.

"Now, that is just not true, Susan. You have some very nice traits about you and you are very sweet. What I need to know, is whether you've had sex recently."

Susan began to cry. "Now, now, Susan, don't cry. Can you just tell me what happened? Did someone force you to have sex?"

Susan cried harder and began to shake. Nurse Markham went over and embraced Susan. "Susan, would you rather talk to me alone?"

She softly whispered, "I ain't supposed to tell nobody."

Dr. Harris said, "He threatened you, Susan? Is that what happened? He cannot hurt you now. You are safe. He will never hurt you again. I can promise you that, but you must tell us what happened."

Susan looked at Doctor Harris and at Nurse Markham and back again, and the tears welled up in her eyes again. "I will talk to her, please. Please make sure Anna Kate is safe too. He can't hurt her either, sir, please." Susan sounded desperate. She had brought her knees up to her chin and had her arms wrapped tightly around them with her chin resting on her knees. She was rocking back and forth from front to back, clinching her eyes tightly shut and breathing heavily.

Doctor Harris laid his hand gently on her shoulder and said, "It is going to be okay now, Susan. Don't worry. I will take care of it. You don't have to worry anymore." Doctor Harris left the two alone to talk. Susan continued to rock.

Nurse Markham sat down in the doctor's chair. "Susan, you are very brave young lady. Did you know that?"

Susan stopped rocking and let her arms and legs go. She sat up and sniffled. She looked over at the nurse puzzled, "I am? Why?"

"You've been through so much and you're so brave to talk to me. I admire that."

Sniffling again and brushing her bushy, unkempt hair away from her face, she said, "Oh. My grandpa came in my room one day when my grandma had gone to town with my sister, Anna Kate. He sat down on my bed next to me and started rubbing my shoulders and told me I was pretty. He kissed me on the cheek."

"Okay, what did you do?"

"I tried to move away. I was playing with my dolls. He kept rubbing on me. He put his hand on my leg and moved it up my skirt. I pushed it away and moved away. He told me that was how girls learned about boys. That it was normal. Next thing I knew, he had me down on the bed and he was holding me down. [Susan began to sob]. He pulled my panties down, and then he…he…."

"And this is your grandfather?"

"Well, he ain't my real grandpa. He's married to my grandma. My real grandpa is dead, but we call him, Paul, grandpa."

"Oh, I see. Well, honey, this won't ever happen to you again, but there is something that I need to tell you. You are going to have a baby. That is why you have been throwing up. That is called morning sickness. It is perfectly normal. Doctor Harris will be back in to check you to make sure everything looks normal with the baby, okay?"

Susan's demeanor brightened. "*A baby*? Sure, I will be right here. I sure hope it is okay. I ain't been eatin' much lately cuz of the throwing up. A baby!"

In another room sat Lily wondering what was going on with her granddaughter. Nurse Markham came out and repeated what Susan told her in the doctor's ear. Doctor Harris went to his office and called the Sheriff to report the crime. Then he went to Lily's room to tell her what was going on. He never imagined the reaction he would get.

"Mrs. Clarke, I apologize for your wait. This is a difficult situation, and we must make certain that we handle this in the best possible way. I am sure that you are aware of your granddaughter's difficulties, right? [Lily nodded in agreement] Now, Susan has a physical age of a 17-year-old girl, but her mental age is that of a 9-year-old. Do you fully understand what that means? She does not have the capacity to understand and to make decisions like a girl of 17 would be able to do. She thinks and behaves like that of a 9-year-old."

"I guess I do. I mean she is smart in many ways. What is all of this about? You are beating around the bush doctor. Get to the point!"

"Ma'am, your granddaughter has been the victim of a sexual assault, and she is pregnant."

Lily jumped out of her seat and screamed, "What! What has that girl gone and done?"

Bewildered by this response, Dr. Harris said, "Ma'am, I just told you that the girl was raped. The girl cannot consent to sexual behavior. Now you need to sit down and listen to me."

Lily sat back down. "Well then, who has done this? Did she tell you?"

"She did, ma'am. She says your husband has been violating her since she returned to your care a couple of years ago."

Lily jumped back up again screaming, "She's a liar. He wouldn't do it. He wouldn't. She's lying. He wouldn't do that unless she enticed him. She's always walking around with her clothes hanging half off. I keep telling her about it. Now look what she's gone and done. I want her out of my house. You call her daddy and tell him to come get her 'cus she ain't going back to my house. Ain't no way. She's gonna accuse my husband of this. He would never do this."

"Ma'am, if you do not calm down and sit down, I will call and have the law come and remove you from this office. The Sheriff is on his way to your home to arrest your husband. The Department of Family and Children is on their way here to get Susan, so you don't have to concern yourself about her either. I must say that I have never been so disappointed in a grandmother in all my years as a doctor. I have repeatedly told you that your granddaughter is unable to make decisions and to consent and, yet you blame her for what has happened to her. This is your husband's fault, ma'am. You should be angry at him and him alone. What you do about that is your business, but you should not take it out on this child. You should be ashamed of yourself!"

Lily got up from the chair and stormed out, going directly to her car. When she arrived home, she called Jonas. Jonas received permission for emergency leave and drove home. After talking with his mother, the doctor, the social worker, Jonas decided that it would be best for Susan to stay in Norfolk but to live in a foster home until the baby's birth. At that time, the baby would be placed for adoption, and they would decide what would be best for Susan after that time.

Jonas also met with the District Attorney. His mother begged him not to prosecute Paul. He knew how difficult life was for his mother and Paul and how much more difficult it would be for her if Paul was in prison. At this time, Paul was 60 years old and putting him in prison did not seem like a wise idea to him. Most likely it would be a death sentence. After much deliberation, Jonas asked the DA not to prosecute.

Susan was placed in a wonderful foster home. The foster parent was an older lady whose sons had a gospel singing group known all through the South. She was kind to Susan. She made sure that Susan went to her doctor's appointments and that she ate well. She even had a baby shower for her with ladies from her church and invited Anna Kate, who was so excited about being an aunt. Of course, Susan had to drop out of school. It was not the worst thing that could happen; Susan wasn't doing well, and she didn't like school. But Mrs. Allison made sure that she kept learning life skills so that she could take care of herself once she left her home. When it was time for the baby to be born, Mrs. Allison called over to the Clarke's to let them know that they were on their way to the hospital. That day came in December 1967, a bouncing, healthy, six-pound little girl screamed her way into the world. Susan did not want to see her baby, but she did name her little girl—Sarah Stewart. When the social worker returned to the hospital to pick up the adoption paperwork, she discovered that Susan had run away.

Four days later, the baby girl would be in the hands of the Department of Family and Children's Services of Virginia.

Part Two

CHAPTER 15

1983

"Dear God, please hear me. I don't want to be here anymore. Nobody wants me. No one cares that I am here anyway. I want to be with you. You love me. I took pills. Please let me go to sleep and wake up with you. I want the pain to stop. Everyone lies to me. They say they love me, but they lie. They hurt me. I just can't take it anymore!" Faith rolled over in her bed, sobbing and drifted off to sleep.

As she slept her head began to race around over all the tragedies and traumas of her life; those events which had brought her to this point in her young, seventeen years. Her mind first went back to the most horrific night of her life because it was still the freshest in her mind; it was her greatest shame. It was her first ski trip to the mountains with her family of the year. The anticipation and excitement were immense. This had been a very cold winter and there was a nice bed of snow in the mountains, great for skiing. She had been so excited about the trip. She loved skiing with her dad. When they arrived at the hotel where they would be staying, Faith noticed a familiar face in the hotel lobby. It was a boy she had dated briefly the previous year of school. She didn't think much of it, and they unloaded their car and went to their room.

Faith and her dad loved to ski. He had been raised in the mountains, so he had experience skiing. Faith was learning, and she had fallen in love with it. Her mother didn't care at all about skiing. She took the time to go shopping in the town where they were staying. On one of her trips down the mountain, Faith heard her name being called from down below.

"Faith! Faith! Over here, it's Brian. Over here!" Faith could see her former boyfriend waiving at her from below. She was not interested in going over to see him, but her dad said, "Go on, Faith. It's no big deal. Just go say hello."

So, Faith went over. Brian Johnson had been the first boy Faith dated when her family moved to Cary. It was a very brief, three-month dating relationship which ended because Faith didn't want to move as fast as Brian. Brian was known to be fast with girls, but Faith had hoped he would not be with her because he knew that she had never dated anyone before. But when she wouldn't cooperate with moving into a more intimate relationship, Brian dumped her. When her family arrived at the sky resort, Brian was at the bottom of the hill with his friend, Robert Davis. Faith liked Robert. He was a few years older; she thought he was funny and outgoing.

Faith's dream seemed very real. She became cold and pulled up the covers around her. She was curled up underneath them as if the temperature were more like 50 degrees than the 72 it was currently. The dream was so vivid she could even smell the pines and dampness of the clay and snow beneath her feet. It was like living it all over again.

"Hey, what are you two doing here? I didn't know you knew how to ski?" inquired Faith.

Robert started laughing, "Uh, not really, but it's okay. You're pretty good. You've been doing this awhile, haven't you?

"Well, yeah, my dad grew up in the mountains and he grew up skiing, so he taught me."

Brian seemed anxious to cut-into the conversation, "Well, uh, I, I mean we were wondering if you had plans for dinner later?" Just about that time, Faith's father came up. "Honey, if you want to hang out with your friends, that's okay. I will take your mother out to a nice dinner."

Faith's heart started to pound because she really didn't want to go. She had a new boyfriend in Cary, and she didn't want to mess that up, but she felt like her dad was pushing her to go, and they were right there looking at her for an answer. "Well, I guessed it would be okay if we just went to eat or something. I want to go to sleep early tonight so that I can be on the slope early."

"Okay, great, just meet us in the lobby at 6:00 pm," said Brian. Then the boys went into the lobby and Faith went back up the mountain to ski.

When Faith returned to her room to get ready for dinner, she didn't want to wear anything that might make it appear like a date, so she just wore jeans and a button up blouse and her cowboy boots. She pulled her hair up into a half pony. She did not go out of her way to appear "dolled" up.

They decided to go a local steak restaurant for dinner. They each ordered and then Faith excused herself to the bathroom. When she returned there was a drink waiting for her. Brian told her it was a strawberry daiquiri. Faith had done some drinking since she had moved to Cary with her friends, but she was by no means sophisticated when it came to alcohol. She knew she could not drink much. She sipped on the daiquiri and ate her dinner. Brian immediately ordered more drinks. He always tried to look more mature, like he knew all the right things to do and was more grown than he actually was. Before she knew it, dinner was finished, and she had consumed two daiquiris. She could feel the buzz in her head, but she still knew what was going on. She didn't think she was drunk.

They decided to go back to the lodge and hang out there. There was a huge living type room with a huge fireplace. When they got there, not many people were hanging around in the lobby. There were a few other kids their age, so they struck up a conversation and everyone was talking and having a good time. One of the kids had snuck in a bottle of Crown Royal and the others were quickly mixing up drinks. Brian and Robert were enjoying more than their share. People started sitting on the sofas and talking to each other about school, football, and other activities. Little by little the crowd started to dwindle down. Robert had been talking to a girl and the two of them had gone to another room to talk. Before they knew it, Brian and Faith were alone. This made Faith feel extremely uncomfortable. She tried to stay away from Brian and to keep the conversation about school, friends, etc., but Brian followed her to sit beside her, and he continued to try to put his arm around her. Faith was feeling very sleepy, and then it happened.

Brian was beside her and he whispered in her ear, "Faith, I love you. I am sorry that I dumped you and hurt you. Let's get back together. Make love to me."

Faith moved her head to look at him and began to laugh. "Hm, Hm (clearing her throat), uh, what? You just dumped me a month ago, and now you want me to believe that you love me? I don't think so, Brian. Not me. You've got plenty of other girls ready to tear of their clothes off for you, but I am not one of them."

Brian was a bit snarky about her response. "Well, that was cold, Faith. I am being serious here. I made a huge mistake breaking up with you." Again, he moved closer and closer to her on the sofa. The next thing she knew, she was flat on her back and Brian was pulling her pants off. Faith squirmed and said, "Brian, stop. Get off me right now! I told you I am not doing this. Brian, stop." Just as the words were leaving her mouth, Brian put his hand over her mouth and pressed down with all his body weight. It was hard and she couldn't wiggle enough to get his hands away so that she could get away. The next thing she knew, it was too late. She began to cry. The crying turned into sobbing, and she tried to speak through his hand. "Stop! Please, stop!" But her words were too muffled to be heard. Her heart broke in two.

She heard a noise come from the back of the room, "Hey, Brian and Faith why don't ya'll come with me and Amber…." Robert walked up to the sofa. Even though it was dark, he could see their figures from the firelight. He quickly turned around and scooted Amber out of the room. It was over. Brian quickly zipped his pants up. He ran off towards where Robert and Amber had gone. "Hey, Robert, wait up!"

Faith was all alone. She pulled herself together and sat for a minute. She was in shock. Then, she wiped her eyes, fixed her hair, and went back to the room she shared with her parents. They were already asleep. She went into the bathroom and softly cried. She changed into her pajamas and crawled into bed. If only she had known that this would not be the end of it all.

When Faith returned home from the trip, her phone was practically ringing off the hook. Her girlfriends were calling her to tell her about gossip they had heard about Brian. Faith was in no mood to hear anything about Brian, but one of her girlfriends told her anyway. "Well, what I heard was that Brian and Robert went to Ski Beach, and they hooked up with these girls from Cary who were there, and they both got laid. Brian is telling everyone at school how crazy this girl was in bed. Robert isn't really saying much. It's probably not true, but I just had to tell you. Everyone is talking about it." Faith became enraged.

Now Faith's dream took a different turn. For a few moments, there were only vivid colors swimming around, but she could hear the voices of children. It was like the voices of children playing. Then the image started to become clearer to her. She was at the playground where she played as a small child. She could see her childhood friends running around. Some were on the monkey bars; some were chasing each other; and another group was playing near a group of trees. She instantly remembered this scene. The scene closed in on little girls playing beneath a group of trees. They were moving around and talking to each other and playing "family". One little girl was sitting quietly in a corner with a piece of pine sweeping the floor. She appeared sad, almost crying. One of the other girls said to the other one dancing around, "See she doesn't look anything like us; she has brown hair, blue eyes, and she's little. She can be the adopted child. She can do the housework while we get ready for school."

"Sure, she can help Momma with her cleaning while we are at school," said the other little girl.

"But I am older than both of you," the child said, "Why wouldn't I go to school before either of you?

"You're like a dwarf or something. You're too small; you'd get stepped on. You cannot go to school. There's something wrong with you." At that very moment, the child sprung up to her feet and she ran from the play area to a bench where her teacher sat and she grabbed the waist of her teacher, sobbing. Faith was sobbing in her sleep. She remembered the deep pain this incident had caused her, and the treatment did not stop with this one incident. It continued each year. Some incidents she could handle, but from fourth grade until eighth when her family moved, the harassment and bullying became much worse. Girls would call her degrading names, and often they would refuse to talk to her at all. Faith would spend her recess time alone. Sometimes it wasn't all bad and she could get by. There were children who didn't know anything about her, and they would talk to her and play with her. She found comfort there. But what hurt her the most, were the times when her family and friends at church were together and she would overhear conversations between her parents and other grownups.

Her mind took her to such an occasion at their church. Everyone was dressed up, more than just a usual Sunday morning church service. There was food being served. People were everywhere in the church hall talking and mingling. Faith and a few of her closer friends were seated on the edge of the stage eating some finger foods. Her parents were just a few steps away talking with two couples. Faith could hear them well. They were doing introductions and talking about their families. Faith's father smiled and told the others that that they had one daughter and motioned over to her. The others spoke of their children and smiling sharing cute stories of fun times. It wasn't long before Faith's mother, though, changed the otherwise charming moment by saying, "Well, you know we've had some issues. We adopted Faith when she was five. It has been a difficult adjustment." Faith wanted to crawl under a rug and never come out. Was she really that horrible? Why would her mother say something so terrible to other people who don't know her? She felt so hurt. How could anyone accept her if her mother does accept her?

After this occasion, Faith noticed this behavior in her mother more and more often. It became commonplace for her mother to identify Faith as adopted. It felt to Faith as her mother dismissing any bad behavior, unattractiveness, or lack of intelligence to that fact rather than anything that could have come from her or her husband. This would forever leave a wide line of demarcation between Faith and her mother.

Faith did have one friend with whom she could feel good about herself; she could be herself. This was Paulina. Paulina and Faith met in elementary school. Although she did not realize Paulina's home situation until she was older, she and Paulina were like kindred spirits. Life at home for Paulina was not good; and, like Faith, she tried to hide it from everyone. Paulina's father had been accused, tried, and convicted for embezzlement just months prior to Faith moving to Boone. She had three siblings—two sisters and a little brother. Faith loved going over to her house because she was able to be around other children. She detested being an only child. Paulina's younger sister, Georgia, was in the same grade as Faith and Paulina. Her parents held her back a grade. Faith was also friends with Georgia, but it was not as close a relationship as she had with Paulina. It was as though Faith could sense that Paulina needed a faithful friend more than Georgia did.

Paulina's mother was a bitter woman. At times when Faith would go the Welch home, her mother would be sweet and kind; but far more often, she was angry and mean. It seemed like she was always angry with Paulina about something. Many times, Paulina would be grounded for some alleged infraction, but often Faith felt like Paulina could never do anything to please her mother. Faith and Paulina would often calculate the risk of breaking her restriction to go off on their bikes or for a walk in the neighborhood woods. There was a large pond that they liked to walk to and just sit and daydream. Other kids in the neighborhood would go there to make out or smoke a joint. Faith never did that, though she suspected Paulina might have been persuaded to join in. Faith never judged Paulina, nor did Paulina judge Faith. Their hearts were broken eight years later when Faith's family would move again. Faith hated the idea of trying to find another friend she could trust like Paulina. It was a relationship which would be broken until the Internet and social media were invented. Once they reconnected, it was like no time had passed. Paulina was the sister Faith never had.

After this period of the night, Faith became visibly afraid. She grasped onto her blanket, and she squeezed it tightly. The colors returned briefly, swirling all around, but then they went black and suddenly she felt her stomach drop. There was an odor she hadn't smelled in a very long time, and it upset her tremendously. "No, no! I don't want to go there. Don't make me go there, please." Faith cried. The scene began to appear through the darkness, and it was a small home, a ranch style home. There was a small girl and a small boy sitting on the front porch with an older boy. "Tomorrow's the day, huh?" said the young boy.

"Maybe," frowned the little boy.

"Oh, Scottie, don't worry so much. I'm sure it is going to be fine. I bet you'll have a great room all for yourself! And you, sweet girl, anyone would be proud to have you. You're like sunshine in the rain."

"But I don't want to go away, Jeb. I want to stay here with you and Scottie and the girls. I don't want to leave. I live here, Jeb."

"Well, now, that is true, but we weren't ever going to be your forever family. Look at us, we got so many kids already."

"But we've been good lately, ain't we, Jeb. Why? Is it 'cuz daddy hates us so much? Is that why…is that why he does mean stuff to us?"

Jeb held his head low, and he was quiet for several minutes. A few minutes later his sister, Rebecca, came out and sat down. "What's going on out here? Hey, Jeb, what's the trouble?"

Faith asked Jeb, "Is this why we are leavin'? 'Cuz daddy hates us and 'cuz of what he's been doin'? We didn't mean to." Faith's little, piercing blue eyes welled up with tears as she looked at Jeb and Rebecca for an answer. "I don't wanna leave you, Jeb, Becky." Faith wrapped her little arms around Jeb's waist as tight as her little body could hold on.

Rebecca, too, became silent. She took Scottie's little head in her hand and held him close to her. She pulled Faith over close to her with her other hand and they all sat cuddled up together in their grief. Rebecca and Jeb both knew that what the young ones had said was true. Their father had beat them, forced them to stay in a closet for hours at a time, kept food from them, and other things to punish them for whatever wrong he thought they had done. He never treated his own children this way. Rebecca, Jeb, and their oldest sister Dawn were hard pressed to do anything about it because he would threaten them if they did. Their mother did as she was told and nothing more, and they hated her for it. They all longed for the day they, too, could escape this nightmare they called "home."

The next morning came, and the social worker arrived early. The children were dressed in clothes they had gotten from Good Will. Jeb, Dawn, and Rebecca were ashamed that their parents wouldn't even purchase new clothes and shoes for Faith and Scottie, and they did not allow the children to take anything from the home. Their parents refused to allow them to say goodbye. They were forced to stay in their rooms as Mrs. Henderson took the children to her car. There were no hugs, no kisses, nothing. The children were placed in the backseat of her car, and, within minutes, they were gone. Faith and Scottie sat holding each other's hand as tight as they could, not saying a word.

The drive to the offices of the Department of Family and Children's Services took about twenty minutes. Every attempt Mrs. Henderson made to engage the children in conversation was met with no response. Once they arrived, she helped the children from the car and attempted to separate them, but she could not get them to release their grip. Her anger at the behavior was apparent as they entered the building and took the elevator to the third floor. This was the only time that she saw any glimmer of interest from the pair. She could tell that they were in awe of the elevator, but neither spoke a word. When the elevator opened, the doors opened to a waiting area with a desk and two chairs. "Now, Faith, Scottie, I need you to wait here for a few minutes. Sit here and be good for me, okay?" The children sat down in one of the chairs but said nothing. Mrs. Henderson looked at the young woman at the desk, "I think they'll be fine here while I go see the director for a minute." The young woman shook her head in acknowledgment.

Mrs. Henderson disappeared down one of the long halls to an office for several minutes before she came back to the children. When she returned, she looked at Scottie, "Okay, Scottie, it is time for you to come with me." She held out her hand toward Scottie. Scottie looked over at Faith and Faith at Scottie. They tightened their grip and refused to let go. The two instantly began to cry and scream, "NO! We're staying together. I'm staying with Faith. No!" The children screamed so loud the entire building could hear them. The children fell to the floor and began to kick and lay on the floor flailing about so that anyone who dared try to get them apart would end up bruised. Others came from their offices to see what was going on and to try to help. The children were distraught. Mrs. Henderson attempted to pick Scottie up from the floor, but he kicked her in the stomach. For a four-year-old, he packed quite a punch. Soon a man arrived who was able to subdue the youngster and take him to another room.

Faith, too, was contained and taken to another room attended by Mrs. Henderson who, by this time had had enough and had been able to regain her composure. "Faith, you better get yourself together, little lady or no one is going to want to take you home today. This is no way to behave little girl." Mrs. Henderson plopped Faith down on a hobby horse. "You better dry those eyes up and put on a happy face right now!" Mrs. Henderson said in a most hateful tone, pointing her finger in Faith's face and shaking it at her. Faith was frightened. She had no idea what was about to happen to her. Where she was going? Who she was going with, and why? She didn't know if they would be nice to her or mean like her dad. How was a five-year-old supposed to understand all of this and why was her brother, Scottie, being taken away from her? What had they done to deserve all of this? She did not understand.

Mrs. Henderson left the room. About three or four minutes later she returned with a man and a lady. Faith was completely terrified. She couldn't move on that hobby horse. She was frozen. Mrs. Henderson looked over at her and said, "Faith, these are the Roberts—Lee and Ellen. They want to be your Momma and Daddy. Faith was confused. Who were the people she just left? Weren't they, her parents? Why did she need new ones? What about Scottie? She didn't say a word. The lady walked over to her, "Hi, Faith, I brought you something. I hope you like it." The lady pulled a small, pink bear out of her purse. At first Faith didn't want to look at it. She was still so frightened. But the lady held her hand out to her, so she looked at it and she looked at the lady. She looked okay. She didn't look scary. The bear was pretty. It had on a dress with a lace collar and a straw hat. Faith smiled and took it. She had never had anything like that before.

Faith got down off the hobby horse. Everyone smiled. Then, the man tried to reach out to Faith. She jumped away and toward Mrs. Roberts. Mrs. Henderson whispered to Mr. Roberts, "Take it slow. She's uncomfortable around men." The adults spoke just a few more minutes and then they decided it was time to go.

"Faith, would you be okay with going with us to a hotel? We could get to know each other a little bit. How does that sound?" Mrs. Roberts asked her.

Faith was quiet for a few minutes. "Are you going to be there the whole time?"

"Yes, I will," answered Mrs. Roberts, "We might go shopping, too. Wouldn't that be fun?"

Faith had a puzzled look on her face, "Yes, I guess so. I guess I could go."

"Alright then," said Mr. Roberts, "We have a bit of a walk. We'd better get started." The three walked to the elevator and down they went to the street. Everything seemed fine until Mr. Roberts started to pick Faith up to carry her to the car. Faith became frightened again. She didn't understand what was happening and she began to scream and cry and hit Mr. Roberts. The Roberts' car was parked some distance from the DFACS office. Faith screamed the entire way to the car. She had screamed and kicked so hard that she wore herself out. Once they were driving, she fell asleep in the backseat of the car.

Faith's traumas had come full circle this night. All of them circling around in her brain. She couldn't take it anymore. Why did she have to endure it? Why couldn't she just be left alone and have a normal life like everyone else? No more. She'd just rather be dead. She'd rather be in heaven than deal with this crap. No more of the gossip; the bullying; the memories; no more torture!

Then the morning came, and she didn't die. She was very much alive--extremely sleepy and covered in sweat, but alive. The dreams Faith had that night were so vivid. She still felt terrified when she woke up, but she managed to get through her normal routine so that her parents wouldn't know anything had happened. She didn't know what to think or how to process anything that had happened the night before. She just went to school and kept her head down and didn't say much to anyone. It hadn't changed the way she felt about herself and her life. All she knew was that God must not have wanted her yet, so she had to do something else to make her life bearable. Graduation was coming so maybe college would make her life better.

When Faith returned home from school that day, she decided not to go out with friends as she normally would on a Friday night. She wanted to think about her life and especially her future. Faith was pragmatic, and she had decided that she was going to come up with a game plan for the rest of her life, a plan that she could stick to so that no one else could ever hurt her. She helped her mother with dinner and as soon as everything was cleaned up, she went to her room and shut the door. She put on music and got out a notebook. She thought about what she wanted to study in college and what she would want to do as her career. At this point, marriage and family for her, although not completely written off, would be well down the road and not a top priority for her. Education would be first. A bachelor's degree and then right into a master's would be her priorities. She wanted to do an internship of some sort. She knew that made getting hired easier after graduation.

Then, she needed to find a way to keep temptation at bay. Since the rape, she had lost control of herself. She had become promiscuous. She felt so awful about herself. She thought that was all she was good for, and that sex was all anyone wanted from her. She began to drink heavily to get through the agony of the sexual encounters and to numb herself from the memories of the rape and the other traumas of her past. She knew that curbing social interactions would be her best bet. If she continued to live at home and only went to school and work and then came home, she thought she would have less temptation to involve herself in those weak areas. She prayed to God to help her to be successful, for God's forgiveness for what she had done with her life thus far, to help her be a better person, and to protect her.

CHAPTER 16

Dangerous Waters

Despite her best intentions, Faith continued to struggle with her demons. After that dreadful night in the mountains and returning home to find her reputation ruined, she clung to her boyfriend Kyle. She had confided in him about what happened, and he had been very kind and compassionate towards her. He even helped her get some revenge for what had happened.

One evening Kyle gathered up three of Faith's guy friends and they made a plan to get revenge on Brian. Brian's parents often allowed him to drive their car, a Mercedes, when they were out-of-town. Brian was wild and drove like a crazy person. He loved to show off the car. The group knew that he couldn't wait to show up at the Key Club meeting that week in his parent's car. The meeting was in the library after school. The boys decided to meet in the parking lot and wait for Brian to leave the car to go into the school for the meeting. It was still summer, and the temperature was still quite hot. Brian was so careless that he had left the car unlocked, so the boys were able to gain access to the car quite easily. This also meant that Brian would be hard pressed to be able to blame anyone for what he was going to find. The boys opened the car doors and unzipped their pants and urinated all over the inside the car and then threw in dog poop that they had collected from their neighbor's yard. They made sure the windows were up and shut the doors. It would be at least an hour before Brian would return. The boys then left the scene.

When the meeting was over, everyone walked outside to get into their cars to leave. When Brian got to his car, he opened the door and was hit with the horrible stench. He was furious. He looked around at everyone staring at him. Most were laughing at him. "Who did this? I am going to get whoever did this!" Brian threw an all-out temper tantrum in the parking lot. Once he calmed down, he asked Robert to take him to the store to get some things to clean up the car. Everyone started to leave and were whispering about who might have done it to him and why. When Faith and Kyle walked by, Brian grabbed Faith by the arm, "Did you do this little girl?"

"Get your hands off of her," said Kyle.

"It's okay, Kyle," Faith looked directly into Brian's eyes as indignant as she could, "I suggest you keep your opinions to yourself, Brian Johnson. I'm sure there are somethings you don't want to get out to the wrong people, right? You don't need me to start talking, but I am ready to start talking, if you are."

"Uh, yeah, sure. See ya'll later."

Faith and Kyle walked to their cars, stopping at Faith's. "Wow, you were pretty strong just now. I didn't know you had it in you."

"I don't, but I had to say something to get him to back off. We can't have him calling the police."

"I know. We don't need that, but maybe he will leave you alone and shut up about all of it now." Kyle leaned over and kissed Faith on the cheek. "Call me when you get home so that I know you are okay."

"I will." Faith got in her car and drove off. She couldn't help thinking how much she just wanted to be alone. Not involved with anyone. It was such a struggle for her. She felt pressure from every angle. Her parents hated Kyle and wanted her break up with him because he was four years older than she. Kyle wanted their relationship to be more, and the boys in her class were always talking to her about breaking up with him so that they could go out with her. Faith was confused and frustrated. That night kept whirling around in her head and she thought she didn't really want to be with any guy who could possibly do something like that. Was it something every guy could do? She just didn't know. She couldn't talk to anyone about it.

When Faith got home, she called Kyle to let him know she was home. Kyle wanted to continue to talk, but Faith was quiet. "What's wrong, Faith?" asked Kyle, "You are so quiet. Is everything okay?"

"Well, I just don't...I...."

"Faith, what is it? Tell me, please."

"I don't want to hurt you, Kyle, but I really just want to be alone right now. I have so much going on at school and my parents are harassing me. I just can't take it."

"Faith, are you breaking up with me? Please don't say that."

"Maybe it won't be forever, but for right now I need some time to myself, Kyle."

"I see. You have been through a lot. I get that, but I love you and you know that I am here for you always."

"I know that Kyle, but right now I just can't…I don't want to be…. Look I need to go. I have a biology test tomorrow." Faith hung up without giving Kyle a chance to say anything else. She spent an hour or so trying to study, but her mind was constantly thrown off track by thoughts of that night. She finally got ready for bed, said good night to her parents, and went to bed.

The next morning when she awoke Faith felt a bit better not feeling tied down to a relationship with expectations. She looked forward to going to school for the first time since the "event". When she got to school, her friends Carrie Anne, Kit, and Marianna were waiting on her. "Hey girls, what's up?" Faith smiled at them.

"Well, aren't we cheerful all the sudden. What brought you out of your funk" asked Kit?

"You are looking at a free woman. Suddenly I feel so relieved. I don't know. I just do."

"Wow, you broke up with Kyle? Why?" asked Marianna

"I'm just bored, I guess. You know my parents have been harassing me about him anyway. My life is so much easier now without them hounding me."

About that time the bell rang, and the girls went into the school and on to their homeroom. When Faith got to homeroom, Trevor Kincaid was there sitting in the desk next to where Faith always sat. "Hey, Faith, how are you today?"

"Well, I guess I am okay. How are you, Trevor? Are you ready for that biology test in fourth period?"

"I will be doing great if you tell me that you dumped that boyfriend of yours. I guess I am as ready as I can be for that stupid test."

Faith giggled, "Do you ever study for anything, Trevor? I wish I was as smart as you and didn't have to study."

"And the boyfriend, Faith? When are you going to get rid of him so we can go out?"

"Well, as a matter of fact, we broke up last night."

"Really? Why?"

"Oh, I dunno, I am just tired of him, I guess." Faith giggled as the bell rang for the end of homeroom. Faith got up and quickly walked towards the door leaving Trevor behind. This same conversation went on for months, but Trevor never seemed to get around to actually asking Faith out, which made her very confused. It was the same with other boys in school who had always told Faith that they wanted to go out with her, but she had a boyfriend. Once Kyle was gone, though, they never asked her out. Some even asked her out, but then stood her up. Once her reputation was ruined, Faith knew that there was little she could do to get it back, correct it, or even get the truth out about what had really happened. She never wanted her parents to know.

Once the weekend came, though, Faith would go out with her girl-friends. One of them would drive while the others drank. They knew they were dangerous territory drinking underage, but everyone did it, but at least they always had a designated driver. There were times, though when they would meet up with boys from school and they would split up for a while. It was during this time when Faith would find herself in precarious posi-tions, especially when she was not the driver, and she was intoxicated. She had an emptiness within herself that she could not explain or understand. The alcohol seemed to make her awareness of it disappear for a brief time, and her intimate encounters with boys gave her a brief feeling of what it felt like to be loved, or so she thought. She knew she was living a very danger-ous life, but somehow, she couldn't find a way to stop it. She could justify it to herself because so many of her friends were doing the same thing, but she hated herself for doing what she was doing. She was deeply ashamed.

CHAPTER 17

Moving On

Once she graduated from high school and moved onto college, Faith felt like she would be able to take control over her life. She made goals and was determined to meet those goals. She was excited about college and what it had to offer her. Mostly she hoped it offered her a way out of Carey and on to something much better. She started school at Appalachian State University. She wanted to travel the world and to find a career that would allow her to do that on someone else's dime. She enrolled with English as her major with art history and photography as her minors. Faith loved being outdoors, taking photographs of landscapes, old barns and wildlife, and to write.

The first year of school went well for Faith. She studied and made the Dean's List. Her father pulled her aside one day and told her, "Faith, I am so proud of how well you have done this year. You have worked so hard, and it is reflected in your grades, but honey, you didn't have much fun. College is as much about the experience as it is about the education. These are the best years of your life, and you deserve to have some fun. When I was in college, I was in a fraternity. I had a great time, and I am still friends with many of my fraternity brothers. Why don't you think about a sorority? Your mother was in a sorority when she was in college, too." Faith had so much respect for her father; she felt she should do what he said, but she knew that sororities and fraternities typically involve partying and that could be a real problem for her. She told her father that she would consider it.

Faith then talked to friends she had made in school about Greek life. She gathered information about each of the organizations and then decided to go out for rush. She was not excited about the idea of rush, but she felt that this was what her parents wanted, so she did it. In the end, she joined Kappa Delta. Several of her friends were already in that sorority, so it seemed the most obvious choice. Over the next few months, she went through the training program and was initiated as a sister.

At the same time, though, the Greek events started to happen and that presented problems for Faith. College and sorority life made it easier for Faith to slip back into her old behaviors. Suddenly, the pain and shame returned, as did her self-hatred. She felt herself spinning out of control. Somehow, she managed to keep her grades up so that her parents would not be the wiser, but it was difficult. She was living a double life and she hated herself for it.

Faith also decided to get a part-time job so that she would not have to ask her parents for money. She got a job in a large bookstore store, and she quickly made friends with several other college students working in the store. One of her friends from Carey, who was also attending school at Appalachian, knew some of the people working in the store and they began spending time together outside of work. Two of the guys who worked in the store, Colin and Hank, were fraternity brothers. Both were incredibly handsome. Colin worked in the stockroom and Hank worked in security. Faith's friend, Josie, had a crush on one of the boys' other fraternity brothers.

One weekend during the summer before school started, Josie and Faith went over to the fraternity house because Josie wanted to see the boy, on whom she had the crush. They were going to play poker. After playing a few hands, the four decided to watch some television, but Josie and her crush did more making out than watching tv. Faith and Colin sat and talked for a few minutes and the next thing Faith knew, Colin leaned over and kissed her. She was completely shocked. It was so unexpected. Faith had not gone with any intentions of doing anything with anyone, and Colin knew that Faith had a crush on Hank. She leaned back, "Colin, where did that come from?"

"I've wanted to do that for a long time, Faith."

Faith did not know what to think. Suddenly, looking into his eyes, she had feelings she did not expect to have. Colin kissed her again. Feelings flooded her from head to toe. She felt dizzy and unbalanced. It felt great and completely terrible all at the same time. She wanted to do it, and she wanted to slap him at the same time. She knew it couldn't end well. Her head was swimming, and her heart was pounding so loud it felt like it was in her head.

A few hours passed, and Josie came to find Faith. Faith and Colin were asleep. "Faith," Josie whispered, "We've got to go, or we will miss curfew." Faith looked up and then, beside to her. Then she looked up at Josie, who was smiling from ear to ear.

"Don't ask me yet. Give me a couple of minutes, ok?"

"Sure." Josie left the room to give Faith time to talk to Colin.

"Colin, Colin, wake up," Faith gently shook Colin to wake him up. "I need to go. I don't want to just leave and not say something to you."

"Oh, sure, Faith. Yeah, I wouldn't like that." Colin sat up and stretched at bit. He looked at Faith and smiled at her. Then he grabbed her quickly and pulled her back down in the couch and kissed all over her face.

"Colin, Colin, we have to go. We're going to have to talk about this at some point. It isn't like I don't know that you have a girlfriend. I don't understand. Can we talk later, please?"

"I know. We will talk about it. I guess I will see you at work later?" Faith shook her head "yes".

This was the beginning of an awkward relationship between Colin and Faith that would last until Colin graduated from college. It almost ended when Colin admitted to Hank that he had had been with Faith. Hank confronted Faith in the store about her betrayal. He told her that he was ready to ask her out when Colin made the confession to him. Now, he said, he would never ask her out. Faith was furious with Colin, but more furious with Hank that he wasn't angry at Colin for his part in the betrayal. Of course, she had no idea how the events of that night were portrayed to Hank. Faith grew to believe over time that Colin may have told Hank because he didn't want Hank to ask Faith out, but instead to keep her for himself.

Faith fell deeply in love with Colin. She would never admit this to him, though. She couldn't because she was the other woman. Colin had been dating the same girl since high school. Faith knew the girl and did not like her. Norah Porter was a snob and she bossed Colin around like a dog.

Faith just couldn't help herself. She saw the best in Colin. He was kind and generous. She loved being with him. As time progressed, she became more and more anxious because she knew their time would quickly come to an end. She hoped that maybe Colin would find the courage to end his relationship with Norah. She never said negative things about Norah, though, she didn't want to put him a position where he felt like she was giving him an ultimatum or would think that she was being spiteful.

As graduation neared there was a party for Colin and his other fraternity brothers who were graduating. For whatever reason, Norah was not coming to the party, so Faith and Josie went. It was a very emotional night for Faith. It would be the last time that she and Colin would ever be together. She found out that Colin had proposed to Norah. It was heartbreaking for Faith. In their talk, it seemed to Faith that Colin felt obligated to propose to Norah because they had been dating for so long, but he didn't have the courage to end a relationship that wasn't working for him. Faith couldn't understand it. Colin told Faith he was sorry, and that he knew he hadn't been fair to her, but he couldn't help his feelings for her either. Faith told him that she was fully aware of what she had been doing and she accepted the consequences. She was on the verge of crying, but she held back. She rested her head on his chest for a few minutes while she was thinking of what to say and how to say it.

Faith lifted her head and looked into Colin's eyes and spoke from her heart, "Colin, I know that this is goodbye. I don't want it to be, but I know it is. I knew from the beginning that this would probably happen. I am a bit used to disappointments in my life; it's all I ever seem to get. So, for tonight can we forget everything else and just be together for right now?"

CHAPTER 18

Learning to Love Again

After the relationship with Colin ended, Faith tried to focus solely on school and less on social activities. She received permission to take extra classes from the university so that she would have too much work to have much for a social life. It worked to a certain degree, but there was a deep desire within Faith that just longed to be loved. She believed that she was not truly loved by anyone, except maybe her dad. Her grades were excellent, but she felt deeply unfulfilled and letting go of Colin was one of the hardest things she had ever done. She had only ever loved one other person, Kyle, and she had really hoped that Colin would find the courage not to marry Norah.

One afternoon, Faith went home for the weekend. Her parents were out-of-town, and she needed to go shopping, so she headed out for the grocery store. While strolling through the store looking for something interesting to have for dinner, she heard a familiar voice come from behind her. She turned around and saw Liam Avery standing behind her. She ran over to him and hugged him. "Liam, what are you doing here? I thought you were in Cuba?"

"I am, but I am home on leave. I came in here to pick up somethings for my mother. I saw you when you came in and I wanted to say hello. How are you?" Liam was a friend from high school. Faith and Liam had gone out a few times, but there was nothing serious and nothing intimate, which Faith felt good about. They had the same group of friends, so they were often at the same parties. He was a couple years older, but he didn't do great in school and graduated just a year ahead of her. He was very handsome. He had light brown hair and hazel eyes. Since he had joined the Marine

Corps, he had gotten muscular and fit. Faith was very impressed. She had liked Liam very much, but he never showed much interest in her. He always seemed to prefer the more popular girls.

"Oh, I am great. I will be graduating soon and going on to graduate school. I am excited about it."

"Wow, where will you be going to graduate school?"

"Well, I am not quite sure just yet; I applied to Rhode Island School of Art & Design and Savannah School of Art & Design. They both have excellent programs in photography. I am going to be interning this summer in New York. I am really excited."

"That is amazing. I didn't know you were interested in all that. I'd really love to see some of your photographs. Hey, maybe we could go to dinner and a movie while I am home, if you aren't dating anyone."

Faith smiled at Liam, "Oh no, no boyfriend; but I'd love to do that. I'm at my parents, so the phone number is the same. Give me a call. I've got to go now."

"I sure will. Say 'hi' to your mom and dad for me." Liam waived goodbye to Faith as she turned back around and strolled away. Faith smiled the rest of the time in the store and couldn't wait to hear from him. She couldn't wait to get home and call Josie and tell her about seeing Liam again.

"That sounds so awesome, Faith, but didn't Liam stand you up the last time ya'll were supposed to go out?" Josie hesitated to ask, but she knew someone had to bring it up. She didn't want Faith to get hurt.

"Well, yeah…yeah, he did. That was three years ago, though. Surely, he's grown up since then, right?" Faith was trying to sound optimistic.

"Sure, it is possible and now that he's been in the Corps a year or so maybe he is more reliable. But, Faith, let's say ya'll go out and you have a really good time, he still has to go back to Cuba, and you'll be going off for grad school. Do you think a long-distance relationship like that is realistic?"

"That is something to think about, but let's not cross our bridges until we come to them. For now, let's just wait and see if he even calls me."

"Yeah, that sounds like a good plan. Well, let me know as soon as he calls, okay? I can't wait to hear about it all. I've got to go to work now. Talk to you later."

"I will call you right away. I promise. Be careful driving to work." She tried not to be too anxious waiting for Liam's call. It was about three days before that call came.

"Hello, Faith? It's Liam. How are you?"

"Hi, Liam, I'm great; you?"

"I'm good. Hey, you want to go to the movie tomorrow night? We can go get a bite to eat and then go to the movie, if you want." Liam sounded sort of nervous. Faith couldn't imagine why he would be, after all she'd never stood him up before.

"Okay, that'd be fine. What time?"

"5:30 okay?"

"Sure, I will be ready. See you then." Faith hung up and called her girl-friends right away to relay the story. They were all very encouraged, except for Josie who always seemed to be the voice of reason.

"Faith, do you think…well, hmm…let's see…okay, I'm just going to say it. Faith, do you think Liam still drinks like he used to do when we were younger?"

"You know I have thought about that, but to be honest, I've never seen Liam like that. I've heard other people talk about it, but I have never seen it, so I don't know. Do you think I should be worried about it?"

"I don't know, Faith. Like you said, I've only heard about it, too. I mean, at those parties we were all drinking, so I didn't notice him acting any different than anyone else who was intoxicated, but I have heard people talk about him. Just be careful, okay. If something happens and you don't feel good about it, you can call me. I will come and get you."

"I will, Josie. I appreciate that. You know I'd do the same for you, too, right?"

"Absolutely! Ok girl, love ya. I gotta get back to work now."

Days passed and then the day came for their date. Faith was so excited, but she didn't want it to show. She wore jeans and a nice shirt. When Liam came to pick her up, she waited just a few minutes before coming down so that she didn't look too anxious. They went to Pizza Hut and ate pizza and talked about everything that had happened with friends over the past three years since Liam had left town. It was great catching up on everything with him. When they finished eating, Liam paid, and they left for the movie.

When they got to the theater, Liam asked Faith if she had any preference about movies. She told him that she did not. "Would Hamburger Hill be okay? You know I love war movies." Faith loved history and she wasn't familiar with what the movie was about, so she agreed. She regretted that decision later. It was a violent film about a key battle in Vietnam War. She was not at all interested in the Vietnam War, but Liam seemed impressed that she stuck it out. When they got back into the car Liam looked over at Faith and said, "You know I think the world of you. You've always been so kind to me. You are very special." He leaned over and kissed her. He took her home and walked her to the door. They promised to write each other while he was away.

Faith kept that wonderful memory close to her heart and in her mind as the next year went by and the time came for her to leave Cary for Savannah. She would be studying for her master's degree at Savannah School of Art and Design, also known as SCAD. She and Liam wrote each other, quite frequently. He told her that he would soon leave Cuba and transfer to Japan. It would be a two-year assignment. He would be able to come home for some extended leave in between the two years. Faith told him that she was excited for him; it sounded so exotic and that she would continue to write him as often as she could, depending on her schoolwork load.

When Faith arrived in Savannah, she was so excited to be there. She was following through on her goals. She had met a couple of girls during orientation, and they had decided to live together in a condominium. It was a very nice place to live, and all three of the young women were looking forward to school and living in Savannah. Faith, Teresa and Kelly were all studying Art in some form or fashion. Faith was focusing more on photography and photojournalism. Caroline wanted to be a curator of an art gallery, so she would have more business and management classes to take in addition to art history courses. Once everyone was moved in and settled, the four young women went grocery shopping and cooked a big dinner together. They sat down together and promised to keep one night a week open for a group meal.

As time went on, the reality of school and life became very real. Faith was disappointed to find young people not as friendly as she had hoped. While she did tend to be somewhat introverted, she made a point to resist that urge by starting conversations with those in her classes. By the middle of the semester, she was feeling out of place and a bit homesick. She made her schoolwork her focus and tried to make a few friends in her program, which made things a bit better for her.

While she was away from home one detail of her life came front and center and seemed to occupy her mind more and more. She had always thought about it, in fact she fantasied about it constantly when she was growing up. She had always wanted to know the truth, but she had never really pressed the issue with her parents because she did not want to make them angry or unhappy, but now she was in a position to dig into the issue without any objections. Faith wanted to know about her birth parents and why she had been put up for adoption. She started writing a letter to the State of Virginia about her adoption, but with school and other activities she never seemed to finish the letter. She had many papers and projects to complete by the end of the semester; and then, she found out that her roommates were planning to move out at the end of the year to separate locations which meant that she either had to find new roommates for the condominium or she would have to move somewhere else. She thought about her options and spoke to her friends and professors; and, in the end she did neither. She decided to move back to North Carolina and to finish her master's degree at the University of North Carolina. With the war in the Persian Gulf going on, her interest had been peaked in photojournalism, so she would use elective hours for additional journalism courses.

CHAPTER 19

Loose Ends & New Beginnings

Faith's parents were happy to have her closer to home. She and her mother drove to Chapel Hill during the summer to find an apartment for her. They decided to help her cover the rent so that she could live alone. They found a nice one-bedroom apartment located close to campus, and Faith was able to find a good part-time job as a receptionist at the Sheriff's Office. Liam was also counting down the days until his leave time when he would be coming home for a brief visit. Faith was very excited

Once school began Faith settled into her new routine and her life was running smoothly. Those ideas of finding her roots crept back into her mind again. She sat down at her computer and typed a letter. This time she finished it, put it in an envelope and put in her purse to mail when she went to work the next morning. Her mind raced over all the scenarios she had come up with over the years. The one scenario that she often went back to, was that her mother was probably a girl, maybe a teenager, from the wrong side of town who "*hooked*" up with the rich boy and got pregnant, but his parents would never let him be associated with a girl like her, so she was forced to give her up. If her mother was the rich one, she dreamed of one day showing up on her doorstep and looking her in the eye and confronting her. She also wondered if, perhaps, her parents died. After all, she was five years and four months old when she was adopted. Maybe they were killed in an accident. Did she have any siblings; and if she did, where were they? Why would they have been separated? The more she thought, the more she needed to know the truth of who she was.

Once the letter was mailed all she could do was wait for a response, which drove her crazy. Faith could be quite impatient. It was about five or so weeks later when she received a letter from the Virginia Department of Family and Children's Services. The letter explained that, under the law in Virginia, adoptees were allowed to obtain a copy of their non-identifying information and asked if she wished to have that information. It also explained that there was no indication in the file that her biological parents wished to have reunification, but that she did have a half-brother who had also been placed for adoption and asked if she would like reunification with him. They could contact his adoptive parents and ask if he would like unification with her. This was a complete shock to Faith, but an answered prayer for her nonetheless. She had always wanted a brother and now she had one. She was disappointed that it seemed she would not have the opportunity to meet her mother, but she resigned herself to that before she mailed the letter. With hope in her heart, Faith immediately sent a letter back to DFACS letting them know that she absolutely wanted to meet her brother.

Two months passed and it was time for Liam's visit. Faith spent two days cleaning and shopping for his overnight visit to Chapel Hill. He would spend most his leave with his family. His mother would drive him there, and Faith would pick him up and then return him to Cary the next afternoon. She was so excited about seeing him again. With time difference between Virginia and Japan, as well as the cost, most of their communication had been through letters. While she cherished those, it just wasn't the same as seeing him and talking to him. She had planned something for them to do around campus and had gotten reservations at a nice restaurant for dinner.

When the time came, she was so excited she could barely contain herself, everyone met at a mini mart just outside of Chapel Hill. Liam hugged his mom and told her they would all see each other the next day. When they arrived at the apartment, Liam was surprised how big it was for a one-bedroom apartment and at how neat Faith had decorated it. He put his arms around her and said, "Wow, this could almost feel like home." And he leaned over and kissed her on the cheek. "So now, what do you have planned for us today?"

"I thought we would just drop your things off and then we could go over to campus. I can give you a tour. I can show you the places I like to hang out. Then I can show you around Chapel Hill a bit, and after that I thought we'd come back here and get ready to go eat dinner. I got a reservation at a nice restaurant. It's not too expensive, though."

Liam laughed. "I may not make a whole lot, but I am not broke, Faith."

"Well, I just didn't want you to think that I was…." They both started laughing. Within twenty minutes or so the two were on their way to the UNC Chapel Hill campus. Faith drove around the campus pointing out sites to Liam. "There's the bookstore. That's, of course, were I get my books, but you can also get UNC clothing and stuff like that there, too." She showed him the library and the chapel, the student union, and the football stadium.

"This campus is really very beautiful, Faith. I can see why you like it here, but there has to be other places you go to have some fun with your school friends."

"Well, Liam, to be quite honest, I stay to myself. There are one or two in my classes that I talk to, and we will meet at the library to study, but I don't really hang out with anyone. I just really like to come home and do my work and watch television."

"Faith, you need to have some fun while you're here. Don't worry about me. You cannot just stay cooped up in this apartment. Please, tell me that you're going to be more sociable? You only have a few more months anyway." Faith did not know it at the time, but those words should have been a clue for her, but she did not hear what she should have heard in them.

"I know. My parents are always saying the same thing. I will. I promise. Are you ready to see more of Chapel Hill than this campus?"

"Yes, I am." Off they went to see the city of Chapel Hill. They laughed as they talked and poked fun at each other. They sang with the radio. It was a wonderful day for them. The time got away and soon they were rushing back to the apartment to get ready for dinner. Faith went to the shower and Liam sat on the sofa watching a football game. Once Faith left the room, however, Liam went to his suitcase and took out a bottle of Gin and took several big swallows. He then went into her kitchen and looked inside her fridge and freezer. He looked through everything. When Faith came out of the shower wrapped in a towel, Liam came out of the kitchen and asked, "Don't you ever eat anything? Look at these pitiful pork chops. I hope you aren't thinking I can eat this shit." Faith was completely taken aback by the change in his attitude and language.

"Those chops are just fine. Put them back. Remember we are going out tonight. You forgot that so fast? That's kinda crazy." Faith was a bit put off by the fact that Liam had gone snooping around her apartment.

"But look at them Faith, they're so thin you could read a newspaper through them. You're going to have to do better than this once we get married. I make enough money that you should be able to buy better food than this. I guess we will have to go out." He then grabbed his bag and went into the bathroom. Faith didn't know what to think, but her feelings were hurt by his criticism. She thought that she had planned a nice dinner. He made her feel so bad about it.

It wasn't too long before Liam was dressed and ready to go. "Now, what's the name of this place where we are eating tonight? I hope they got bigger chops that shit you got!"

Faith recommended a place just outside Chapel Hill known for its steaks and seafood called Chez Nous. Once there it seemed that Liam had wound down some and he was kinder and more conversational. They talked about school and what Faith's goals were. Liam told Faith that he would be coming back to the U.S. for his next assignment, but he did not know when he would get his orders or where he would be assigned. Faith was happy to hear this news. Liam reached across the table and took Faith's hand. They continued to talk.

About five minutes later, a family sitting at a large table just beside the couple had gotten a bit louder and the staff brought out a large cake. People stood up and took pictures of the older couple sitting at the end of the table. It was an anniversary. Liam and Faith looked on with smiles acknowledging the special nature of the event. Faith stood up and offered to take a photo of everyone so that the entire party could be in the photo. The older gentleman leaned over and asked Liam, "So when you gonna marry that gal"? Liam smiled and whispered to him, "Hold on, don't ruin the surprise," and Liam gave the gentleman a big smile.

Faith returned to the table and looked at Liam, "Isn't that wonderful. They remind me of our grandparents. They've stood the test of time."

"You are so right. Do you think we will?"

"Make it? Oh, I dunn…." Just then Liam dropped to his knee, which caught the attention of the family at the next table and opened a small box. "Faith, will you marry me?" The family at the next table were all looking at the couple waiting to hear the response.

Faith's eyes were opened as wide as they could get. She looked at Liam and reached out to touch his face. "Yes…yes, Liam, I will marry you." Everyone in the room began to clap for the couple. The older gentleman bought the couple a glass of champagne to celebrate. It was the most wonderful evening of Faith's life. She looked at the beautiful ring and looked at Liam.

"I hope it's okay. I don't know anything about this stuff. I had a couple of my buddies go with me to pick it out. It's not terrible, is it?"

"Oh no, Liam, it is the most beautiful thing I have ever seen. She leaned over and gave him a quick kiss." Everyone hung around for a while and talked and shared stories of love, happy times, and even some hard times. The couple listened intently trying to take it all in. It was truly a beautiful night, until the couple returned to Faith's apartment.

CHAPTER 20
Jekyl & Hyde

After the wonderful dinner and night of celebration at Chez Nous, Faith and Liam returned to her apartment. Faith was feeling sleepy from the champagne; Liam was feeling amorous. He kept telling her how beautiful she was and how he had always loved her; but that, until that moment, he never realized how much. Faith was swept up in the emotion as they entered her apartment. She planned for him to sleep on her couch and her in her bed, but it did not turn out that way.

It all seemed so wonderfully, splendid; and then, it came crashing down. Liam asked Faith to do something she didn't really want to do. She had never done it before, and she really didn't want to do it...ever. Liam became enraged when she avoided his advances in that direction. She tried everything she could to redirect him to something else, but he was persistent. Finally, he had had enough, and he sat up in the bed, "What's wrong with you? Don't you want to be with me? We just got engaged. You can't make me believe that you've never done this before with all the guys you've screwed. I could go out right now and pay a hooker fifty bucks and get better sex than this!" He pushed her out of his way as he jumped out of bed and went to the sofa.

Faith was dumbfounded, angry, and sad at all the same time. Why was this such a big issue? He knew that she really wanted to wait until their honeymoon so that it would be special, but emotions had taken over that night. His voice was mean spirited. She laid back down in her bed and cried herself to sleep. She thought to herself, "how could such a beautiful night have turned so ugly? How could a man she loved make her feel so low?"

The next morning when he awoke, Liam went into the bedroom and crawled into bed with Faith. "I am so sorry for what I said to you last night. I didn't mean a word of it. It was all the drinks last night. I don't handle it well sometimes. I am really very sorry. Will you forgive me, please?"

Faith did not move right away. She kept her back towards him, and her eyes closed so that he wouldn't know for sure if she was awake. Alcohol should not be an excuse for such horrible behavior, but she understood it. She had done it herself. To not forgive him, she thought, would be hypocritical, but he had been so mean. After about five minutes of making him hang in the lurch, she rolled over and looked at him. "You hurt me with what you said last night. You shouldn't hurt the people who love you, but I will forgive this time." They hugged tightly and kissed.

"Oh, no, look at the time. We've got to get on the road." The two hurried to get dressed and eat some cereal before they left for Cary.

"Love you too, Faith. I am truly sorry for last night. I didn't mean to ruin our special night. It won't happen again; I promise." Then, he was gone. Faith stood and watched as he walked up the driveway to his parent's home.

That weekend the two families, Roberts and Avery, planned a barbeque to celebrate the couples' engagement. Liam's grandparents were also included. Faith loved Liam's grandparents. His grandfather always had a funny story to tell. Faith could listen to Mr. Avery tell stories all night just to keep the night from ending and Liam leaving the next day. Unfortunately, the night did come to an end and Faith and Liam had to say goodbye. Goodbyes were not easy for Faith. She had grown up with a fear of abandonment and rejection, so she tried to hold back her fear and disappointment that Liam could not stay. Like the blink of an eye, the goodbyes had been said and Faith was in the backseat of her father's car headed home. Tears streamed down her cheeks as she gazed out the car window.

Sweet Surprises

As quickly as Faith returned to school, her graduation was fast approaching. She had papers to write, research to be done, and photos to be taken, as well as studying for her comprehensive exams. At the same time, she anxiously awaited a response to her letter to DFACS regarding her brother. Faith threw herself into her work and focused on nothing else. Her exam was scheduled for April 2nd. The night before the exam Faith's apartment was covered from one end to the other with books, papers, and photographs, not to mention dozens of empty cups of Diet Coke. Faith found herself in an all-out panic. Her neighbors downstairs were having yet another party. The noise was loud, and it sounded like the party was in her apartment. Her heart raced in fear of failing. As the night drug on, Faith's head began to pound; and before she knew it, she was vomiting. She tried to sleep, but it escaped her. Her mind racing through each subject matter and the details that she would have to remember. Her head continued to pound, and she found herself in and out of the bathroom all night. Before she knew it, it was morning.

Faith showered, got dressed, and raced to the university. She was still throwing up and her headache was stronger than ever. When she arrived at the school, she inquired of the proctor what the rules were regarding bathroom breaks, explaining to the proctor about her migraine headache and nausea. The proctor reassured Faith that all would be fine and that she could excuse herself to the restroom whenever the need arose. Just those words alone seemed to calm Faith's stomach. She sat down and began her exam. The exam took her five hours to complete. As soon as she finished, she raced home to sleep.

It seemed to Faith like she had slept for days. She finally felt relief from the migraine as well as the demands of school. She sat up in her bed and took a good, long, deep breath, and then blew it all back out. Finally, the only demand she had on her at this moment was to think about the planning of her wedding to Liam. She jumped from the bed and into the shower almost in one jump. She got herself dressed and drove to the closest bookstore to purchase every bridal magazine she could find. She then went back to her apartment, checking the mail on her way in. As she flipped through the pieces of junk mail, there it was. The letter she had been waiting for. She held it to her chest as she threw open her apartment door and flopped herself down at her dining room table.

At first all she could do was look at the envelope. She was afraid to open it because it might say that her brother did not want to meet her. She didn't think she could handle that, so she sat motionless staring at the envelope. She took a deep breath, opened the envelope and removed the letter from inside. Her eyes raced all over the letter looking for the response about her brother. As she read, overwhelming joy filled her body. He had said yes.

However, there was a provision which had not been mentioned in the previous letter. The letter indicated that she was required to meet with a social worker in Raleigh to be interviewed regarding her request to be re-united with her brother. Faith did not understand why she needed to meet with someone from DFACS in North Carolina, but she went; she did not want to risk not being able to meet her brother. It took her a couple of days to get the nerve to go to DFACS. After all, her last experience in a DFACS office was traumatic. She drove to downtown Raleigh and parked on the street. Her heart was thumping like a snare drum, so loud she thought for certain it could be heard by others. It took her five minutes to get the nerve to get out of the car and to walk to the office. When she entered the office, there was so much going on she could no longer hear her heart. Ladies were running around like mice who just got a whiff of cheese. The room was large and there were desks scattered around the room as if they were thrown about in a hurricane. Men and women were working on their computers.

Some were on the phone. She could understand why they didn't seem to notice her come into the room. Papers and file folders seemed to be stacked and strewn everywhere. The office was a complete mess.

As she stood there waiting, that memory came rushing back to her. There she was again in an instant on that horrible day. It was as if every minute came rushing through her brain in the flash of a camera and all the pain and emotion with it. A tear came to Faith's eyes as she stood looking around the office, and anger began to fill her. The resentment she felt for how she and Scottie had been treated welled up inside her. As she wiped the tear from her eyes, she heard, "Hello, I'm sorry, may I help you with something?"

Faith turned around, "Um, yes, I received a letter that said I needed to come to this office for an interview." She held her hand out with the letter.

The gentleman took the letter and briefly read it over. "Oh yes, I see. Well, I can help you. If you'll just come this way." The gentleman directed her to a private office. He sat down in the chair at the desk and held his hand out for her to sit in one of the chairs in front of the desk. "Well, it says here that you wrote to the DFACS office in Norfolk about your biological family and they told you about a half-sibling and asked if you wished to be united with this brother."

"Yes, that is correct. I wrote back saying that I wanted to meet him, and they were to contact his family or him, I guess, to ask if he wanted to meet me. According to that letter, he said that he does."

"Yes, well, in these sorts of matters, we find it best to speak with the parties before reunification. We need to know why you've come forward now after…you're how old, miss?"

"I am twenty-four years old, sir. I don't see what it matters that I am just coming here now."

"Well, you became a legal adult at eighteen, so why didn't you start your search then?"

"Well, a number of reasons which are really none of your concern; I do not understand what that has to do with anything. Why should it matter why I wish to meet my only sibling, my brother?" Faith was becoming visibly angry. "Some people never search. Hell, some people never even know that they were adopted until they're old, so why does this matter?"

"That is true. How long have you known that you were adopted?"

"Day one, sir. I was five years old when I was finally adopted."

"I see. We need to make sure that you have only good intentions for wanting to meet your brother. So, that is why we have these meetings."

"Why would have ill intentions towards someone I never knew existed? It certainly isn't his fault that any of this happened to us. I'm sorry but this is just asinine. I want to meet my brother because he is the only blood relative that I have in the world as far as I know. We should never have been kept apart as far as I am concerned, but then that's on DFACS now isn't it."

"Ma'am, there is no need to become hostile."

"I guess it is out of the question to ask about locating my foster parents?"

"Oh yes, I am afraid we don't do that. Foster parents are kept in anonymity. There is always the fear that adoptees may come back with a grudge and want to sue their foster parents for this or that." Faith was blown away by this revelation. Her experience in the foster care system was like that of many foster kids. She changed foster homes almost as often as she changed her socks, and she wasn't treated like one of the family. In fact, she had been abused. For him to state that the agency is going to protect foster parents from lawsuits brought by adoptees for Faith was a declaration of war. She could not get out of that office fast enough.

"We would never have anyone who would want to be foster parents if we didn't keep them anonymous. I will call the counselor in Norfolk and let her know that we have met and that everything is okay for the unification. I wish you luck, ma'am." Faith sneered at him as she stood up and left the office.

CHAPTER 22

A Bright Future

After the meeting at DFACS and having taken her final exams, Faith was ready to concentrate of more pleasant things. She was eager to start making wedding plans. She spoke to Liam almost daily now that he was back in the States. They were both very anxious to get the wedding done so that Faith could move. Their future together seemed full of promise and excitement.

The first task was to find a dress. After looking through the magazines, she just wasn't excited about what she saw. Faith was sentimental and liked antiques and other traditional things. She thought the perfect dress for her to wear would be her mother's. That dress had a simple elegance which she adored. It was ivory crepe with an empire waistline. Faith called her mother to ask her about wearing her dress.

"Are you sure, honey. My dress is so plain. Wouldn't you like to have your own dress?"

"No, Momma, I want to wear your dress; but, if it is ok with you, I would like to change some things on it."

"Okay, I will get it out and take it to the cleaners to make sure it is okay for you to wear. I will let you know when I get it back. We need to start looking at the invitation list. I will talk with Liam's mother and see if she's ready to start working on that and we'll come up with a maximum number of invitations. I don't want it to get out of control, but I also don't want to miss anyone either."

The date for the wedding was set for May 16th which was the anniversary of her father's parents. She was so excited about the symbolism because her grandparents had been married sixty years. Faith wanted to incorporate all kinds of symbols of successful relationships in her wedding. Her mother had other ideas. Faith trusted her mother implicitly to carry out her wishes while she finished school and graduated. That would turn out to be a bad decision.

Just after graduation, Faith came home to work on wedding plans. She happened to run into a member of the church staff while out shopping. "Hi Faith! I just saw on the church calendar that you are getting married on June 8th. How exciting! Are you excited?" asked Helen, the church secretary who had known Faith since she was a little girl.

"What? Did you say June 8th?" Faith was confused.

Helen looked at Faith with a puzzled expression. "Yes, that is what is marked on the church calendar. Is there a problem?"

"Uh yes, it is supposed to be May 16th. Maybe the church made a mistake?"

"I don't think so; your mother was in the office when they wrote it on the calendar."

Faith's blood started to boil. She blew it off as not a big deal and said goodbye to Helen. Her next stop was their local department store to look over her Bridal Registry selections again. When she got to the store, she asked for the department manager who was working just down the aisle. Mary Margaret came over and greeted Faith. She seemed surprised to see her.

"Your mother was just here a few days ago and we went over the list. Is there a problem or a change?"

"My mother was here? Why was she here? I didn't ask her to come and worry over this. I am capable." Faith was now angry with her mother…very angry. As she talked to Mary Margaret, she discovered that her mother had changed some of her selections because she didn't like them. Faith never wanted to pick out these items in the first place, but once she did, she had no plans to change her selections. Faith thanked Mary Margaret for the information, and she left. Faith drove back to her apartment in Chapel Hill. She was so angry with her mother that she needed ample time to cool down before seeing her or talking with her.

When she got home, she called Liam and related the day's events to him. Liam laughed which did not help matters; but in talking with him, Faith was able to cool down and to see the issue as not a big deal. Liam, then, brought up another issue which took Faith aback.

"Why don't we just blow off this wedding thing. Our mothers are out of control with all these plans. We could just elope. You can come out here or I can come there, and we can just go off and get married. It would be much cheaper!" Once Faith actually listened closely to Liam, she could tell that something was off in his voice and his speech. She couldn't really put her finger on what it was, but she knew something was wrong."

"You know we can't do that. We would both be disowned. I couldn't just jump in the car and start driving not knowing where I was going and not tell somebody. What if I got in a wreck or something? It would destroy our families. We cannot do that, Liam."

"Oh, nothing like that is going to happen. I can get some leave and come to Chapel Hill and we can get married there."

"Liam, you don't own a car! How do you think you can get here? Stop it. We can't and we won't do that."

"Alright, but you know your mother is just going to keep up her tricks and my mom isn't much better. She wants to invite the who's who of Cary whether I know them or not."

"That's no big deal. They each have a limit of 150 people."

"So, we are sending out 300 invitations? That is crazy, Faith."

"No, it isn't. Don't worry about that."

"Oh, okay. Well, I hate to say this, but I need to go. I need to run an errand for my CO. I love you. I guess this craziness will work out somehow. Quit stressing about it. I will call you in a few days. Love you!"

"Okay, I love you too."

At the same time, Faith was anxiously waiting for a letter from DFACS with her brother's information. Every day she hit the mailbox hoping for a letter. When the letter finally came, Faith rushed inside her apartment to read it. His name was David Klein, and he grew up in Wilson, North Carolina, which was not that far away, but he had joined the Army was stationed at Fort Bragg. She could hardly believe it, could it be that he had been that close all along and she never knew? She ran to get paper and to write him right away. She wanted to meet him as soon as possible. She wished that she could have him at her wedding, but that would be too soon, and her mother would have a stroke. Her father knew that she had written the letter to DFACS, but neither of them had told her mother because they knew how she would react; it would not be positive. All she could do is write the letter and wait for his response.

To her amazement, David responded quickly to Faith's letter. She received his response in a week's time. He told her in the letter about his adoption and his adoptive parents. His adoptive parents divorced when he was in his early teens and his father had moved away. His mother had remarried several times. He had a sister with his father and his new wife and a sister with his adoptive parents. Neither sister had been adopted. Faith was his only blood relative. He said he wanted to meet as soon as she wanted. He included his phone number and asked her to call. Faith was thrilled. She couldn't wait to tell Liam.

When Faith spoke to Liam, he was supportive of her meeting her brother. She told him that she was going to have to do in secret; her mother could never know where she was going. Liam told her to at least tell her father so that someone would know where she was when she decided to go. Faith thought that was good advice.

Then, she decided to pick up the phone and call David. She was so nervous. What would she say? She didn't want to sound like an idiot. She thought it over and over, but finally decided she would just have to go with whatever came out once he answered because she couldn't come up with anything. She wondered what he would sound like on the other end of the phone. He had also included a photo in the letter. He was handsome, she thought. Did not look like her, though, except that they both had blue eyes and brown hair. Of course, she realized that they did not have the same fathers, so the fact that they didn't resemble each other did not really account for much.

Faith dialed the number. It rang three times and then an answer…

"Hello?"

"Uh, hello, is this David? David Klein? This is Faith…Faith Roberts, your sister."

Almost immediately, he responded, "Oh, hello, how are you?"

"I am great. How about you? Are you okay?" Faith was still very nervous; she had no idea what to say.

"I'm good. Just hanging out here at the base. Some of the guys just went out for pizza, but I decided to stay in my room and watch television for a little while before we have to go back to work tonight. Where are you?"

"Oh, I am in Cary right now. After my wedding, I will be living in Havelock. My fiancé is in the Marine Corps."

"Oh, that's cool. I work on the helicopter flight line here at Fort Bragg. I wanted to be mechanic, but they made me a fueler. It's okay. I was hoping to get stationed somewhere other than North Carolina after school, but they sent me right back here. I like it, I guess. What do you do?"

"Oh, I just finished graduate school at UNC. I guess it won't really matter because I will probably never use my degree. I am photographer. I studied to be a photojournalist. I don't know what I will do once I get there. We will just have to see."

They went on to talk about their parents. David's life did not sound very nice to Faith. She was sad that they had not been adopted together because he was adopted just a few months before she was. If only, DFACS had done their job and put them together. David told her that he knew what his birth name was, "John Morgan Stewart". This was amazing information for Faith. She now knew what her last name was. She rolled it over and over in her head. She was amazed that his parents were so forthcoming with information since hers were anything but. That, too, made her sad. They had always claimed that they were not told anything about her or the situation from which she came. She never had a reason to doubt that; at least, not until now. If David's parents knew his name, did her parents know hers? Why wouldn't they tell her?

As the conversation came to an end, they planned to meet in person the next week at the Fayetteville Mall. Faith felt like she was going to meet a prince, she was so excited. This was the brother she had always dreamed of and wanted so much. She never imaged it would ever happen. She missed Scottie so much. She dreamed of seeing him again, but she knew that would never happen. It was a hole in her heart that had never been filled. Now it felt like it could finally be.

The days flew passed and the day came for Faith to drive to Fayetteville. She told her father where she was going. He was almost as excited as she was, and he assured her that he would make sure that her mother didn't concern herself about Faith that day. He would keep her busy with other chores. He went out to Faith's car and checked it over to make sure it was working well before her drive. He asked Faith to call him when she got back; he wanted to know how it went. It was just over an hour from Cary to Fayetteville. She would be able to stay a couple of hours before she would need to leave for home. She tried to stay calm. She didn't want to have a panic attack from her nerves. She turned the radio up and set out.

Before she knew it, she was pulling into the parking lot of the Fayetteville Mall. She parked and walked to the atrium. Her heart was pounding so hard it felt like it might just bounce out of her body. As she walked into the center of the mall, she was surveying the area for someone who she might recognize, though she didn't know why; she had only seen one photo of him. There were soldiers in uniform everywhere, so it wasn't as if he would be the only one and easily picked out either. She kept looking until she noticed someone who looked like he was looking for someone too, and then, they caught eyes. Faith smiled.

As he approached her, he put his arms out to hug her. She reached out and grabbed him back and they hugged for several seconds. "Hi, David. I'm Faith." Faith was beaming from ear to ear with a huge, albeit probably goofy, smile across her face. "You are so tall! That isn't fair. I got the short genes," Faith said to him. David chuckled.

"Looks like it, but it is better for girls to be small and petite like you. You're perfect. You ever been here before?"

"Just a couple of times as a kid. We came to Pope once or twice for an air show, I think. Then once my school came because they had some sort of archeological dig going on downtown and we came to see it. All the boys were all ga-ga because we had to go down Hay Street, a street known for prostitution, to get to it. Like they thought they were going to see something during the day. Little boys, ha!"

"Oh, that's funny. They cleaned that area up and it isn't like that any-more. I don't know about that archeology thing, though. That sounds pretty cool, actually. I have been here for about four months, not too long. I will probably be here for most of my enlistment. I don't know if I will re-enlist."

"It's not that bad, is it? I hope not. I have to live with military life for a while. I think Liam wants to stay in and retire. So, I am curious about what your parents told you about your adoption. I hope you don't mind talking about it."

"Oh, no, I don't. I don't remember it. I was just a few months old. All I really know is that she was pregnant, and the dude didn't want no part of it, so he told her to put me up for adoption. She was living in Richmond at the time. One thing I did forget to tell you, though, is that she wanted me to be raised Jewish. Are you Jewish?"

Faith was completely puzzled by that revelation. As far as she knew there was no such demand for her to be raised in any specific religion, but she would ask her father. "No, I was raised Presbyterian. That is very interesting, so your parents were Jewish. And you were adopted just a few months after you were born, where I was almost six years old. Wow, it's too bad we could not have been adopted together."

"Why do you think we weren't together?"

"I have no idea. I was in Norfolk, and you were in Richmond. Maybe one didn't know about the other? I wish they had, though, because you would've loved my parents. I'm sorry your father flaked out on you. That's tough. I had friends growing up whose parents got divorced, but their dads didn't just move away. What about your sister who you grew up with? What's she like?"

"Oh, my goodness, she is a complete mess. She's been married a few times. No children, though. She's been on drugs. I don't see her much. She always has so much drama. I don't like drama."

"Man, I hate that for you. I would've loved to be your big sister all this time."

"Well, we have each other now. Do you know anything about your father?"

"No, I don't. I really don't know anything other than what that stupid "non-identifying" information gave me, which was almost nothing. It said he was an "older" man. It also said our mother was "institutionalized" at some point and that she was schizophrenic. Does not really sound good to me."

"Any idea why you were in foster care so long? Almost six?" David grimaced.

"Not really. The paperwork said that I had been in foster care since the age of 4 days. I guess she had me the first four? I don't know. Maybe she abandoned me and there wasn't paperwork done? It's crazy. I am just glad to be here now. Do you want to go get something to eat? I love Chick-Fil-A."

"Yes, let's do it." They stood up and began walking towards the food court. They ate and talked for another half hour before David looked at his watch. "It looks like you need to get back on the road, there sis. You want to get home before dark."

Faith smiled, "But, I don't want to go yet. I guess you are right. I will call you and we'll get together again. We won't ever be strangers again." They hugged and Faith walked back to her car. She ran over every word of their conversation again in her head as she drove home. She was determined that she would solve the mystery of their past if it took her until the day she died; and, if possible, she would do it without the help of DFACS.

CHAPTER 23

The Wedding

Before they both knew it, June had arrived, and the families were marking the days to the wedding with parties and last minute chores. Liam took a week and a half of leave so that he could attend all the parties with Faith. They had a grand time and they received beautiful gifts for their life ahead. Before they could get married, however, the minister required that they meet with him for counseling. They didn't know what to expect but surmised that it must be to see how well they knew each other. Faith was nervous, but Liam didn't seem to care much about it.

When the day came to meet with the minister, Faith picked up Liam and they drove to the minister's home where he asked to meet. They both knew Reverent Maxwell well. He had been the minister at their church for several years and was well loved. The couple went into his study to meet. Rev. Maxwell was casually dressed; something they were not used to seeing. "Well, hello, I am so glad to see you both. Please, have a seat," he motioned to the two chairs sitting just in front of his desk. "I guess you two have been plenty busy in the past week, haven't you?"

Liam smiled, "We sure have. We've been carted all over town trying to get this thing done and that thing done." Both men chuckled.

"Well, Liam, you know this wedding thing is really for the ladies. Men don't usually understand all the pomp and circumstance. However, it is a serious business getting married." Both Liam and Faith shook their heads in affirmation. "I wanted to talk with you both today about that serious side of marriage. It is important that we look beyond the emotional part of falling in love and understand that marriage is far different than just being in love. We know that this early stage of love, passion is fleeting. How long does it take to settle in? it is different in every relationship, but if you do not have a firm foundation and put your relationship first, it may not last. How long have you two known each other?"

"Since my family moved to Cary and we started attending this church. We have gotten to know each other better in the past two years because we have been writing to each other and talking about the things that really matter to us," said Faith.

"Yes, I mean, we talk about everything. I don't think that there is anything I cannot tell her. I trust her more than I have ever trusted anyone. She has been there for me as a friend over the years when I had some issues. I appreciate and love that about her."

"That is great to hear. Have you experienced any issues between you in which you had to work through them?"

"Yes, being so far apart and not being able to see each other has been very difficult. When Faith was in school in Savannah and was struggling with some problems, we talked about those problems. She wanted to quit school altogether, but I told she didn't have to give up her dream just because this specific university had not lived up to her expectations."

"That is very true. I was at my wit's end. My roommates were all moving out and I didn't have anyone else to move in with me and school was not going the way I wanted it to. I was overwhelmed. Those phone calls were very expensive, but worth it. He encouraged me to talk with my advisor from undergraduate school and find out what he thought of the situation. That is why I came back to Chapel Hill to finish my master's." Faith squeezed Liam's hand and smiled at him.

"That is nice to hear. You know just about half of all marriages end in divorce these days. Most couples are now going into marriage with the perception that 'if we can't get along, we'll just get divorced,' not a great way to go into a marriage if you want it to be successful. You must wake up every day wanting to be married to this person next to you. It takes work. If you go into this marriage with the mutual understanding that divorce is not an option and that you will put the other person's needs before your own, you will be successful. Put the *'we'* first, then the *'you'* and last should always be the *I*. That's '*we*', '*you*', and '*I*'. Remember that always. Is there anything that you would like to ask me?"

The couple looked at each other and shook their heads "no" but asked if they could call him if anything ever arose that they needed his help with. Rev. Maxwell gave them his numbers so that they would always have them.

"I guess I will see you both down front in a couple of days, then!" He stood up and reached out to shake both of their hands. Then they walked to the front door talking about how beautiful the weather had been since Liam had gotten home. Rev. Maxwell thanked them for coming and Faith and Liam thanked him for his advice. They then walked back to Faith's car.

"Okay, so how do you feel about that conversation, Liam?"

"I thought it was a great talk, especially the 'we', 'you'. 'I', thing. That is a great way to look at it. I know that we will find ourselves in disagreements some time, but if we can focus on that maybe it won't be so bad. You know I love you."

"I like that idea, too. There's just one thing we need to talk about."

"What's that, Faith?" Liam looked at her seriously.

"You know. Your drinking, Liam. You know if anything comes between us, it will be that. You know that you need to stop. I don't want to come across as a domineering wife, but I have to be honest. It scares me. Any time we have had a disagreement it has been because you were drinking."

"I know, honeybunches, I will. I promise. I can't really drink that much because of my job. You will see when you get there. Sometimes I just get ahead of myself when I am trying to blow off some steam."

"Okay, so I will drop you off at your parents and go home to get ready for the party tonight."

"Sounds good." The couple went their separate ways to get ready for the last party before the rehearsal dinner and wedding. After the rehearsal Liam and Faith decided to meet some friends out at a local bar. Faith wanted to dance. When they got there, her friend was already there. Liam had met her friend the day before. Liam stepped aside to talk with his groomsmen for a few minutes. Faith and Sunny talked at the bar.

"So, you really going to marry this guy tomorrow?" Sunny asked Faith in a peculiar tone of voice.

"Yes, I am. Why?" Faith looked puzzled.

"Well, I probably shouldn't..." just then Liam came back and threw his arm around Sunny.

"Hey, good to see you again. What are you girls talking about?"

"Nothing, honey," replied Faith. She noticed that Liam was standing rather close to Sunny. Faith had taken Liam to meet Sunny the day before. They spent a few minutes at her home talking and then they left. Faith had become friends with Sunny her last semester of school at Appalachian. They had a couple of classes together. Sunny had a reputation for being loud and a flirt with men. Faith had always found it to be funny, until now. She was not quite sure what was going on.

As she stood there looking at the two, who were talking in whispers, Faith saw Liam run his hand up Sunny's skirt. Faith's blood shot right up. She grabbed Liam's arm and pulled him away. "What are you doing right now? How could you do that right in front of me?"

"I was just teasing. It's nothing. We're just playing around, that's all."

"You don't play like that. That's my friend. You don't treat my friends like that."

"You're being a bitch right now, Faith." Liam walked away to go back to his groomsmen.

Faith looked over at Sunny. "Why would Liam do that to you? Why would he think that would be okay?"

"That's what I was trying to tell you before he came over here. When you guys left yesterday, Liam came back over to my house. I couldn't believe it. I asked him why he came back without you. He said he wanted to talk to me without you there. He came in the house and the next thing I know he is hitting on me. He made innuendos about having sex with me. I turned him back around right quick and made him leave. I am sorry, Faith. You shouldn't marry this guy if he's like that. You deserve better."

"Sunny, I am only going to ask this once, so please tell me the truth. Did you have sex with Liam? I know how he can be. Was he drunk?"

"No, of course, I did not! Yes, I think he was. It was about an hour or so after ya'll left, so he had time to get tanked. I don't think it will work out for you if you marry this guy. He's a snake."

Faith took a deep breath and walked quickly to the door. "I have to go. I have to figure this out." Liam was waiting for her there.

"What did she tell you, Faith? You cannot believe her. You know when you went to the bathroom at her house, she had the nerve to hit on me. That's no friend, Faith. It is a good thing you won't be around her anymore after tomorrow."

"Get away from me. I am going home."

The Wedding Day.

With the blink of an eye, their wedding day arrived. Liam looked forward to seeing old friends and Faith enjoyed girl time with her bridesmaids. Her mother loved the changes that she had made to her dress and veil. Faith decided to just ignore the little things her mother did and said that were derogatory. Faith's father was there holding her hand and talking to her about how proud he was of her and what she had accomplished. She was a full-fledged daddy's girl.

Then the music began, and the wedding coordinator directed the bridesmaids to the back of the church. Faith and her dad stood waiting for their cue. Before she knew it, they were walking down the aisle and tears welled up in Faith's eyes when she saw her family and friends looking on as she walked to the front of the church. And then, it was over. Where had the time gone? What had just happened? It seemed like she was in a whirlwind, and she felt dizzy.

Liam held her hand tightly as they walked quickly out of the door of the church to a waiting vintage car. They drove around the city sitting perched on the back of the convertible. It was fabulous! They arrived about ten minutes later at their reception site, which was just across the street from the church. Pictures were being taken as they got out of the car and walked up the stairs to meet their friends and family, and inside the antebellum home. It seemed like a million photos were taken and then the guests began coming up and greeting the newly married couple. Faith's mother and mother-in-law brought food to them to eat as they met with their guests. The hour flew by fast. The couple excused themselves so that they could change clothes for their trip to the beach. When they returned, they were dressed in bright colored, Hawaiian inspired shorts and t-shirts. The crowd loved it and clapped for them. They ran to Faith's car which had been decorated by the wedding party. They jumped into the car and drove away, waving out the windows.

CHAPTER 24

A Brand-New Life

Their time at the beach was wonderful. A mutual friend had loaned them the use of their condo for their honeymoon. They spent time on the beach, bike riding, and eating wonderful meals together. Unfortunately, that couldn't last forever, and they had to return to Chapel Hill to pick up the last of Faith's things for the drive to air station at Cherry Point, North Carolina.

It wasn't a long drive; it was just boring. Liam did not like to drive, so Faith drove. She enjoyed driving. She was excited to see the apartment that Liam had rented for them. They talked and sang with the radio, and Liam napped. While he napped, Faith daydreamed about their life together. She was full of hope.

Once they arrived in Havelock, they drove right to the apartment to unload. The apartment complex was nice and had gated access. They pulled right up and parked in front of their apartment. Liam told Faith to cover her eyes and he led her to the door. Once he had opened the door, she uncovered her eyes. Faith looked to the left and looked to the right. She began to cry.

"What's wrong? Why are you crying, Faith?" Liam was confused and worried.

"Our furniture is never going to fit in here. Liam, this is the smallest apartment I have ever seen. Do you remember my apartment at all?"

"Oh, honey, I am sorry. We'll make do with what we have for now. It will be okay. Don't worry. This is what we could afford on my income. Once you get a job and we've been here a year, we can look for a bigger place."

Faith realized quickly how she sounded--unappreciative. She immediately dried up her eyes and gave Liam a hug. "You are right. It will work out. I will make it work. I'm sorry."

Liam hugged her and patted her on the back. "I will go get the stuff from the car. You stay here. It won't take me long."

"No, I am coming with you to help." As the couple was unloading their car, a neighbor from an adjoining apartment came out. She was a Hispanic woman about Faith's age.

"Hey, Liam. You're back already?"

"Yep, we just drove in. Lieutenant Teresa Hernandez, this is my wife, Faith."

"Very nice to meet you, Faith. Liam has been told me a lot about you. I hope you will like it here."

Faith smiled, "Thank you. I hope so too." Liam and Faith continued to unload the car, and Lt Hernandez left in her car.

Once they had finished unloading, they both collapsed on the floor. Faith looked over at Liam, "I think we need to find a Walmart so we can get an air mattress to sleep on until our furniture arrives, and maybe we can get some food, too. I'm starving. We can go grocery shopping tomorrow."

Liam looked over at her, "Sure, that sounds fine."

After they had returned to the apartment to eat dinner, they blew up the air mattress and had a good time jumping around on it. Liam had purchased a small television, so they had something to watch to pass the time. While they were watching *Mad About You*, Liam said, "Faith, there is something that I need to tell you. I wanted to wait until after everything was over and we were settled in, but I think I should tell you now."

Faith became worried. "What is it? What do you need to tell me, Liam?"

"Well, two things really. Just before I left to come home for our wedding, I got orders."

"What kind of orders?" Faith didn't know what that meant.

"I have to go to Persian Gulf for a four to five-month deployment. I leave in two weeks."

"WHAT? How could you not tell me this before? I am going to be here alone? I don't know anyone."

"I know but I didn't choose this. I have no choice. It's my job."

"So, what is the other thing you need to tell me, Liam." Liam could tell that Faith's patience was wearing thin.

"Well, I haven't paid my phone bill in two months. They have cut me off. I need to get that paid so we can get phone service." Liam's face was crunched up as if he was expecting Faith to explode.

"Really, Liam? How much money are we talking about?"

"Well, you know we have been talking a lot, and I have been paying on your ring." Liam sighed, "It's 150 dollars."

"Oh my gosh, Liam. If you didn't have the money, you should have told me. We didn't have to talk every day. And you didn't have to get me an expensive ring. I would have been happy with just a wedding band. You need to be responsible about these things. I will do it, but it cannot happen again. I have always paid my bills and paid them on time, Liam."

Liam walked over to her and put his arms around her, "I know. I will do better. Now I have you to help me learn about money management. You are much smarter about that kind of stuff than I am."

Later that night, they laid on the mattress and watched some more tv in their bedroom. It did not take long for Faith to fall asleep. She was exhausted from driving and unpacking. Faith didn't know how much time had passed when she woke up needing a bathroom break. When she awoke, she was shocked for find herself alone. Instead of going to the bathroom, she walked out into the living room looking for Liam. He wasn't there. Faith had no idea where he might be. She looked in the second bedroom and bathroom, but he was not there. She went back into their bedroom and threw on some clothes. She headed outside to see if she could find Liam.

The night was very quiet. She barely heard the crickets chirping. She looked around for which way to start looking first. She looked to see if the car was still there, and it was. She walked just around the corner of the apartment when she heard a television playing. She knew that someone was still up. She realized that the sound was coming from Lt. Hernandez's apartment. While she had no reason to think Liam would be there, Faith decided just to go ask Teresa if she had seen Liam. She walked to the top of the stairs and knocked on the door. In a few minutes, the door opened.

"Hi, Teresa, I am sorry to bother you. I am looking for Liam. Have you…." Teresa tried to keep the door just behind her so that Faith could not see in, but she heard his voice. Faith pushed the door open. "What's going on?" she heard Liam say.

"Faith, it isn't what it looks like," said Teresa.

"How do you know what I think it looks like, Teresa? Liam get up! You wake up right now!!" Faith shook Liam trying to wake him up. Faith looked over and saw an open bottle of liquor on a nearby table. She turned and looked at Teresa, "So you two have been drinking together? What else have you been doing?" Faith noticed that Liam's fly was undone, and Teresa was wearing a night gown.

"I promise, Faith. We just had a few drinks. That's all. I promise. He said you were asleep, and he wasn't tired yet."

"So, you thought it would be okay to invite him in? A man who has just gotten married…a newlywed, what about that seemed like a good idea? Explain to me how I shouldn't get the wrong idea with what I see here?"

Teresa said nothing.

"Well, I am going home. When he wakes up, you should inform him of exactly what has happened here and let him know that I know. He might want to find somewhere else to sleep." Faith left.

She was home about twenty minutes when Liam returned, staggering in the door. Faith was seated on the floor, silent.

"Hey, baby, why you so mad? I wasn't doing anything wrong. I couldn't sleep so I went over to Teresa's for a little while. We were just talking about you."

"Really. Is that the story you are going to stick with Liam? How did your pants get unzipped, then? Huh? I walk up there and open that door to see my husband laid out on another woman's sofa with his pants undone. What did you think…did you think about it at all? What if that had been me, Liam? Would you be angry with me?"

"You're being stupid. I am not answering any of this shit. I couldn't sleep so I went outside. I heard Teresa's tv on, so I went up there. Yeah, we had a couple of drinks. I am sorry, but I am a grown damn man; and, if I want to drink, I am going to."

Faith and Liam were standing face to face, only about a foot apart. Faith raised her hand to slap him, but he grabbed her hand before she could make contact. Liam laughed. "Really, you think you can slap me, Faith? Do you really think you could do that?"

Faith was so angry. She couldn't speak. She went into the bedroom, slammed the door, and locked it.

The next morning Faith woke up early and decided to go to the grocery store. Liam was still asleep on the living room floor. Faith stepped over him to get to the front door. Faith's mind was reassessing the events of the previous night and she hardly recognized what she was placing in her grocery cart. When she returned home, she found Liam sitting outside of the apartment smoking a cigarette. "Why didn't you wake me? I would've gone with you."

"Yeah, right," Faith said in the most indignant tone she could muster.

Liam followed her into the kitchen. "Faith, I am sorry about last night. Tell me what to do and I will do it. I love you."

Faith stopped unloading the groceries and turned to look at Liam. "Tell YOU what exactly? Not to cheat on your new wife? We've been here less than 24 hours and I find you half-dressed on the couch of another woman, who I might add, was wearing very little! So, you want me to tell *you* what to do? You can start by not going into other women's apartments. I would never go to another man's apartment that you didn't know why I was going. I would tell you before, if I would go even then! You can stop your drinking. Vacation is over. It's time to get back to work."

"I am sorry. I made a big mistake by going up there. It will never happen again. I swear." Liam moved closer to Faith. "I love YOU. I married YOU. YOU can trust me."

CHAPTER 25

Challenges & Disappointments

Two weeks passed quickly, and, for the first time, Faith had to leave Liam at the base and return home alone. She decided to prepare her resume and to look for a job. Faith spent hours looking through the classified for a lead but was not successful. A neighbor told her to go the local employment office and to register there. She immediately did that but was told that the market was slow due to troop deployments. Many had lost their homes and returned home to their families. To get through the long days, Faith took up decoupage. She sat for hours working on this or that in between eating lunch and watching soaps. The silence and loneliness were driving her crazy. She decided to call home.

Once Faith told her parents of the deployment and the slow economy, her parents asked her to come home and visit until Liam's return. Lee Roberts had a friend who owned a small airplane. His friend offered to fly over to Havelock and pick her up, and then return her a few weeks later. She took them up on the offer right away. Liam called her twice a week to check in on her, but the calls came at 4 a.m. Faith didn't mind, though. It was good to know that he was okay. During one conversation, Liam told Faith that he was completely sober. The troops were not allowed to drink during a deployment, not the mention that most Middle Eastern countries forbid drinking. He promised her that since he was alcohol free, he would never drink again. This promise, however, would never be true.

Faith's flight home was due to arrive just two hours after Liam's. They had spoken before she left for the airport, and he said he would pick her up so that she wouldn't have to call a cab. When Faith's flight arrived, she was anxious and excited to see Liam. Faith looked around the airport but didn't see him. She waited for her luggage, thinking he might just be running a bit late. Once she had her luggage, she went over to the waiting area and sat down. An hour passed and no Liam. Faith looked through her purse for change so that she could call home and find out if he was on his way or not. When she called, she got no answer. She left a message on the machine so that he would hear it if he was out smoking a cigarette. Faith rolled her luggage outside and sat on it waiting for Liam to arrive. Another half-hour passed; Faith was worried. What could've happened? She finally decided to call a cab.

When Faith arrived home, she found her car parked right where she had left it, and Liam was not home. She couldn't imagine what was going on. She called his unit to find out if they had been delayed for some reason. She was told by the man on the other end of the phone that there was no delay, they had arrived back at the post at 2 o'clock. It was 5 o'clock and Liam was nowhere to be found. Faith unpacked her suitcase and began washing clothes. At 7 o'clock the door opened and Liam staggered in.

"Hey Faith! I'm home. I am so glad to be home."

"Really. Is that right? I am too, but you know I wouldn't be here if I was still waiting for you to pick me up at the airport!"

"Wait, I was supposed to pick you up? Oh, I am so sorry. I forgot. Some of the guys wanted to go to the NCO club when we got back, so I went with them. I was so tired that I fell asleep on the sofa in the club."

"Liam, do you really expect me to believe that story? You were tired? More like you got drunk and passed out. Then you thought up this cover story hoping I would buy it, and you'd get off Scot free for forgetting me. Well, it's not happening!"

"I really did fall asleep. When I woke up no one else was there so I had to call a buddy to come get me and bring me home. I didn't do anything wrong, Faith."

Faith's temper was flaring. "How do you forget, Liam, that you spoke to me when you were in that airport? You said you would be home around 2 and that you'd come and get me? How do you forget you wife, Liam?"

Liam moved over towards Faith and reached out his hands to touch her arms and bring her close to him, so that he could apologize again. Faith grabbed her arms away from him and began to walk towards the living room having to squeeze between the kitchen counter and a table. When she did this, her elbow hit Liam in his side. Liam violently grabbed Faith and threw her to the ground. He was on top of her looking down into her face, one arm across her chest holding her down and the other above her head with fist clinched ready to strike her. Faith flinched and turned her head away expecting Liam to hit her in the face. "Don't you **ever** do that again to me. You hear me little girl. I could kill you right now and believe me, no one would know. I have given up my career for you and you want to treat me like this? Your degrees don't mean crap. They aren't worth the paper they're written on. Everybody knows that. That's why you can't find a job. You are such a bitch."

Faith twisted her waist attempting to wiggle away from Liam, terrified of what might happen next. Liam looked up toward the ceiling and tightly closed his eyes and clinched his jaw. When he opened his eyes again, he looked at Faith again and then got off her. Faith slowly got up off the floor and ran to the bedroom. She shut and locked the door. Faith decided to take a shower. She sobbed uncontrollably in the shower. She couldn't understand this situation. She had no experience with anyone who had a serious drinking problem. She felt helpless and ashamed, but more than anything she was afraid—afraid of just what her husband was capable of, drunk or not. She reminded herself, though, that she took vows and those vows included, "for better *Or* worse". This situation felt more like "better *And* worse". It was her responsibility to make sure she kept her vows and to pray for her husband and their marriage. She could disappoint herself and Liam, but she could not live with disappointing God.

Within a few weeks, Faith interviewed for a position with a marketing company. It wasn't her ideal choice, but she felt like she needed to take any job that was offered. On the day of the interview, she was feeling hopeful. If she had a job, she would have somewhere to be while Liam was at work. It would help keep her mind off how bad things seemed. She was overjoyed when she was offered the job. She started the following Monday.

In the months to come, this scene would be re-enacted many, many times, sometimes worse and sometimes not so bad. Liam also presented her with more financial issues she had not anticipated. He frequently bounced checks and Faith had to pay for those checks. Before she knew it, all the money she had saved, several thousand dollars, was gone and their credit card debt was increasing. Faith never dreamed that she would end up paying for her own engagement ring and honeymoon, but that was what happened. She tried not to focus on these negative things and to look for the good. There were days when that was almost impossible.

One of the activities that Faith and Liam enjoyed together was antique shopping. They never really bought anything expensive, but they enjoyed walking through shops and looking at antique furniture, coin collections, jewelry; anything that was old. They both loved history. There were many cities in North Carolina where they could drive in a few hours to go antiquing. On one trip, they went to a flea market. It seemed like there were hundreds of vendors. Faith and Liam separated for a while so that they could see the items they were most interested in. They agreed to meet back in an hour. Faith went towards the china, jewelry, furniture and Liam went towards the guns and coins. They agreed not to buy anything without consulting the other first.

An hour passed quickly, and Faith returned to the meeting place. A few minutes later Liam appeared, and he was overly excited. "Look what I found, Faith," Liam pulled out a gun from a bag. "It's a Colt Single Action Revolver. Do you know how rare these are? The guy only wanted $150 for it." Liam looked so pleased with himself, but Faith was astounded.

"I thought we weren't going to buy anything without talking to each other first?"

"I couldn't let this go. There were other guys looking at it. I should be able to re-sell it for more after I get it cleaned up."

"You don't know that. Spending that much doesn't leave us much money for the rest of the month. What's going to happen if something bad happens and we need money?"

"Then I will sell it. I promise this is a great deal." Faith was angry but she didn't feel like continuing to argue about it. They left the market and drove home.

A month passed and Faith was happy that things had been drama free for a while. But that calm was not to last. One Friday afternoon as Faith arrived at home from work, she noticed that Liam's car was already home, and it was parked oddly. He hadn't pulled all the way up to the sidewalk and it was crooked, taking up almost 2 spaces. She walked into the apartment and Liam was on the sofa watching television. "What's up with that parking job, Liam?"

"What? Oh, I was in a hurry, I guess. What's wrong with it?"

"Really, Liam? The car is sticking out into the drive, and it is crooked. Are you blind?"

"Don't be such a nag, Faith. It's fine. What are you making for supper tonight?"

"Well with that attitude I am not sure I want to cook YOU anything. You've been drinking already, haven't you?"

"Yes, Faith. I am a grown man, and I will drink if I want to. You aren't my mother." Liam went outside to smoke a cigarette.

Faith went on with cooking dinner. After they had eaten, Faith got showered and got into bed to watch tv. Liam stayed on the couch. When she was ready to go to sleep, Faith got up and shut the door so that the sound of the television would not keep her awake. She must have slept for about three hours when she got up to go to the bathroom. She noticed that the bedroom door was not completely shut as it was when she went to bed. Liam was not in bed either.

Faith went into the living room only to find the television off and Liam nowhere to be found. She knew that Lt Hernandez was gone on an exercise, so she would not be there. Faith went back inside and put on some clothes and then went back outside. She went to the complex swimming pool to see if he was there. He was not. Then, she walked around to the hot tub area. To her surprise and disgust, there was Liam passed out just beside the hot tub with his shorts down at his ankles. Faith immediately looked around to see if anyone was around. She was so ashamed, embarrassed, and humiliated.

She went over to him and shook him. "Liam…Liam…Liam, you've got to wake up. You're undressed by the hot tub! People can see you, Liam! Wake up! She shook him hard until he finally awoke. "How could you do this? Who has been here with you?"

Liam was extremely groggy. He looked up at Faith, but it was like he was in a trance. He didn't seem to recognize her at first. Then he shook his head and open and closed his eyes. He finally seemed to recognize his condition. "Oh my God!" Liam quickly ran to catch up with Faith. Faith was already halfway back to their apartment. She was quietly sobbing, and her mind was running through all the scenarios that could have put Liam in that place and in that condition. She knew it wasn't good and it was another slap in her face and to their marriage.

Liam tried to run towards Faith as fast as he could in his condition. He followed her into their apartment. He begged her to listen to him, but Faith walked into the bedroom and slammed the door, locking it behind her. Liam stood at the door. "Faith, please listen to me. It isn't like what it looked like. I promise." When his pleading didn't seem to work, Liam got angry. The more she didn't respond to him, the angrier he became. In a few minutes, Faith opened the door and, not saying a word or making eye contact with Liam, she grabbed her purse, walked out of the apartment, got in her car and left.

While Faith was gone, Liam managed to find more liquor and kept drinking. He hid the bottle under the sofa. Faith drove around the city and county to calm herself down and to think about what she was willing to do or not to do. Her mind always came back to those words, *"better or worse; in sickness and in health."* She had gotten an overabundance of both. As she had done in the past, she went home determined not to argue with Liam anymore that night. You cannot reason with a drunk person, so the best thing she knew to do was just not to talk to him at all.

When she arrived back at the apartment, she walked in to find Liam not in the living room. The television was on, so she sat down on the sofa. A few seconds later, Liam came barreling out of the bedroom holding the Colt revolver. Faith saw it and was confused. Liam said, "Faith, I am so sorry. I promise it wasn't what it looked like." He began to sob. He fell to his knees and began to beg Faith for her forgiveness. "If you don't forgive me, I don't know what I will do. I love you. You are the only person who really loves me. My mom and dad never cared about me. My grandparents were the only ones who took care of me when I was growing up. They knew how my parents were and they took me in when I needed it. My dad beat me so bad. He hated me for being born. My mother never had time for me. She was too busy with her stupid church. She had her friends lay hands on me because she thought I was crazy. Please, Faith, don't leave me." Liam lifted the gun to his temple.

Faith, panicked inside, calmly said, "Liam, put the gun down. This is crazy. You don't know what you are saying. We just need to get some sleep."

"I don't want to live if I cannot be with you, Faith."

"Look, let's just talk about it tomorrow. Do you know how embarrassing what you did is? My God, Liam! Your pants were down exposing yourself. Someone had to have been there with you. Who was it? No, I don't want to know. All I need to understand is that you've cheated once again. This madness has to stop, Liam."

At that moment, it was like a switch had been flipped in Liam's brain. He put his hand down, stood up and looked at Faith with utter contempt. "Well, if you were good in bed, I wouldn't have to go looking, now, would I? You are so damn self-righteous. I gave up the career I wanted to marry you, and this is the thanks I get. You think you're so damn smart. You ain't shit, whore!" He raised his hand again; but this time he pointed the gun right at the center of Faith's head. "You don't know what I can do. I could kill you right now and no one would ever find you. You don't even know whether this gun is loaded or not. I've killed people and I can kill you."

Liam was so serious and cold. His voice was deep, almost growling, and his eyes were black. Faith was looking down the barrel of a gun and had no idea what to do, not do, or say. She said nothing for a few minutes, so she could think. "So, you kill me, and you lose it all. It won't matter what your dreams were. Is that what you want?" Liam was still for a moment, and then he lowered the gun and sat down in a chair. His brain switched again, in an instant.

"You need to think about what it is that you really want because I won't take this forever, Liam. I know your parents disappointed you, but that's over. You are a grown man. You need to stop dwelling on the past and move on."

"Oh, like you have, huh? What about you, Miss Perfect? How do I know what you do all day? I am at work, working hard to make a living, going to war and getting shot." Liam pulled up his shirt and turned slightly towards Faith. "You see his right here? This is a scar from when I got shot." Then he pointed towards his knee, "Here's another scar from another bullet. You're such a fucking bitch, Faith. You have no idea what I have been through. And, hell, you could be cheating on me for all I know!"

"While I am at work, Liam? Listen to yourself. You know I am not that kind of person, Liam. Have I made mistakes? Yes, absolutely I have, but you know what happened to me. You know what Brian did to me."

"You are so full of shit. Brian didn't do anything to you that you didn't want. You just got mad because he didn't take you back. He couldn't rape you. If you don't want a guy's dick in there, you can keep it out. You're a liar, Faith."

Faith could not believe her ears. She hadn't told anyone except Kyle and Liam. How could someone who was supposed to love her think that she *wanted* to be raped? Her heart sank. She got up from the sofa, went into the bedroom, and went to bed to cry herself to sleep.

CHAPTER 26

Hanging On For Dear Life

F aith and Liam soon found themselves at their first anniversary. Liam had a special surprise for Faith. He felt he needed to do something special because Faith had endured many negative circumstances that he had caused. He made sure to get home that evening before she did and had the surprise waiting for her in their guest room. Faith also planned a nice dinner for the two of them. She went to the grocery store right after work to get what she needed and then she headed home.

When she parked, she saw that Liam was already home. Faith had a reoccurrence of panic attacks over the past year. She never knew what to expect from Liam. Some days would be perfect. He was sober and they would have a nice time spending time together. But, there were as many other days when she would come home to find him sloppy drunk. Liam could be a silly drunk, but more often, he was a violent drunk. This caused Faith immense anxiety and panic attacks. This day was no different. She didn't know how long he had been home and what condition she would find him in.

When she walked through the door, Liam was sitting on the sofa watching tv. "Hi, honey, you're home early. Is everything okay?"

Liam replied, "Sure, you don't have to worry. I had a good day at work, and I am ready to celebrate our anniversary. What do you have there?"

"Well, since we don't have much money to go out and eat, I went to the store and got some nice steaks to grill and some other stuff to make us a nice dinner. Is that alright?"

"Well, sure it is. I have something to show you."

"Liam, we agreed that we wouldn't spend any money this year. We're supposed to be saving to get a bigger place."

"I know, but you've put up with so much from me and you're still here. I had to get you something special. I will be right back. Close your eyes."

Faith frowned, "Okay. I hope you aren't about to make me mad, Liam."

"I highly doubt that honey." Liam went into the guest room and returned a few minutes later. "Okay, now you can open your eyes."

Faith opened her eyes and saw Liam standing in front of her with the most adorable Yorkshire Terrier puppy she had ever seen. "Oh my gosh, you're totally right, Liam. Oh, she is so adorable. Where on earth did you get her?"

"I saw an ad in the base newspaper. I called to find out if there were any puppies left to adopt and the lady said yes. I went right over there to pick one out for you. She doesn't have papers because her father was born in Germany and her mother was born here."

"Oh, who cares? We aren't going to breed her anyway. I love her. Thank you!" Faith stood up and gave Liam a kiss. Liam had bought her a bed, leash, a couple of toys and puppy food. "I have to make dinner, so you are going to have to entertain her for a while."

"That's fine, but don't you want to name her?"

"Oh my gosh, yes, I do. She needs a grand name for such a little girl. I know what I want to call her—Princess Isabella! We'll call her Bella!" Liam agreed.

This gift did much to get Faith to look away when Liam came home drunk, but it could never last. The only time Faith was happy was when Liam was away from home. She could come home and not have a panic attack not knowing what kind of mood she would find him in; and she could go out with her girlfriends to the movies or shopping without him laying a guilt trip on her. Most of all she liked the peace and quiet of her home. She knew that this was no way to live, but she made her vows, and she was determined to keep them.

Before she knew it another year had passed. Faith and Liam had agreed that their apartment was just too small, so they decided to look for something larger. They were fortunate that Liam had gotten a promotion and a pay raise. They drove around and looked at houses and neighborhoods.

They looked at apartments and they looked at houses. There were only a few apartment complexes to choose from and when they considered the increased cost, a house looked like a better option. However, Faith did not want to buy a house because she knew that they would only live in the house a short while before Liam would get orders to move. Liam wanted to buy a house with a yard for Bella. They finally found a house that they could afford, and it was a new home. They were thrilled.

Liam's parents helped them with their closing fees and before they knew it, they were gathering up their things and packing them for the move. The enthusiasm and joy did not last long. Liam's drinking escalated after he had taken a desk job in his unit. He seemed to have some difficulty learning his job, which made him feel inferior and he believed that his superiors were being unjustly hard on him. Faith often waited until he was out of the house to scour it looking for liquor bottles. One week she found over 20 bottles hidden around the house in varying levels of consumption. She confronted Liam with the evidence, thinking if he could see just how bad it was that he would do something about it. On the contrary, Liam became defensive and angry, and then he would storm out of the house and stay gone all day and into the night. Faith didn't where he went when he left, but she had a good idea where he was. She worried for him being on the streets driving, but what was she to do? She often tried to hide his keys, but he would get violent with her until she gave them back. Faith tried locking herself in the bathroom to get away from him, but he would pound on the door so hard it sounded like he was going to break it down. Once she hid in a closet in their guest room to get away. She was in the closet so long that she fell asleep.

Liam had come up with a new way to harass her, too. While working at the marketing firm, Faith had encountered an issue that she never dreamed would happen in a solid, reputable business. The first Christmas that she worked there, the company threw a Christmas party in the office after hours. Everyone brought food and dressed in their finest Christmas wear. At some point during the party, the management asked for all the ladies to come into the conference room. One of the sales representatives, Denise Landrum (the only lady in the office), told the ladies that she had a special gift for the newest hired employee. That lady went over to where was standing. Denise then told everyone listening that the gift was passed to the newest employee each year to show that this person was very special to the office. All the other ladies standing around had no idea what it was but were anxious to see. Andrea, who fit Denise's description, put her hand out to receive the wrapped gift. Denise told her to go ahead and open it, that everyone would be opening gifts later. So, Andrea preceded to open the gift. Once she opened it and looked, a look of shear embarrassment came over her face and she turned pale. The crowd began to shout, "Show it; Show it, Andrea!" Andrea slowly reached into the box and pulled it out. There was a gasp in the room from the ladies and they all looked at each other in horror. The men, who were standing in the hall just outside of the conference room were laughing and joking around. They whistled and shouted comments. The gift, if you could call it that, was a life-sized, rubber penis. Faith made a beeline out of the conference room. Faith felt this was uncalled for and disrespectful to the ladies in the office.

She made her way back to the sofa in the reception area. She could not believe what had happened. She was so glad that it wasn't her who got "it" because she would have embarrassed everyone who participated in the gag. Not only did she find it repulsive, but she also believed it was not done to show appreciation to the newest employee, but to get back at the ones who stood up for themselves. Andrea was a hard worker, and she was smart. If someone got out of line, she would pipe right up, putting him or her in their place. Faith waited for Liam to get to the party so that she could tell him what had happened. When he did finally show up, he was drunk, and he was talking all kinds of crazy nonsense. Faith could not get out of there fast enough.

The event at the Christmas party weighed on Faith's mind. She was a strong, independent woman who knew right from wrong; this was wrong and should never have happened. Faith knew she couldn't go to the manager because he was out-of-town. The office manager was in on it, so she would be of no use. Faith decided to write a letter to the regional manager to let him know what had happened. She sent the letter unsigned because she certainly did not want any repercussions.

It did not take long for the phones to start ringing from the regional office once the letter had been received and read. The manager was called on the carpet for allowing the prank. Although the letter had been unsigned, it seemed that everyone in the office believed that Faith had written the letter. Faith denied any involvement. Denise pulled her into her office to read her the riot act for "*threatening*" her position in the office. Faith was not the type of person to take this type of behavior from Denise. "Denise, I did not write that letter. If I had, I would have been well within my rights to do so, it was inappropriate, and, quite frankly, beneath you. I was offended and so were a lot of other people in this office. You *have* heard of sexual harassment, right?" Denise became very defensive. She said, "Honey, I have lived sexual harassment long before you were born. I have had to work three times as hard as these men in here to get where I am, and I don't appreciate you or whoever may have written that letter threatening my position. It is a setback for women in this office."

Faith looked at Denise as if she had two heads, "Denise, you are the worst example for the women in this office. You have been completely co-opted into believing that this kind of behavior is necessary to be accepted in the workplace. Women should never have to accept this kind of behavior in order to feel a part of the workplace. It is beneath us. I feel bad for you that you think you must behave like a childish man in order to belong." Faith got up and left the room.

Then her boss, Lamar, called her into his office. He proceeded the conversation with the assumption that Faith was guilty. He chastised her for the letter and called her a back stabber. Faith had had enough. She, again, denied writing the letter, but said she approved of the contents of the letter. She told Lamar that she was embarrassed and angry by how the ladies had been treated. She told him that she considered it unprofessional and told Lamar she would have no part of it. He continued to press her trying to get her to admit to the letter. He told her that he did not appreciate her holier-than-thou attitude and told her that she was fired. Faith got up and walked to her desk and picked her purse. She took the office key out and laid it on Andrea's desk. Andrea was sitting at her desk.

"What's up? Why are you taking your key off the chain?"

Faith looked at Andrea with an expressionless face and said, "Because he just fired me. Andrea, we may have had some differences, but I want you to know that I think you are an awesome person and I hope your life goes well."

Andrea stood up and gave Faith a big hug. Faith left.

Liam was proud of Faith's determination to stop the practice of sending this gift around. "They just better be glad you didn't get that thing because they would had to deal with me. Have they never heard of sexual harassment?"

"I know, right? I could file a lawsuit and I would probably win because none of the girls were happy about it, least of all Andrea. None of those girls would lie to protect any of those men up there. They're just angry that someone stood up to them. They didn't expect to be challenged."

Liam, however, would turn this around on Faith later. When she was unable to get immediate re-employment. He started back with the "your degree is worthless…blah, blah, blah." He wouldn't let it go. It was a daily, unending assault on her self-esteem. He knew how smart she was, but he just had to let her have it because she was unable to find a job. He just couldn't admit that the real reason was because of where they were living, a military base with little to no jobs for highly educated individuals. Most of the jobs only required a high school diploma and only paid what a high school diploma would get you—minimum wage. There were some Civil Service jobs, but those had been filled long ago and, in fact, some of those jobs had been eliminated in the past few years, so the best jobs went to career individuals.

Liam also managed to work in abuse about her student loan debt and how *his* money was going to pay *her* debt. Faith knew she could come back at him about the thousands of dollars she spent in the first few months of their marriage paying for his debts, for her ring, and for the honeymoon, but she wasn't that kind of "tit-for-tat" kind of person, so she kept her mouth shut. She had to listen to his constant berating about how useless she was; how he had given up the job of his dreams for her; how he was carrying her and she was doing nothing; how she would never last a day in the Navy or Marines. It all was becoming too much. She felt as if her head were going to explode listening to him say over and over, "You need to join up and do what I do. We'd make good money together. But you're too damn scared, aren't ya? You're such a loser. Why I married you is beyond me. I guess it was so I could have a free piece of ass any time I want, but you don't even want to do that anymore."

Faith was almost at her limit. She felt bad enough about not being able to find a job. Every day was a nightmare waiting for their mutually assured destruction, it seemed like to her. She desperately needed a way to get through to Liam. She loved him so much and hated seeing him ruin himself. As much as she was hurt by his infidelities, the violence, and mounting debt, she had no desire to leave him. One night in bed as she lay trying to go to sleep, she devised a plan that she thought might just work. Years later as she looked back on things, she did not understand why she thought this was a good idea. Was she really trying to show him, or was she really just trying to ease her pain?

One afternoon, she went to the grocery store to pick up a few things. While she was out, she decided that she would go to a park and sit and drink some Vodka. After she had a buzz, she'd go home and "show" Liam how stupid he looked when he was drunk. What actually happened was quite different from what she had expected, and it scared her. Once she began drinking, it started to feel too good to not feel anything. She drank far more than she had intended. When she left the park to drive home, she realized that she was in real trouble. She knew she had no business driving a car, but she had to get home. The entire drive home, Faith sobbed and prayed for God to get her home safely, that she not have an accident and hurt herself or someone else. Her prayers were answered.

When she got inside the house, Liam was waiting. "Where on earth have you been? You're never this late getting home." He looked at her and he could tell something was wrong. Faith didn't drink alcohol anymore since she married Liam. "What's wrong with you, Faith?

She looked at him and fell into his arms. "I'm drunk. That's what the hell is wrong with me. I'm sorry. I didn't mean it…. I think I'm gonna be sick!" Liam helped her to the bathroom and held her hair as she vomited.

"Oh, Lord, Faith. Why would you do this to yourself? You aren't me. You can't be drinking like this. Why? I know I am an asshole, Faith. I cannot lose you. I love you." Liam genuinely sounded concerned and Faith was surprised that her condition hadn't made him angry.

"Because this is how you look. I'm sick of it. Do you like seeing me like this? Because I hate every day when you come home drunk. I clean up your vomit. I've cleaned pee off the walls where you've peed in the middle of the night thinking you were in the bathroom. It's ridiculous, Liam. I may deserve many things, Liam, but I don't deserve this!" Although she let Liam have it about his poor behavior when he was intoxicated, she felt ashamed for her behavior that night. She was, however, more frightened of it. She could tell within herself that drinking could become a problem for her, too, especially if she allowed herself to give in to the detachment she felt when intoxicated. Faith did not like not being in control. It was bad enough that she could not control her marital circumstances with Liam, but she could control herself. She swore she would never allow herself to become addicted to any substance, much less alcohol.

"You are right, Faith. I know I have disappointed you. I am sorry for it all. Please do not ever do this again. I don't think I could take losing you." He helped Faith into bed and got her medicine for the headache she would surely have the next day. Unfortunately, Liam's words were flat because within days, he was drunk again and harassing her about not having found a job. What else could she do, but give in to his demands?

"Fine, Liam. What do you want me to do? I will go to the recruiter if that's what you want, but I will tell you this right here, right now, if they won't give me the job that I want, I will not do it. With the education I have, I better get the job I want!" Faith was emphatic.

"Okay, that's my girl. Let's go. I've got to get a quick shower and you do whatever you need to do, and we will go down there. They will want you to take the ASVAB. I am sure you will blow that test out of the water, though."

Liam was correct. They arrived at the recruiting station and the first thing the recruiting station manager did was to sign Faith up to take the test early the next day. After Faith took the test, he would be able to score it immediately and they could discuss what she career path she wanted and what her options were. Sure enough, Faith blew the test away.

"Now Sergeant, I respect your opinion, but as I told my husband when I agreed to come here, I will not go through with anything here today unless I can have the job I want."

"Ma'am, with this score, and barring any unforeseen problems, I don't see why that would be an issue. What job is it that you want?"

"I want to be a combat photographer. My degrees are in photography and journalism, so I think that would translate nicely."

"Yeah, sure it would. It is a small career field, but with your education, we should be able to get you in. Now, do you have any criminal record of any kind?"

"No, sir. I got a ticket once, but I have never been arrested for anything."

"Have you ever been a party to a lawsuit of any kind?"

"No, sir."

"Ok, I am going to give you some paperwork that I need you to work quickly, but as thoroughly as you can and try to get it back to me in the next two to three days. When did you want to leave for boot camp?"

"Well, Liam is already scheduled to go to NCO school next month, so I would like to wait until he gets back, if I could. We have a dog, and I don't want to have to leave her in a kennel."

"Oh, sure, that's no problem. It looks like the next class we can get you in actually is in September, so that's three months away. Is that doable?"

Faith looked over at Liam. Both nodding and speaking together, "Sure."

"You will also need to work on your push-ups, sit-ups, pull-ups, and running. It's better to get there already physically fit. It makes it less painful and stressful."

"I will make every effort to do that, Sergeant."

CHAPTER 27

Wits End

For Faith the next month seemed to fly by. She was busy working at a temporary job in the marketing department of the local hospital and taking photographs on the side at weddings and parties for extra money. Liam had run up significant debt in the first three years of their marriage and Faith needed to make extra money to try to make extra payments on those debts. Before Liam left for NCO school, he spent time with Faith teaching her much of what she would be learning at boot camp. He wanted her to have a leg up on those skills. He exercised with her to get her ready for the physical nature of boot camp also. While Faith was no athlete, Liam worked with her so that he felt like she could pass. Faith enjoyed the time that Liam spent with her, teaching her. She felt closer to him.

When the day came for Faith to get on the bus to head off for Parris Island, the couple found parting more difficult than they had imagined. Liam began to have second thoughts about pushing Faith into joining the Corps. He started telling her she could stay if she wanted and not go, but Faith knew that, although it wasn't the job she would have chosen, it was the best paying, secure job she could have at the moment. Her enlistment was not long—three years, and those years would pass quickly. "I need to go, Liam. I will call as soon as I am allowed," Faith leaned over and kissed him on the cheek, "Don't worry. I will be fine. You've taught me everything I need to know. I will keep my head down and blend in. You just take care of my baby and yourself and before you know it, I will be back."

"I know. I am just panicking. I love you, Faith." Faith turned and walked up the steps into the bus. Liam stood and waiting until the bus was completely out of sight before he got back in his car and drove home.

The bus ride to Parris Island, South Carolina, from Cherry Point was excruciatingly long. What only takes six hours by car is almost twelve and half by bus because of all the stops along the way. Faith didn't seem to mind, though. She enjoyed looking at the countryside along the way, the small towns, the people and activities were interesting to her. It took her back again to thinking about her birth family. Who are they? Could any of these people belong to her? This was normal for Faith-- to wonder whether she could belong to someone in a crowd at a concert or a football or basketball game, if they might recognize her face.

Before she knew it, she was asleep with her head leaning against the window of the bus. She was curled up with a blanket around her and her feet pulled up underneath her. Then, the bus came to a stop and all the lights came on. The driver came on the speaker, "Welcome to Parris Island, South Carolina, Home of the Marine Corps Training Academy." Just then Faith, jumped up and began gathering her gear. "If you are here for training, please stay seated until one of the DIs comes on the bus and gives you instructions. Good luck to you all and thank you for wanting to serve your country." He turned and walked off the bus. Faith could feel the anxiety welling up inside her. Her head was getting light.

"Hey, are you alright? You look a bit pale and sweaty," said the girl sitting in the seat just behind her. She was standing, looking toward the front of the bus for the DI to come aboard. "I guess you are as nervous as I am. The Marines are no joke."

"Yeah, I know. I married one," responded Faith.

"Crazy, and now you're joining up, too. Wow, what are you going to do in the Marines? Oh, I am Jessie, by the way."

"I'm Faith. I am going to be a Combat Photographer. What about you? What brings you to the Marine Corps, Jessie?"

"Nice to meet you, Faith. That's a real nice name. I am going to be a personnel clerk. Not quite as exciting as Combat Photographer, but it will help me get a job when I get out, and that's what I was looking for when I enlisted."

"That is very wise of you, Jessie. You will be able to do something with that when you get out, and you should be able to make decent money, too." Just then the DI showed up and stomped on board the bus.

The DI quickly unloaded the bus and had the troops sit and wait for further instructions on the sidewalk. Jessie and Faith sat together. "Do you think we'll all go together, the girls, I mean"?

"I have no idea," responded Faith, "but I hope so." About twenty minutes passed before the DI returned and yelled for everyone to stand up. "Okay, you slugs! Move like you've got a purpose! Single file. Hup, 2, 3, 4; hup, 2, 3, 4…."

The group marched to a building about a thousand feet from where they had been waiting on the sidewalk. "And halt," yelled the DI. The group stopped. Another DI came out of the building and spoke their DI. "Ok, when I call your name fall out and stand in this area over here, pointing to his left." Both Jessie and Faith's names were called, so they moved over to the left side. When the DI had finished calling names, he announced that everyone in that group would be in his company and that they were to stay put until another DI came to get the remaining soldiers. This lasted about half an hour.

"Alright, everyone, I will call your name and you file quietly inside. You will move to the left and fill up all the bunks on the left side prior to moving to the right. Every bunk should be filled. This will be your home for the next eight weeks. Stand at the foot of your bunk and wait for further instruction."

Once everyone filed in and filled the room, the DI walked up and down each aisle looking at each recruit. Some stood as still as possible and stared straight forward trying not to blink. Those recruits were passed by. Those recruits who smirked or giggled, the DI would stop in front, and proceed to scream into the face of that recruit. "Just what do you find amusing there troop? Do I have something on my face? Huh?" The recruit almost instantly washed the smirk from her face and a look of terror took its place.

"No, Drill Instructor, no."

"I think you are making fun of me, troop. Drop and give me forty! One, two…those are some sorry push-ups! Start over…."

After that recruit, the DI stepped in front of Faith. "Well, well, well, what is this? How do you have E4 rank on your uniform there, troop?"

Faith felt unsettled by the question. She did not want to stand out in any way from the other Marines, but she had to answer the question. "I went to college, Drill Instructor."

"Is that so? What kind of degree do you have, fancy?"

"I have a BFA in Photograph and Art History and a master's in Photojournalism."

The DI was visibly impressed, but not too impressed. "Drop and give me thirty sit-ups, Avery. One-two-three…." The DI continued this routine all around the barracks. Some recruits received more or less depending on their responses to the questions. After the DI finished, the troops were allowed to unpack their belongings. The DIs instructed them on how to roll their clothing and how to properly store them in their drawers. Once that was completed, they were allowed to shower and to go to bed.

Over the next several weeks, the recruits worked out, learned map reading, had weapons training, continued grueling mental and physical training. Some of the younger recruits had difficulty with the mental challenges. They rebelled against the authority of the Drill Instructors and often became entangled in legal issues. Others broke down physically and were sent home. Faith did not care for any of it, but given her situation at home, she knew she had no other choice but to make it. She kept her head down, did everything she was told to do and did not make waves. She earned the respect of her leaders for behaving this way. They often gave her some leeway when she didn't quite make the mark on some of the physical challenges. Sometimes she got a third and fourth try to make the challenge. She usually made it by then. She was always very appreciative and kept her head down.

The day came for the unit to get their dress uniforms and Faith was not feeling well. Her ears ached and her throat was so sore that she could not bear to swallow food. She did not want to say or do anything about it because she had already been to sick call once. She went on with the day as best she could; but, as the day went on, she felt worse and worse. She knew she had a fever, but she was not certain how high. As the day passed on, she began to feel so badly that she did not make sense when she spoke. Her friends told her that she need to say something to one of the D.I.s, but she refused. So, instead her friends went to one of the D.Is. The D.I. asked Faith, "Do you feel bad, troop?" Faith looked up at her from the floor and immediately the D.I. knew they had to get her to the Emergency Room, "Okay, get up. We need to get you to the hospital." She felt Faith's head. "Troop, you must have a fever over 102. You should have said something. This is dangerous." When they got to the Emergency Room, Faith's fever was 105°. The doctor at the emergency room examined Faith thoroughly. She was diagnosed with a severe upper respiratory infection and double ear infections. She was admitted to the hospital.

Faith believed that she would be taken care of in the hospital and would be able to return to duty quickly; and, in a way she was, but not in the matter she had assumed. Unlike most hospitals, she did not receive the round the clock care she thought was custom. She received medication on a time schedule, but she rarely saw a nurse or doctor otherwise. When it came time for housekeeping, she was shocked to find out that she was the housekeeper! Even with a fever of over 103°. She took cold showers to lower her fever, which took three days. She received a huge shot of penicillin in her hip to beat the virus. When she was finally able to leave the hospital, she was required to walk back to her unit. She felt almost as tired going back as she had felt going into the hospital, but at least she could swallow and eat again.

Once she returned to her unit, things went back to normal, except that Faith had missed her final PT test. Because of this, she would have to stay two weeks longer. She would be assigned to another unit, and she would be there like an active-duty soldier rather than an trainee. She would help trainees during the day with whatever the DI's needed, and she would have time to work on getting ready for her final test.

Two weeks passed quickly, and the morning of her test came. Faith was nervous because, even though she had been doing well, she was always afraid of failure. The DI looked at Faith, "Troop, you have nothing to worry about. You've worked hard these ten weeks and you are ready for this. You got this. You gotta believe in yourself. Now get out there and let's get this over with!" That is just what Faith did. She blew it away. Doing far better than she had ever done. The whole place was yelling for her. She had never felt so good. The next day she would be on a plane headed for her photojournalism training unit in Maryland. She almost couldn't hold back her excitement. She couldn't wait to call Liam.

When Liam answered the phone, it was an immediate blow to her self-esteem. Liam sounded as if he had been on a week-long bender. He was angry with her because he hadn't heard from her. She tried to explain to him that she was under the phone restrictions for the new group of girls she was housed with and they were newbies. He began to rant and rave about how unfair that was and how he was going to call so-and-so. Faith told him to not to call anyone as he had already gotten her into trouble once doing that and claiming he was of higher rank than he was and demanding to speak to her. Faith finally screamed, "Liam shut up; I am trying to tell you that I passed. I passed the PT test. I am leaving tomorrow for Fort Meade."

"Oh, oh, oh, okay. So, it won't be too long until you will get some leave then. That's good. I'm sorry. We had an exercise, and I am just still tired. Well, just let me know when you can what all the details are. I'm real proud of you, Faith. I knew you could do it. I love you, honeybunches."

"I love you, too. Thanks for believing in me. I will see you sometime real soon. Liam, lay off the liquor. We need the money if we want to go home for Christmas."

"Yeah, I know. I will."

Faith arrived at Fort Meade, Maryland, in November 1994, eager to learn what makes combat photography so compelling while trying not to get oneself killed at the same time. It seemed that from the time she stepped off the plane at Baltimore Washington International Airport, she was the interest of the Drill Instructors. It wasn't that they did not speak to the other troops, but their eyes and whispering seemed to be pointed at her, which made her exceedingly nervous. She had to wonder if Liam had done something stupid again that would hurt her before she'd even had the chance to get started. She tried to make herself a wallflower and hoped they'd move on to someone else. They were a class of about twenty.

Roll call was done, and they were put at ease so that room assignments could be handed out. Faith stood quietly until her name and the name of another female recruit was called. She nervously walked forward. "Corporal Avery, Sergeant," said Faith anxiously. The DI stared at her for a few seconds while he handed her the room assignment, and then smiled.

"Tell me, Avery, how is it that you stand before me as a Corporal?"

Faith swallowing hard and looking past the DI responded emotionless, "I have a bachelor's degree and a master's degree, Drill Instructor."

The DI's interests were peaked. "Oh really? Well, now, where did you go to school and what are those degrees in Corporal?"

"Sergeant, I have a Bachelor's in Fine Arts from Appalachian State University and my Master's in Fine Arts from the University of North Carolina."

The DI laughed at bit. "Sounds a bit yuppy to me. What are you doing here, exactly?"

"My degrees were in photography and journalism, Sergeant. I wanted experience in combat photography, and I grew up as a foster child for part of my life…," Faith looked up into the DI's face, "this is my way of paying back the government for taking care of me for those few years."

The DI was silent, looking right into Faith's eyes. "That's impressive, Corporal. Keep up the good work." He took a step back. Yelling at the top of his lungs, he called everyone to fall into order. "Grab your bags and, on my command, you will fall out and move to your rooms and begin unpacking your things. At 1730 we will meet back out here, and the cadre will take you all to the dining facility for dinner. At 1930 we will have a brief meeting in the day room on the first floor to go over the events for tomorrow. ATTENTION ON DECK! FALL OUT."

Faith's time in training seemed to fly by because she found it interesting and fun. She enjoyed the others in the class. Many of them were intelligent and witty and fun to be around. She found herself actually enjoying herself for the first time in a very long time.

She also performed well in the course. She was in the top two in her class. The instructors liked her and often allowed her to aid in the instruction because of the knowledge she had from her education. Her favorite part was going out into the woods and photographing the environment and doing mock scenes. Everyone eagerly awaited the development of the photographs as they developed in the dark room and to see whose photograph would be selected as the best for that mock event. The final exam for the course was similar in that the base had a post wide exercise, and the students were to go out and photograph the event. Each student would be graded on their photographs of the exercise. It was no surprise to anyone when Faith received the highest score.

In the blink of an eye, graduation had arrived, and Faith was an honor graduate. She told Liam and her family not to come because she just wanted it to be over and to get home as quickly as possible. She had gotten orders to Cherry Point to serve in the Public Affairs Office. There would be plenty of time for her to visit with family once she got home because she had built up leave time. Though it would not be the best or easiest way to get home, Faith chose to take a bus back to Cherry Point to save money because she knew that Liam had spent about every dime they had while she was gone, so she did not want to ask her parents for money for a plane ticket. She told Liam what time the bus would arrive so that he could be there to pick her up. She couldn't wait to finally sleep in her own bed again. Twenty-two weeks was a long time to be gone from the person you love.

C H A P T E R 2 8

Homeward Bound

When the bus arrived in Cherry Point that Friday afternoon, Faith looked around and did not see Liam anywhere. She went to the baggage area and retrieved her bags and then went out front to see if he might be waiting out there. Once again, Liam was nowhere to be found. Faith was furious. This was the second time she had gone somewhere, and he failed to pick her up as he promised. No doubt in her mind that he was most likely drunk somewhere instead of being where he was supposed to be. The more she thought about it, the angrier she became. She looked around and within a few minutes a cab pulled up. She looked in her wallet and, thankfully, it looked like she had just enough cash to pay for a cab to take her home. She hailed the cab and asked the driver to take her home. As she sat in the back of the cab, her anger turned to disappointment and humiliation that her husband could forget her after being separated for over twenty-two weeks, and she began to cry.

When the cab pulled up to her home, she stepped out and paid the driver. As he drove off, she walked up the driveway and her sadness turned to fear. What if he was dead? What if he left her? What if he's in there with someone else? All the *"what ifs"* were killing her. But she straightened up her back, and she marched up the driveway and she opened the front door ready to lay into him, and what she saw blew her mind, though she really didn't know why; it wasn't the first time.

Liam was laying passed out on the sofa. One leg was hanging off. One arm was up against the side of the sofa and he was snoring like a freight train. In the floor next to the sofa was a female passed out face down. There was a liquor bottle lying next to her. Faith immediately walked over and kicked her with her foot. The woman looked up at Faith. "You need to get out of here, honey. This ain't your house or that ain't your man."

Without saying a word, the woman got up, grabbed the bottle and ran out. Faith had no idea where she went or how she got there because there were no other cars in the driveway other than Liam's and Faith's.

Then, Faith walked over to the sofa, and she tapped Liam on the arm several times to wake him up, each time tapping harder. He finally opened his eyes. When he finally realized who it was that he was looking at, one could see the light bulb go off in his head when the realization hit him of what his wife had just seen and what he had forgotten to do. "Oh my God! I…I…I…I am so, so, so sorry Faith. It wasn't at all what it looked like. We were just talking. Nothing happened, I swear."

"Yeah, okay, Liam. You forget to pick your wife up from the bus station after being separated for over twenty-two weeks so that you can do God knows what with some other woman in our home. Yeah, that's believable."

"Faith, I swear. I'm so sorry. I thought your bus was tomorrow. Please forgive me. I didn't do it. I swear. I've been waiting for you. I love you. Look, I am going to go get a shower and get cleaned up, and we'll get you all unpacked and we'll get some food and talk about everything. We've got to go sign you in at the base."

"I really don't have much to say to you, Liam, but I do have to go sign in, so we might as well get that done."

After they got cleaned up, Faith and Liam drove to the base to the In-Processing Center. When they entered the building there were not many soldiers there. Faith walked over to the line and Liam sat down in one of the chairs to wait. When it was Faith's turn at the counter, the soldier looked at her name and looked at her, "Oh yes, I think we've been notified about you. Let me go see." Faith was puzzled. The Clerk walked to the back to someone at another desk and spoke with a higher-ranking soldier. That soldier returned with the Clerk.

"Hello, Corporal Avery, I am Staff Sergeant Willis. We received notification that you would be reporting for duty soon and your first sergeant asked that he be notified as soon as you signed in. I have just called him to let him know that you are here. He will be here soon. If you will just have a seat. We'll get you in processed as quickly as possible."

"Sergeant, is there a problem that I need to be aware of? My husband and I did complete the all the paperwork so that we could be assigned together. I believe it was done correctly."

"Oh, no, there's no problem. He'll explain when he gets here. No need to worry."

"Thank you."

Faith walked over to where Liam was sitting and told him what had just transpired. Liam was curious also about why the first sergeant would want to see Faith right away. He had never been treated that way when he arrived at a duty station.

About half an hour passed before the first sergeant arrived. He came into the building huffing and puffing and apologizing, "Corporal Avery, I am so sorry it has taken me so long to get here," stretching his arm out to shake Faith's hand, "I am your first sergeant, Howard Schmidt." He looked over at Liam and put his hand out to shake Liam's hand as well.

"Hello, I am Liam, uh, Sergeant Liam Avery, her husband."

"Nice to meet you, too. Let's sit down. I was in the middle of my garden when they called me, so I had to do some things to make myself presentable before I could come up here. I do apologize. Corporal Avery, I must tell you, your leaders and instructors in training were most impressed with your level of accomplishment in photography and that is why you have received the duty assignment you have received here at Cherry Point. You are going to be working for the Base Commander's public relations staff. This is highly significant because you will be the most junior soldier in that staff. I don't want you to feel intimidated by that because you have all the necessary skills. Do you understand?"

"I do, First Sergeant. My education, both in college and graduate school, has been in photography and journalism, so I probably have more background than most, but that certainly does not mean that I know it all."

"That's right and because you have the education behind you, rather than just on-the-job training like most get in the military, you have a skill set that really cannot be matched. The Commander wants to make use of that. This also means, however, that you will be traveling with him from time-to-time. Do ya'll have children yet?"

"No, not yet."

"Good, then it won't be a problem just yet. Now, Sergeant Avery, how long have you been stationed at Cherry Point?"

"This is my fourth year."

"Hmmm, well, we know she will have to be here at least a full year before she would be eligible to PCS anywhere. We'll cross that hurdle when we come to it. Okay, let's go check on your processing and get you home, so you can relax and get ready to be at work Monday morning! Glad to have you're here, Corporal Avery."

"Thank you very much, First Sergeant." When they returned to the desk, Sergeant Willis was waiting with the paperwork Faith needed and all was completed except for her to get her gear. First Sergeant told her that she would do this after formation on Monday morning. She thanked Sergeant Willis for making everything so easy and she and Liam left to go home.

Liam was very quiet in the drive home. Faith didn't notice at first because she was lost in her own thoughts of what her job was going to be like; what the people were going to be like, especially the base commander. Then, she noticed some tension in the air. "Liam, is something wrong? You seem a bit tense."

"Nope. It's fine," Liam barked.

Faith suspected the "green-eyed monster" was poking at Liam. She could tell from his tone that he did not like how she had been treated by the first sergeant. "You aren't fine. What is it," retorted Faith?

"I guess you're just over the moon to be working with all these officers and high-ranking NCOs, not with grunts like me. Soon, I won't be good enough for you."

"Oh my God, are you serious right now?" said Faith, "Are you really going to behave like a jealous child? You don't get it at all because you are too busy thinking about yourself all the time. Do you know what kind of pressure putting me into that environment will be for me? You heard the first sergeant, there will be someone who will, no doubt, believe that I don't belong there because I haven't earned my way there. They'll be angry because

I have the education and they don't. They'll make it twice as hard on me as everyone else; you wait and see. You're such an ass sometimes, Liam!"

"You're right. I wasn't seeing it that way. Well, no one better give you any shit, or they'll have to deal with me."

"Oh, no, you have to stay out of it. I have to make my own way. That's the only way to earn respect, Liam."

Liam chuckled. "You are my smart girl, aren't you?"

"It's why you married me." They both laughed.

CHAPTER 29

Good Times & Good People

The day to report to duty soon arrived and Faith was a bit nervous. She entered her new unit alone, feeling anxious and not sure what exactly to do. An NCO came running by her, "Hey, you the new girl? Follow me!" Faith turned around and followed the NCO to formation, just outside of the office building. First Sergeant Willis caught up with her and told her that once they finished with formation, he would take her to get her gear and then bring her back to the unit. Faith fell in at the back of the formation. During the announcements, First Sergeant introduced Faith to the rest of the unit. He had nice things to say which made her feel a bit insecure. She certainly did not want to be put on some pedestal she might just very well fall off of.

When formation was over, everyone came and introduced themselves to Faith and told her that she would like it in this unit. Within a few minutes, everyone had moved on to their jobs and Faith was left waiting for the First Sergeant. About five minutes or so later, he came driving up in a truck to take her to get her gear. On the drive, they had a great talk about her education and about Liam…how they met, how long they'd been married, etc. She felt a feeling of security welling up inside of her.

The next few months Faith spent getting to know the base and her job. She built relationships with her co-workers that felt satisfying. She enjoyed going to work every day. The other female soldiers were helpful and encouraging with her continued efforts to improve her physical fitness. Overall, life at work seemed rewarding.

There was one obstacle at work, however. Faith almost immediately noticed tension between herself and an NCO in her unit. Unfortunately, this NCO was her next line supervisor and he controlled everything about her time, assignments, reviews, etc. Almost immediately, he began making snide comments about her advanced education and his lack of education but his having OJT. Faith had never been one to brag about her education to make anyone feel lesser, after all her own husband did not have a college education. She had not mentioned anything to anyone about her background; the First Sergeant chose to do that. On an almost daily basis, he tried to do something to make Faith look incompetent. However, it did not work. Faith either noticed the error or she caught it in advance by double checking information with others in her unit.

There was a class Faith was required to take for driving a military vehicle. Staff Sergeant Clifton intentionally told her the wrong place and time or the course. Faith had already decided that she would never put her trust in this NCO, so when she was eating lunch a few days prior to the class, she asked another NCO about it, not acting as if she knew anything about it. When Faith showed up at the class at the right time and place and in the correct uniform, Staff Sergeant Clifton's face showed his shock and his rage. He almost immediately walked over to another NCO and began talking to him. Faith supposed that he was probably asking him if he had spoken to her about the class. She watched him as they spoke. His face turned dark red. He was incensed that Faith had gotten the better of him. This behavior would continue until Faith was reassigned to another unit on the post a year and half later.

CHAPTER 30

Disappointments & Surprises

Unfortunately for Faith not much changed at home after she returned from school. There was a very brief honeymoon period between she and Liam. They got along wonderfully. He went for a period of not drinking and they were having a great time together. However, that situation almost never seemed to last for the couple. Faith never knew what would set bad times into motion because Liam so rarely told her the truth about anything. But one thing she did know, the bad times were not just bad, they were horrific. Things were different now. She wasn't just hiding the truth from her family, now she had to hide it from the military. She couldn't let them know that anything was ever wrong at home.

There were days when she went to work that she had no sleep because of his middle-of-the-night tirades. She often found herself locking herself in the guest bathroom or hiding in one of the closets to get away from him.

She made sure that her watch had an alarm so that she would always be at work or PT on time. Liam, however, did not act up as much during the week as he did on the weekends because he, too, had to be at work on time.

When Fridays came, however, all bets were off on whether he'd be sober or not about 98 percent of the time. He would start as soon as his unit was dismissed from work, whatever time that might be. Within an hour he would've consumed at least one fifth of a liter of gin or vodka, and that was just getting him started. Over the years of excessive drinking, Liam's tolerance was quite high. Faith never really knew how much he drank in a single day, but she knew it was too much. Sometimes she didn't want to know because she knew that it would make her sick. She feared that she would wake up one day and he would just be dead; or worse, he would drive and kill an innocent person. Either way, their lives would be over.

In order to survive the constant drama and terror, Faith chose to live in denial. She tried sneaking off to an Al-A-Non meeting a few times, but it didn't work. Liam found out and it wasn't worth his berating; and she couldn't relate to the people there because they were so far ahead of where she was. Denial was easier, though dangerous.

The time came for Faith and Liam's fourth anniversary. Liam promised to be good and to take her to a restaurant out on the water. It was a dress-up restaurant. She was hesitantly looking forward to it. They decided to pretend it was a date and to get dressed in separate rooms and that Liam would "pick her up" from her room for the date night. When Faith opened the door, her heart melted. There stood in his best suit stood Liam looking like the day they got married. Tears welled up in her eyes. "Oh no, don't you do that," said Liam, "I promise, tonight will be a good night. I won't screw it up. I swear."

Faith put her hand out towards Liam, "Hi, I am Faith. I just moved here. Have you lived here long?" Liam chuckled and agreed to play along.

The night went so well, Faith wasn't sure if she should allow herself to enjoy it. They had a great conversation during dinner. Their food was amazing. They held hands across the table. It was one of those nights that most girls go home and write about in their diaries—one they never forget. Faith just knew the other foot was going to drop at any moment, but it didn't. They went home and made love all night. Liam stayed in the bed all night, not getting up to go drink in secret, passing out on the sofa. Faith almost wanted to believe the night might last, but could she do that? This would be a night that they would never forget.

CHAPTER 31

Making New Plans

For a few weeks after their anniversary, Liam seemed to be taking a break from his drinking. It felt nice to come home and not be confronted with an angry, drunk man. At this time, Faith's unit came up to their annual training certification time and she had to go to the range for qualification. Because this area of North Carolina is swampy and hot in the summer, it could be unpleasant. Faith started hydrating herself a few days before because she tended to dehydrate in extreme heat; but it seemed, that on this particular day, it did not matter. After shooting at the range in biological warfare gear, Faith became very ill. She believed that she was just dehydrated, and a fellow soldier drove her home. Liam met them at the door and helped get her into bed and brought her some cold water.

After doting on her for a little while, Liam looked at Faith and said, "I know this might sound crazy, but you don't think you could be pregnant, do you?"

"Are you serious? Of course, not. Why would you think that? I don't think so. It shouldn't have been the right time."

"Well, but maybe you should just check to see. You aren't on birth control anymore."

"Just because I got sick at the range? You know I don't handle heat well."

"True, but it might be…it could be? It couldn't hurt to check? I will go to the store." Liam came back with not one home pregnancy test, but three home pregnancy tests. After Faith laughed about him wanting her to take any of them because she had always been very regular in her cycles and she was sure that she should not have been ready to ovulate yet, she agreed to take a test. Much to her surprise, she was absolutely wrong! She was pregnant. 214

CHAPTER 32

Changed Priorities

Once Faith knew she was pregnant, she made a promise to her little one. She promised for better or worse to Liam, but this baby had not. She would not tolerate Liam's bad behavior anymore after this baby was born. She prayed that Liam would turn over a new leaf and make a commitment to be a better person for his child. He believed that his parents failed him, so maybe he would change so that he would be a different father to his child. She prayed every day for that.

The first few months into the pregnancy went well. To Faith it seemed like her prayers had been answered. They were trying out churches. They were doing things together at home to get the nursery ready. They were picking out names together. It seemed like all was well. Faith enjoyed Liam so much when he was sober. He made her laugh, and it felt so good.

Unfortunately, good times never lasted for this couple. Inevitably the day came when Faith came home to find Liam passed out on the sofa. She had no idea how long he had been there. She tried to tread lightly, but it never really mattered because if he was going to go off, it didn't matter what she did. She went back to the bedroom to change out of her uniform and put on more comfortable clothes and go back to make something to eat. While she was changing clothes, Liam showed up in the bedroom ranting about something. He was slurring his word so badly that she couldn't understand what he was talking about. Faith was tired and in no mood for Liam's nonsense, so she brushed by in the doorway and rolled her eyes. She motions for her dog to come on so that they could go out. Liam grabbed her by the arm and swung her around and pushed her up against the wall, "Who do you think you are rollin' your eyes at, bitch?"

"Liam, let go of my arm. I'm not doing this with you right now. You are just looking for a reason to fight and I am not doing it. I am taking the dog out. Let me go." Liam let her go at that point, but he wasn't done with her. At that point, he went back to the sofa and went back to watching television. Faith took Bella out and then made dinner. She did what she could to keep things on an even keel; but as the night went on, Liam did what he always did. He would sneak out and continue drinking for hours. It rarely failed that his anger and resentment would escalate to the point of verbal and physical abuse against Faith.

Faith went to sleep that night around 10 o'clock. Around 2 a.m. Liam woke Faith up ranting about something. She could not understand what he was talking about. He pulled her out of the bedroom to yell at her about whatever it was that he thought she had done wrong. He kept yelling and yelling and yelling. Faith tried to calm him down, but he refused. He was slinging his arms around trying to hit her. Faith tried to hide in the guest bathroom, locking the door. Liam all but knocked the door down. After an hour of yelling and attempts to fight, Liam finally gave up and Faith slept in the bathtub that night. Faith was five months pregnant. Faith continued to worry about whether this baby would make it, given all the stress Liam was putting on her. All she could do was pray.

When it came time for Faith to deliver (a week before her due date), she returned home from work and went to the bedroom to change out of her uniform. She wanted to go back to base to walk the track before they went to go get something to eat. Liam said, "Hey, give me a hug before you go back." Just as she went to wrap her arms around him to give him a hug, Faith's water broke." Faith was shocked. She had no idea what to expect.

"Go get my bag. It is time to go to the hospital. My water just broke." Faith had no idea at this point that Liam had been at home drinking all afternoon. Liam went back to the bedroom and got the suitcase they had prepacked for the hospital. When he came back, Faith looked at him and asked him a couple of questions. He slurred his words and his breath proved to her that he was drunk. She was furious, but she had no other choice. They could not afford an ambulance ride. Faith prayed to God that he would deliver her and her baby safely to the hospital. She was so angry that she did not speak the entire way to the hospital.

Once they were in the delivery room, Faith needed to let the nurse know that there was a problem with Liam. She had to do so delicately because she could not risk Liam losing his job. Because she never actually went into labor, labor had to be induced. It wasn't too difficult for Faith to get her point across because Liam wreaked of alcohol. In addition, the epidural had not worked. Faith was completely unprepared for the pain. The labor was long and painful. The nurse was more attentive to her because of this situation and so, Faith made some facial expressions to the nurse to get Liam out of the way. The nurse kindly asked Liam to step aside because Faith was in such pain. From that moment on, the nurse held her hand to help Faith through the rest of birthing process. She didn't see Liam again until after their son Stewart was born. At that point, she let him have it about his behavior, but it had no effect. He returned the next day to drive them home, again intoxicated. Not wanting anyone to know that there was a problem. Faith said nothing out of shame, humiliation, and fear.

When little Stewart Neil Avery was three months old the Averys moved to California. Faith wasn't happy about the move because she hadn't been at Cherry Point very long and she loved her assignment there. Liam insisted that he *had* to PCS because he had been at Cherry Point too long and that he was due for a move, but Faith didn't believe him. She believed that Liam's bad behavior was beginning to catch up with him. She knew that there were many days when he went to work hungover, still smelling of alcohol. She couldn't understand how he could drink as much as he did and function at work. Maybe he wasn't functioning as well as he thought he was.

When Faith got the Camp Pendleton, she was not received very well and the people that she worked with were not nice. It made her very unhappy. The NCO she reported to, was much like the NCO at Cherry Point. He did not seem to like her. But Faith had learned from her last position how to handle it. She kept her head down and did her best, no matter how childish he behaved. Her job was to write public service announcements about the base and to take any necessary photographs to go along with it. Sometimes she would be called on to take photographs and write a story when the base commander gave speeches. SSG Stephens became visibly resentful when she received accolades for her writing and photographs. At this point, Faith did not care about his childishness, she had bigger problems at home.

Little Stewart also was not doing well. From the time he was born, Stewart seemed to be sick with an ear infection or a respiratory infection or both. He would get over one only to get the other. He would be well for one to two weeks, then be sick again. It was wearing Faith out. When they arrived in California, Liam's first sergeant told him not to bother asking for time off to take care of his child; that was Faith's job. Faith's first sergeant, on the other hand, told her that it was both of their responsibilities, or they could send the child back to their parents! Faith was devastated and terrified. She would never give up custody of her child for her career. Both Stewart's health and Liam's drinking would prove to be a career ender for Faith.

They had just been in California two months when Liam's birthday came around. Faith had been doing a combat driving course that week and she wanted to do something special because they had had some late nights. She got off work early, so she picked up Stewart early and went to the Commissary to buy some steaks for dinner. She and Stewart went to the store to buy Liam his favorite movie, *Braveheart*. Then, they headed for home. When they got home, Stewart was already hungry, so Faith quickly put him down in his carrier in front of the television so that she could run into the kitchen to make his food first. Liam was on the computer. "Liam, I am going to feed Stewart first. Then, I will get your birthday dinner started, okay? He is already hungry."

"Yeah. Whatever." Faith thought the response was odd, but she let it go because she was hyper focused on getting Stewart's food ready. Just then Stewart started to cry because he was hungry. His tears quickly turned into screams.

"Shut up the hell up!" Liam yelled at the top of his lungs at Stewart. Faith's motherly instinct to protect her child sent her flying into the room. All Faith could see in her mind was Liam about to grab Stewart and shake him. Terrified, she slapped him lightly on the back to get away. She was terrified that Liam might shake her child and she could not allow that to happen. She didn't tap him hard. Just a quick slap on the back to get away and let her take over. In another instant, however, Liam grabbed Faith and slammed her up against the wall with his hand around her throat holding her up against the wall with rage in his eyes. "I will kill you, you cunt! Don't you ever touch me again! I will fucking kill you! Do you understand me? I will fucking kill you! You don't know who you are messing with."

Faith's first thought was for Stewart, who could see what was happening. Her second was for the neighbors who might call the police if they could hear what was happening. She had to get through to him.

"Yes, yes, I understand. *Stewart* can see you. Stop, Liam! Please, stop! Liam! Please, stop! Liam…*Stewart* can see you!" Fear penetrated her eyes as he choked her. Liam finally realized what Faith was saying about Stewart seeing what he was doing, and he stopped, dropping her to the floor. Faith didn't say anything else. She picked up Stewart and took him to the kitchen to feed him. She cooked dinner, acted as if nothing had happened, and then she waited for Liam to pass out.

Once Liam was passed out, she packed up hers and Stewart's clothes. They left in the wee hours of the night and went to the home of a Master Sergeant she worked with. She asked for her help getting emergency leave to go home for a week so that she could file for divorce. Then, Faith made a phone call to a friend back home in Cary to ask for help to buy a plane ticket home; she could hardly compose herself while talking to her friend as the reality of her situation was setting in. Her friend bought the ticket, and within eight hours she and baby Stewart were on a plane home.

When they arrived home, Faith couldn't bring herself to tell anyone the details of what had happened. To this day, she has only told a few people the exact details. It was still too horrific for her to talk about. She still wanted to try to work it out, but Liam wasn't interested. She went to his grandparents for help. They were the only people Liam ever listened to. Without giving them the blow by blow of what had happened, she told them that Liam's drinking was out of control. His grandmother asked the question she had not wanted to answer—was Liam violent? All Faith could do was lower her head with tears running down her face. His grandfather asked Faith to call Liam. At this point, Liam did not know that Faith and Stewart were no longer in California. When he answered the phone, he was irate, "Where the hell are you, Faith? Where is my son? You need to get your ass back home!" His grandfather, who was listening in, responded, "Now son, that is no way to speak to your wife." There was dead silence for several minutes. "Son, you need to make this right with your wife. You have behaved irresponsibly and terribly towards Faith." Liam paid lip service to his family that he would try; but he lied to her, and he lied to them about changing his behavior. If anything, the conversation with his grandfather only made him angrier.

Faith also went to see the minister who had married them. As they sat in the study of his home, Faith told him the story of what had transpired in her marriage. He was exceptionally kind to Faith. She told him that divorce had not been a choice before Stewart was born, but now she felt his protection was more important. Through her tears, she asked if God would forgive her for a divorce. The minister conveyed a story in Matthew in which the disciples asked Jesus why divorce had been allowed when the Jews were in the desert. "It was because their hearts had become hardened. God knows your circumstances and He knows your heart." While she still had reservations, she found comfort in his guidance that day.

When they returned to California, Faith thought that she and Liam might still have a chance, but Liam was angrier than ever. Faith ended up kicking him out. She felt like her life and Stewart's was in constant danger. Even after Liam moved into the barracks, he did not leave Faith alone. He would call her three or four times a day, or he might show up at the apartment unannounced. One afternoon, Faith came home to find Liam there washing clothes. She was determined that she would not engage in any conversation that might lead to an argument. Liam started questioning her about what she was doing, who she was hanging around, etc. Faith wasn't going to go there with Liam.

"Liam, I do not have time to go anywhere and do anything except work and take care of Stewart. I think it would be best if you just left now. I am not going to argue with you."

"I am not ready to leave. I want to know how you plan to handle all of this. Hmmm? What is the plan, Faith? You have a three-year contract."

"We will split everything in half. You get your truck. I get my car. I get custody of Stewart and you get visitation. I am taking a hardship chapter to leave the Corps, and I will be going home to Cary. Now, I want you to leave." Liam became enraged at what Faith was saying, and the more she asked him to leave, the more he resisted. "Ok, I have had enough. I am calling your mother so she can talk sense into you. This is ridiculous." Faith picked up the phone and dialed Liam's mother. Liam reached over and grabbed the phone out of her hand and threw it across the room. Little did either of them know that the call had gone through and that his mother had heard the entire incident, and little did Faith know that Liam had been in their bedroom and had taken all of her jewelry from her jewelry box. He pawned the jewelry for cash to buy alcohol.

Stewart continued to be sick. By Christmas, it hit a critical point. He went into respiratory distress on Christmas Day. Faith and Stewart spent 6 hours in the Emergency Room trying to get him stabilized and then four days in the hospital. By this time, Liam had decided to try and get sober, and he was in rehab in the same hospital. However, he never bothered to see his son. Faith only left her son's side to get food. Faith inquired from the nurses if anyone had been to see Stewart. They told her that no one had come.

During the time Stewart was hospitalized, Faith's unit harassed her about missing work to care for her child. She was told that if she did not show up to work, she would be court martialed for dereliction of duty. Because she was scared, Faith called a chaplain on the base to ask for help. The chaplain assured her that she would not be court martialed for taking care of her sick child. After Stewart was released from the hospital, she went to her First Sergeant and asked to be released from Marine Corps because she would not agree to give up custody of her child now that she would be a single parent and that he was an unwell child. She needed to go home. She knew that she could give Stewart a better life in North Carolina around his family and friends than so far away. She also knew that her marriage was over. Liam was not going to change for her or for Stewart; he had proven it over and over. The last thing she wanted was to raise Stewart with a father who he would only learn to hate. Even if he only saw him once and awhile, maybe it would be a better relationship than seeing the selfish, drunken behavior of his father, and especially his violent behavior. Faith's greatest fear, though, was that something would happen in a moment of desperation and she, or Liam, or Stewart, or all three would end up dead. This was not a situation she was going to let happen.

CHAPTER 33

Homecoming

Faith and Stewart arrived back home in March 1997. Stewart was nine months old and still struggling with respiratory problems. Faith's parents, though concerned for their daughter and grandson, were happy to have them back home with them. Faith's parents had never been happy about Faith joining the Marine Corps or moving to California. They supported their daughter in coming to terms with her divorce and raising her son on her own.

Faith would also have to confront the Averys about what had happened between she and Liam. She had gone to them when she came home, but she never told them or her parents the full extent of the problems with Liam. Faith wanted to maintain a good relationship with Liam's parents for Stewart's sake. Faith never had the opportunity to grow up with her grandparents. Both sides of her parent's families lived outside of North Carolina; so, Faith was never able to be around her grandparents, aunts, uncles, or cousins long enough to really know them. She wanted that for Stewart. Even if it meant tolerating the intolerable, she would do it for Stewart.

Within two months Faith had found a job as a photographer for a local newspaper. It wasn't the best job or the job she really wanted, but it would do until she found something better. She would be able to save money by living with her parents so that she could find a place for she and Stewart to live in a year or so. That was her plan. She always had a plan.

Faith knew she needed to get her head back on straight, too. With the verbal, emotional, and physical abuse heaped on her by Liam over the four and half years they were married, she needed to regroup. Faith felt that she needed to find out what attracted her to someone like Liam in the first place. She wanted to make sure that she never allowed someone like Lam into her life again. She wasn't certain she wanted to get married again, but if she did, she didn't want anyone like Liam Avery. She made a list of priorities for what she wanted in a spouse—no drugs, no alcohol, hard worker with life goals, a Christian, etc. Until she found someone who met her criteria, she would not get into a committed relationship, and she would not allow the person to meet Stewart. She also made a commitment to herself that she would not date for at least a year from the divorce. She wanted to feel mentally ready and not be on the "rebound". At this point she wasn't good for anyone either.

Living at home with her parents, Faith and Stewart began attending her childhood church. It was so easy. Everyone there knew them, and it felt like home, except that the Averys went there also. Liam's parents, grandparents, aunts and uncles all went to the same church as Faith. They were all so kind to her. Still, it felt a bit awkward. They welcomed her home and asked her to sit with them at church because her mother sang in the choir and her father was a deacon.

One Sunday a group of lay leaders came to lead a special weekend of activities at the church. Faith couldn't attend because Stewart had not been feeling well, but she was able to go that Sunday morning. The lay leaders led the Sunday morning worship service. One of the gentlemen leading the service gave his testimony and Faith was moved to tears. Something spoke deeply to Faith's heart that morning. She heard his words speaking of how his life was changed when his young daughter was diagnosed with cancer and what that experience of going through treatment was like, not know from one day to the next what would happen and whether his child would survive. The Holy Spirit touched her. Tears welled up in her eyes and she even began to shake. All her life Faith thought that God was punishing her with all the bad things that had happened to her. Faith had been so angry and resentful towards God, her foster parents, her adoptive parents, the bullies, Liam, everyone. She never realized it until just then how self-centered and angry her world was. Here was this man talking about something so much worse and he was full of joy and love. Faith had accepted Jesus as her

Lord and Savior when she was 14. She had always prayed to God, but there was always a certain amount of anger and resentment about her early years and her failed relationship with Liam hadn't helped. This day changed that for her. Faith finally understood that bad things happen, but those things happen because of humans and their poor decisions; humans are flawed and could never be perfect and, because of this humans will always disappoint in one way or another. She suddenly understood that, as a Christian, joy comes in the morning because Jesus died for the sins of humanity so that we could receive salvation—something we could never deserve. It finally all made sense. Faith closed her eyes and quietly she prayed, *"Thank you, Jesus, for showing me this today. Thank you for forgiving me. Forgive me for the sins I haven't yet asked forgiveness for. I am so sorry for being so angry and resentful all these years. I have wasted so much time. Thank you for these people today. Thank you for my parents. Thank you for my son. Help me to be a good daughter, sister, and mother, the kind of mother he needs me to be. Thank you, God, for saving me…again."*

CHAPTER 34

Settling In

Faith began to feel settled into her life with Stewart back in Cary. She and Stewart were getting into a routine with work, daycare, eating dinner with her parents every night; life seemed normal finally. As life would go, though, nothing good can last too long. Faith always felt close to her Aunt Elizabeth, her mother's younger sister. Her aunt had never married or had any children. She was beautiful and smart. She worked as a paralegal in a large law firm in Charlottesville. Faith looked up to her. Faith had always imagined that when she was older, that she, her mother, and her Aunt Elizabeth would travel and do fun things together because they enjoyed many of the same things.

It wasn't long after Faith started working at the newspaper that her grandfather, Ola Larson, passed away suddenly of a heart attack in his sleep. He had heart problems, so it did not come as shock. However, Faith's grandmother was devastated; she was the one who found him dead. It was traumatizing for her. Faith was closer to her mother's parents than to her father's because she would spend summers with her mother's parents. She loved them dearly, but especially her grandfather. He was a second generation American. She loved to ask him questions about his childhood and his family. Her Aunt Elizabeth would come to their home while she was there, and they would do special things together.

Faith's grandmother had always been a hardworking woman. She worked outside of the home only briefly when her girls were young. Her aunt once told her that the family once speculated that they believed there were side effects she suffered after having typhoid fever which left her with social anxiety. She rarely left home except to get her hair done or, on occasion, to eat out with a few special family friends. Faith remembered that her grandmother was always doing something except during lunch when she stopped long enough for a sandwich and to watch her favorite "stories" on television; but, as soon as they were finished, she was quickly back to work until bedtime. She put Faith to work too. She taught Faith to bake, how to dust and mop, to make beds, and to do laundry. While Faith didn't appreciate much of that at the time, looking back as a mother, she appreciated the hard work her grandmother did for her. Faith did not like seeing her grandmother in such pain after her grandfather died. She would often cry out of nowhere. She became depressed and would sit for hours doing nothing. Leaving her there alone wasn't something Faith, her mother, or her Aunt Elizabeth enjoyed doing.

Faith's mother, Ellen Roberts, like her father Lee, were both still actively working when Faith and Stewart moved backed into their home, though Lee was close to retirement. Ellen worked as manager for a travel agency. She often traveled between the many offices the agency owned. This allowed her to stop by her mother's home and check in on her on a somewhat regular basis. This situation worked for quite some time as Mrs. Larson's health remained good.

Lee Roberts worked at a bank in Cary. He had been in banking most of his life. He had worked for a large, national bank for most of his career, but about fifteen years back he decided to move to a smaller, local bank because of an ethical issue that arose in the bank. The bank leaders asked Mr. Roberts to do something he believed to be improper, and Mr. Roberts refused. The bank officials told him that he could either leave on his own or be fired. This was soul crushing for Mr. Roberts who was a Christian man and refused to compromise himself. When he came home the day he resigned, Faith was fifteen. She sat in his lap and put her arms around his neck, kissed him on the cheek. "Daddy, you'll never go wrong choosing God first. It will all work out. You'll see."

Mr. Roberts was an outgoing, likeable kind of guy. He got along with everyone. He enjoyed being around people and socializing. He was a member of several civic groups and always seemed to be doing something for some cause. He was also on boards at their church. He and Mrs. Roberts had a supper club that they had dinner with one night every month; and with Mrs. Roberts' job, they often got to take exciting trips to try out new hotels or cruises. The Roberts were a good family. Faith just didn't know how good they were.

Faith decided that, now that she and Stewart had settled in and he was well, she wanted to find a way to do some community service. Because of her experience as a foster child, albeit a bad experience, she thought maybe she could find some way to use that experience to help her community. She found out about being a volunteer to the juvenile court as an advocate for children. This excited her. She immediately found out what she needed to do to become a volunteer and gathered all the necessary information.

As soon as she had everything she needed to know, Faith went to her parents. She told them that she wanted to volunteer, but she understood that, to do that, she would need help from them with Stewart. If they couldn't help or wouldn't, she would understand, and she would just have to figure out another way to make it happen. She then went through the information with them about becoming a volunteer. Her father thought it was a wonderful idea. Her mother thought it was a horrible idea. Her mother went off on a tirade about the types of children who get caught up in these cases and how she might get called out in the middle of the night. Faith tried to explain that she wasn't a social worker, just a volunteer to represent the child in court. She tried to explain that she remembered her CASA representative from when they adopted her. She had only seen the woman once, the day before court. Her mother was irate and would not listen to Faith. Faith looked over at her father in despair. "Go ahead. We will work it out. I will talk to her."

"I have to talk to Stewart about this, too, Daddy. We will give it some time before I do anything. It isn't like I have to do it tomorrow." Faith patted him on the shoulder and went to pick Stewart up off the floor to take him upstairs.

Faith took Stewart upstairs to get him ready for bed. She got his pajamas and took him to the bathroom to get him bathed. While he was in the tub, Faith said, "Stewart, I want to talk to you about something."

"Ok, Momma."

"You are getting to be a big boy now. You are going to be 2 years old soon. Did you know that when I was your age, I didn't live with Nona and Poppy?"

Stewart stopped playing and looked his mother puzzled, "You didn't? Where did you live, Momma?"

"Well, Stewart, my mommy and daddy couldn't take care of me, so I went to a place called a foster home when I was a baby. I stayed there until I was 5-years old. Then your Nona and Poppy came and got me, and I became their little girl. Do you understand that?"

"Yes, Mommy." Stewart went back to playing with his toys in the bathtub.

"When Nona and Poppy came to get me there was a special lady that was there to be with me at the court to speak for me since I was very little. I think I might like to do that for some little children. What would you think if I did that, Stewart? Would you be okay with that?"

"If you help the children, Mommy?"

"Yes, Stewart. It might mean that you might need to stay with Nona and Poppy while I go to court to be with the children, but I hope not too much. But, Stewart, these little children don't have parents and they need someone to help them so that they can get parents. You'd like that?"

"Yes, Mommy. Why don't they have parents, Mommy?"

"Oh, honey, lots of different reasons, but Mommy might be able to help them, like the special lady who helped me."

"Okay, Mommy."

"I love you, Stewart. You look like a prune. Let's get out of this tub."

A few weeks later, Faith enrolled in the training course for the CASA volunteers and a month later she was on her way. There was no looking back after that. Faith worked as hard as her schedule would permit to help children in her county. Anything that was needed, CASA knew that they could look to Faith. If she could not help, she would find someone who could. She made it priority to never let a CASA child, or her child, if she could help it, down.

This work often left her with little time for herself. This was a situation that for some time did not bother Faith, but a time came when other people started to ask her why she wasn't dating. Wasn't she interested in getting married again? Didn't she want a positive male influence in Stewart's life? Faith had put so much emphasis on improving herself, taking care of Stewart, that a relationship had not factored into her schedule.

After a year and a half of living under her parent's roof, Lee assisted Faith in locating some property that she could afford in a nice neighborhood. Faith was excited to finally be moving out of her parent's house and into a home that she built and owned herself. Her friends thought that, since she was finally out of the prying eyes of her mother, maybe she would consider dating. Faith finally gave in and decided to let one of her friends set her up on a date. He seemed to be a nice person, good-looking and they had a wonderful time together. He made her laugh and she enjoyed being out with an adult for the first time in almost two years. It took some time, but Faith finally allowed herself to have fun and to have a relationship with someone over the age of two. She allowed herself to trust someone again. Unfortunately, she trusted someone who turned out not to deserve her trust. After five months of dating, instead of breaking up with her, the guy cheated on Faith. One evening Faith took Stewart out to eat at a local restaurant only to walk in and see the guy with another girl cozied up in a corner table looking romantic. Her heart was broken, and she took Stewart and ran out of the restaurant.

Faith was hurt, not because she had feelings for him, but because she had let her guard down. She did not have any real feelings for him. She liked him, but what she finally realized was that she was terrified of being alone after Stewart grew up. For whatever reason she had kept those feeling buried, but after this disappointment, those emotions exploded out of her like a volcano. For several hours she had no control over her emotions; she was a complete mess. As soon as it came on, it also passed. Once the emotions came out, she was fine. It was over. She had forgotten about her list. She got it back out and she put it on her mirror in her bedroom so that she would not forget again.

CHAPTER 35

Revelations

Moving back to Cary also meant that she could reconnect with her brother, David. She couldn't wait to get to a point where she could contact him and let him know that she was back in North Carolina. She was hoping that they could get back together so that David could meet Stewart. Finally, she felt like she had a real family and she belonged, except that she still didn't know what her name was like David did. She wanted to know that. She did know the last name thanks to David. So, she decided to start with that.

About this time the internet was just becoming a more common household tool. Most people had personal computers, and now people were signing up for internet access and obtaining email addresses. Faith learned to use the internet and email while on active duty. She decided one night to sit down and try out some web searches on her last name around Norfolk, Virginia, to see what she might come up with. It was not common at this time to have large responses on browser searches, but what was possible at the time were phone book databases. For a reasonable fee in larger metropolitan areas, you could purchase a list of names. So, she was able to purchase a list of everyone with her last name in Norfolk.

After getting the list of names, about 30, she planned to write a letter with her background information asking if any of these people might be related to her and to David. She typed a form letter on her computer and mailed one to each of the names on the list. She had no idea if she would ever get a response. She prayed that God would answer her kindly and not with rebuke because she didn't think she could handle any ugly responses.

To Faith's surprise the first response came rather quickly, about a week. The letter was from a lovely, young lady who responded that she could not be a relative because the story did not relate to anyone she knew of in her family. However, she said, she worked in the Department of Family and Children's Services and was willing to help in any way. This was exciting to Faith because she knew it wasn't allowed and to offer was exceptional. She put the letter away and hoped for the best. The second response came about two weeks from the first. It was from a gentleman who responded that he was not completely certain. He knew that no one in his immediate line was involved in any adoptions, but that there was a larger, extended family wherein it could have happened, but that he was unaware. He used kind words and wished her the best in her search. It was the third letter that answered her prayers.

The third letter came a few days later. The writing on the front of the letter was that of a much older person. It was difficult to read and seemed strained. Faith walked into the living room and sat down on the sofa to open the letter. It was the perfect day because she was alone. Her father was at work and her mother had taken Stewart shopping. As she opened the letter, it was almost as if she could feel the pain pouring out of the letter. She began to read the letter. He began the letter by answering her questions, "Yes, I am your family," so-to-speak. He began to lay out the story of how Faith came to be one step at a time, and as she read Faith's shoulders gradually began to droop from her sadness. The story, as it unfolded, was one of absolute tragedy; one no one could make up, not even a soap opera. Tears began to fall from her eyes as she continued to read. One page after another telling a tale of horror that no one should ever have to repeat.

When Faith came to the end of the letter, the gentleman left his phone number and welcomed her to call if she wished to speak to him but said he understood if she did not. He thanked her for seeking her family out but suggested that she probably wasn't expecting what was lying in store for her and David. He begged her for her forgiveness for what was contained within the letter. He signed it, "With Love, your granddaddy".

Faith sat for several minutes taking it all in. Never in all her life could she have imagined what was in that letter. She was horrified and relieved at the same time. All her life she thought it was her fault that she was abandoned. Every story she had contemplated made it in some way her fault, but it really wasn't about her at all. However, what it was about was disgusting and despicable. What it was about was far more heinous than anything she was ready to deal with, and it did affect her. It affected her deeply. She needed God's help to deal with these revelations. She knew she could not do it alone.

After a few hours of allowing the truth to sink in, Faith decided that the best thing for her would be to talk through it with someone she was close to. Her father was the person she trusted the most. Lee had become ill from food poisoning. He had gone to the emergency room and was admitted to the hospital. Faith and her mother were taking turns staying with him and taking care of Stewart. Faith thought this was a good situation because she could talk with her dad without having her mother there also. When she arrived at the hospital, her father was sitting up and laughing with a nurse who had come in to check his vitals. He was happy to see his girl. Faith went over and kissed her dad on the forehead and asked him how he was feeling. Mr. Roberts said that while he was feeling better, he still had a headache and stomachache. The doctors had diagnosed him with salmonella.

"Daddy, I got something today that I need to read to you. I might need some of your awesome advice about it," Faith said to her father holding his hand.

"My goodness, I am sure it cannot be that bad, Faith. Go on and read it to me." Faith opened the letter from her biological grandfather and began to read. As she read tears flowed down her cheeks.

Dear Faith and David,

This is in answer to your inquiry about our relationship with you, Susan & myself & the Stewart family. We are the correct 'Stewart' family in regards to the questions you asked in your letter.

To begin with, I must tell you up front that Susan is deceased; having taken her own life in February 1993, and is buried in Richmond, Virginia. The complete story of her life, though tragic it was and how it began with her birth, life and subsequent death. It is heart rendering to bring it to present merely the bad details of her life. I will tell you the absolute truth in this matter, who it involves and some of the sad details as I recall them.

Susan was born much prematurely in Sumpter, South Carolina. She was born in the ambulance on the way to the hospital. I was in the Army at that time. Susan barely lived, but in an incubator for about 2 months, did make it.

We had a small apartment and lived on a limited income but the primary fault that existed in Susan's regard was the lack of bonding with her mother. This never occurred even throughout Susan's life and always had a major bearing on Susan's mental state thru-out her life, even to the end of her life.

Susan's life did not improve to much a degree even after my stint in the military ended in late 1960. We lived in Norfolk where I had employment with the U. S. Civil Service at Langley Air Force Base. Things continued bad for Susan and her little sister, Anna Katherine, as their mother just wasn't a mother at all! I finally divorced their mother in 1961 but soon re-married to a woman with other children. Things did improve for a year or so but then took a turn for the much worse; even made worse by my absence to long away-from-home assignments required by my job. Some assignments took me back overseas again and again, and then required a complete change of careers for me, affecting the family likewise. During these years things were so difficult for Susan and Anna Katherine that I chose to enlist my mother for them to live with and go to school apart from the rest of the family, i.e. wife, step-kids and even a daughter of this marriage. We had to re-locate to the Washington, D.C.

area near the military base where my new job took me. I was the only provider in this family also.

During this period, Susan became pregnant while living in Norfolk with her grandmother and step-grandfather. Susan's step-grandfather was the father of Susan's yet to be born baby; he admitted to this right away. After conferring with all the legal authorities, we all agreed not to seek prosecution of the grandfather due to the many circumstances involving the lives of the grandmother, her advanced age and health, etc. As Susan's pregnancy advanced, she was finally placed into foster care in Norfolk. To my knowledge this may or may not have been a 'Jewish' home and I was not aware of any requirement imposed on Susan to agree to a 'Jewish' upbringing. I also was not aware that Susan had refused to sign any documents for the adoption. She did subsequently come to live with me and my then family in Warner Robins, Georgia. The year was 1970, I believe.

Things did not improve much for any of us, and I even had to re-locate to Columbus, Mississippi, where my new assignment with the government took me. Susan was enrolled in a special school and did well in those studies. She later became employed at a restaurant in Roanoke, Virginia, and managed to live alone in a small apartment. The years were 1971-1972. There she apparently met a fellow named Dawson Dees, a married man, and was soon pregnant again. He abandoned her after finding out about the child, and she returned to live with me in Arlington, Virginia. Susan, Anna Katherine, and Colleen lived with me as I was divorced now from Colleen's mother. It was Colleen's mother's decision not to have custody of Colleen, though I desperately tried to convince her that it was in Colleen's best interest that she live with her. I made generous offers of child support for Colleen, but her mother refused and consequently, Colleen continued to live with me, Susan, and Anna Katherine.

Soon Susan's time of delivery approached. Her doctor in Roanoke arranged for a home for girls and was sent to live in such a facility in Richmond until the birth of her baby. This occurred and the boy-baby was born in November 1972. This child was placed for adoption at that time.

Later, Susan was allowed to go back to Norfolk to live with her grandmother and, yes, her step-grandfather too. Susan loved her grandmother deeply and really was the only mother figure Susan ever had. Susan was now aware of how to exist in that home even though the events of her first pregnancy was apparent. She handled this problem though and soon met a young man and wanted desperately to get married. This was done although we all feared she was not capable of understanding and functioning in a married state with all its components and problems. It soon occurred much to the sadness of all involved! Susan became pregnant again and soon gave birth to a son, Richard Dean Brown Jr. Her husband was immature and unable to understand Susan's problems and troubles that soon cropped up in their marriage. Susan was unable to cope; she was unable to communicate with her husband; and he was immature and soon abandoned Susan and her baby.

Susan became distraught and panicked. Susan killed her baby smothering him and was promptly arrested and jailed awaiting trial. The trial was held, and she was found guilty and sentenced to twenty years. She was imprisoned at the state prison for women in Goochland, Virginia. She served 7 years there and was a model prisoner. She was given a full pardon in 1986 or 1987, I believe.

Susan met a man who worked at the prison while she was incarcerated, and she married again which seemed okay for a while. She then had episodes of mental illness, deep mood changes and much depression. She was on medications throughout this period, but she had difficulty staying on them. She had a good husband who provided well for her, but he was at a loss as to how to handle all the problems arising from time to time. She left him at times, where she went, only she knew. Finally, in early 93 she took her own life with a firearm and that now brings us up to this date, 2002.

I remarried in 1974 to a wonderful person to whom Susan loved and felt comfortable with and trusted. Susan finally had someone to understand her and that she could talk to. She really loved Julia, my wife and one that supported me in our monthly visits to Susan when she was imprisoned. During those years and in the years that followed, we tried to be there for Susan, but obviously we failed.

You mentioned and/or questioned Susan's mental conditions and 'schizophrenic' possibilities in your letter. In my opinion, she did suffer from that in her life, as we review and contemplate the probability of those mental heath issues. I firmly believe that she suffered from parental deprecation as much as anything, and as such she never really had a chance in life. I was as much at fault as her mother for failing to act when she was very young and in need of bonding and affection. I failed her! Oh! Yeah! I did provide material things in her life but not the sound basic love and foundational things she really needed and deserved. I'm sorry for all these failures that I now see and truly sorry for the early hardships suffered by you Faith and David. I missed your childhoods and growing up and all the in-betweens. Again, I'm really sorry for all these circumstances.

If I can be of further help, please call or write.
I remain, sincerely,
Jonas Stewart

"Well, Faith, that's a terribly sad story, and he sounds hurt and ashamed about it. What happened is just terrible, but you cannot allow that to influence who you are. Your mother did the right thing, and she was very brave, especially for someone in her situation. In another time, things could have turned out much differently. You are *the* best thing to come out of a horrific circumstance. That should give him some joy. It gives me joy. Look, God took something terrible and made something so wonderful and beautiful out of it—you!"

"I guess you are right…and my brother, David, is too."

"That's right. There are two blessings that came out of something awful. That is a miracle in my mind. Try not to focus on just the bad part of this situation; focus on the good that came from it. That is all you can do with this information; all you should do with it."

"I will try daddy. I love you," Faith said to her dad.

After spending some time with her father, Faith went home to Stewart and spent time with him but thinking about everything in the letter in her mind. Her dad had something interesting that kept coming back to her mind— "in another time, it could have come out differently". He was right about that. She hadn't realized until that very moment that, if the situation had happened today, instead of 1967, she'd probably have been aborted. After all, this poor child would have believed anything the old man told her. She didn't know not to trust him. He could have told her she was having her appendix out. How truly blessed it made her feel to know that her birth mother had been brave enough to give birth to her and to make the decision to place her for adoption, and the same for David. Neither of them would probably be here now if this had all happened ten years in the future.

These details consumed her mind, and so, she sat down to write another letter to her biological grandfather. In her letter, she assured him that she had no ill will or anger at him for what had happened because he had apologized. She asked him for more information about the step-grandfather, grandmother, and himself. Faith loved history, especially family history, so her letter was filled with questions about his family's history. She remained as positive as she could, not wanting him to feel at all sad about anything else. She told him all about herself and how her life had transpired since her birth. She told him about David and what he was doing in his life. She wanted to help him feel better about how their situation had come out. She also explained her marital situation and how it was that she was now a single parent. She put in photographs of she, Stewart, and her parents. She couldn't wait to get the follow-up letter in the mail, so that she could await his response. She, then, called David to read him the letter.

David was quiet after hearing the letter. He understood the situation, but he was not as ready to forgive as Faith. He believed that these situations could have been different if Susan had behaved differently; and so, he blamed her. Faith tried to help him understand that what had happened in Susan's life may not have been within her control; certainly, the events that brought her to life were not. Faith had to admit that she was angry that the step-grandfather had not been prosecuted for his crime against their mother. She was also angry at the grandmother for not choosing her granddaughter over her husband. As a mother, Faith knew that she would not, could not ever choose a spouse over her child if that spouse had hurt that child.

Faith told David about her follow-up letter and the questions she had asked, especially those that asked for more explanation of the events described in his first letter. David approved and said he would await her call when she received a reply. After the call was over, Faith took Stewart into her room to sleep. She felt like she didn't want to let him go. As he drifted off to sleep, Faith's mind raced through all the details in the letter. She realized how bad her mother had it. It didn't seem like anyone in her family wanted to help her, especially after the situation with her step-grandfather. Faith began to weep silently thinking about how her mother must have felt going through all she went through. Faith felt ashamed for all the years she had wasted being angry and resentful, when, in actuality, she was very much blessed. She prayed for God's continued help because she knew her emotions were running deep. Before long, she drifted off to sleep.

Making A Connection

It was not long after the receipt of the first letter, that letters began to flow back and forth between Faith and her grandfather. He always tried to answer her questions, but it never seemed to be a complete answer. She found out that her biological great-grandfather, not to be confused with the step-great-grandfather who hurt her mother, was also not a good man. He treated his family, especially his wife, terribly. In fact, she found out that the last name to which all descendants, including herself, call themselves wasn't even their real name. His father had taken the name of his stepfather, Donald Stewart, but his real name was "Kramer". His biological father was a Jewish immigrant from Germany. Apparently, he either ran away from his family, or he was killed while away from the family. No one in the family knew the truth. Faith found this fact extremely intriguing, and she was anxious to use her investigative skills to see if she could find out what had become of this ancestor. Perhaps it was this fact that led her mother to request that her son be raised Jewish. Her grandfather certainly didn't understand the request since he and his siblings were not raised in that faith.

Moreover, she also found out that her name at birth was Sarah Faith Stewart. She was surprised because she could not recall being called anything other than Faith her whole life. How could that be? She knew that the Roberts had given her a different middle name, Rose, and, obviously, their last name; but why would they change her first name? She was not happy about that. She loved the name Sarah Faith. She learned that "Faith" came from her great-grandmother, the one who treated her mother so awfully when she became pregnant; however, her grandfather told her that Susan adored her grandmother in spite of her treatment of her during that time. Faith thought to herself, "Well, she may not have understood the situation properly because of her problems. Susan may have forgiven her, but I'm not ready to do that!"

Faith also learned that her baby brother, Richard Dean Brown, Jr, had been born in January 1973 and died in June of that year. Faith felt such grief about little Richard. She so wanted a little brother growing up and she had missed out on growing up with David, and now, little Richard. She would have been such a terrific big sister. It wasn't until the third or fourth letter from her grandfather that she was finally able to understand what the issues were with her mother. She had the "non-identifying" information from DFACS and now the explanations from her grandfather which allowed her to put a full picture together, and it seemed that the majority of what had transpired was due to her premature birth. Susan had an IQ of less than 70, making her legally mentally disabled. She also found out that her mother had repeated the 8th grade three times and still did not pass. Susan had mental health needs that this family did not understand. She wondered if they even cared to understand. Her grandfather seemed to be a smart man from the letters he had written, but somehow, he and everyone else in Susan's life did not seem to comprehend that she was not intelligent enough to make reasonable, meaningful decisions by herself, and that she would've never been able to do so. It was this lack of intelligence that allowed her stepbrothers and grandfather to take advantage of her and to continue to do so for several years. It made Faith nauseous.

Jonas also conveyed the shocking demise of her biological father. He told her that, after his mother died, Paul became depressed and began drinking. He had lost money and property to a couple of grifters who conned him. Paul could not handle it. One day he began drinking and became severely intoxicated. He had gone outside, for what reason Jonas did not know. He fell and was knocked unconscious; and he landed in a large fire ant mound. He died from exposure and the toxicity of the ant bites. He lain in the yard for two days before being found. It took a few minutes for Faith to process the information. For the first time since hearing Susan's and her story, she felt awkwardly relieved. She could see firsthand how God's Word had become true and faithful. She did not need to hate Paul for what he had done because God had taken care of it. It was such a weight lifted off her. She truly had everything she had ever needed.

In June of 2002, Faith received a letter from her mother's sister, Anna Katherine. Faith was surprised because she was unaware that her grandfather had spoken to Anna Katherine. The letter was brief, telling Faith that she was happy to be found and that she was open to meeting Faith. The letter explained that all Susan ever wanted was to be loved and that, unfortunately, she was unable to distinguish between sex and love. "Of course, she couldn't," thought Faith; She was an easy target because she couldn't comprehend what sex was and was not. She was led to believe that sex was love. Faith was put off by her aunt's making excuses. It seemed to Faith that her aunt was blaming the victim, rather than the guilty grandfather and stepbrothers. If her aunt knew all of this at the time, why hadn't *she* told anyone about it? Perhaps because it wasn't in her interest to do so?

The letter also invited Faith and Stewart to come to their home and provided a phone number to call, if she chose to do so. This must have meant that her grandfather had, indeed, spoken to Anna Katherine and Colleen. However, she never received any communication from Colleen. Her grandfather did not speak well of his daughter, Colleen. In his letters he explained that, while Colleen was very intelligent, she had not made good decisions regarding life. She had been married and divorced and had a son who lived with her. They lived in Arkansas. Faith found out later from her aunt Anna Katherine that Colleen also had a child out-of-wedlock in her late teens, a daughter. She explained to Faith that the child had been raised by her paternal grandparents and that Colleen had no relationship with her whatsoever. Colleen's son had developmental issues and was not able to live on his own. Colleen and Anthony, her son, lived in a single-wide mobile home and neither worked. Colleen, she was told, was a Wiccan and had serious alcohol and drug problems. As far as they knew, Anthony did drugs as well. They lived off welfare and food stamps. Faith made a conscious decision not to pursue a relationship with Colleen due to her connection to Wiccans; but she decided to pray for her aunt and cousin that they might find a way out of this lifestyle.

At this point, Faith had not spoken on the phone with either her grandfather or her aunt. She was unsure how she felt about talking to them on the phone. She had to give it thought because she knew herself and knew that, under the right circumstances, she could say something that she didn't mean out of frustration or anger and might, thus, alienate them from her. It was going to take some time to work it all out in her head.

CHAPTER 37

Sweet Surprises

At the same time Faith was making connections with her biological family, she had also ended a relationship. It was a difficult situation because she like him very much, but he did not have any feelings for Faith. Early into the relationship, he had made a decision to enter into a relationship with someone else but didn't bother to tell Faith. He kept seeing Faith for some time before he decided to break up with her on her birthday. Faith's heart was hurt, not because she cared, but because he lied to her. She took him at his word when he told her that he was fine with Stewart and loved children. In the end, she discovered that he did not want to raise another man's child and that he took issue with Faith's continued relationship with Stewart's paternal grandparents. She shared her deep hurt from her divorce, and she thought that he would have enough respect for her to be honest about what he wanted and how he felt. For whatever reason, he did none of that. It hurt, but she was not going to let that get the better of her.

Faith went on with her life. She took a job working as a secretary at Stewart's school after being let go from the newspaper due to budget cuts. It was perfect for her now that Stewart was in school. She could have the same schedule that he had. She also continued her photography to make a little money on the side, as well as volunteering as a CASA representative. Her life seemed so full that she decided to not worry about whether or not a man came into her life. She was happy. Stewart was happy. She needed to learn to just be happy with what she had; so, she did.

Now Faith learned that, just when you think you know what God's will is for your life, He can turn it upside down. It had been a year since the breakup and Faith had not dated anyone. She was not looking for any-one. She had made a conscious decision to be happy with how her life was and to leave it to God to change it, if He so chose. One day after school, Stewart came running into the house with the mail. He threw it down and said, "All junk, Momma." Faith chuckled and said, "Well, that would be nice for a change." Looking through the mail she found a letter from the county. Faith had never gotten a letter like this before, so she opened it im-mediately. It was a letter which gave notice of a hearing regarding the vacant lot behind Faith's home. It notified her that someone purchasing the land had petitioned for rezoning of the lot for a daycare center. Faith thought to herself, "That's just great. It will be noisy all day and the traffic will be horrendous." Faith took the letter to her dad to see what he thought of the notice. He instructed her to go to the meeting to find out the details of the project and to make sure that, if the day care was to be built, there would be a substantial fence and barrier built between her home and the day care. She agreed that she would go to the meeting.

Faith walked into the county zoning board room not knowing any-thing about how the process would go. The room was filled with people. She looked around and found a printed agenda for the meeting, and then she sat on the last row nearest to the door in the very last seat. As she was perusing the agenda, a handsome man came in and sat at the far end of the row on which Faith sat. Faith glanced over and noticed how handsome he was. A few minutes passed, and the gentleman leaned over towards Faith and asked, "Do you know how this thing works?"

Faith smiled and responded, "Not really. I have never been to one of these before."

"Do you know anyone else here? What are you here for?" He asked.

"Oh, I am here for a hearing on the rezoning of a vacant lot behind my house. I see a few people I know who own houses around me."

"Oh, that is what I am here for too. Where is your house located?"

"I live behind the lot nearest to the supermarket."

"Oh, do you think we should all get together before this starts and come up with a plan?"

"That sounds like a smart idea to me." Then, Faith and the gentleman rose from their seats and walked forward to one of the people Faith knew. They all spoke for a few minutes and decided to go to the foyer and discuss a plan for the meeting. Faith couldn't help but look at the guy. He seemed smart and articulate during the hearing. She was very taken by the gentleman. After the hearing was over, the group returned to the foyer and exchanged names and phone numbers. They decided to get back together before the next hearing to strategize again.

The time of the second and final hearing came, and Faith realized that she would not be able to go because she had a previous engagement that she had to attend. When she got home that evening, the phone rang, and it was the gentleman from the county hearing. He was calling to let her know that he could not attend the hearing and to ask if she would let him know what happened. She told him that she wouldn't be able to go either, but she would call and find out what happened and let him know. He had a death in his family, and he was driving back from out-of-town and would not make it back in time. Faith told him that he was welcome to call her later that evening and she would be able to tell him what had happened.

About eight-thirty or so, the phone rang. Faith had just gotten into bed to watch some television before going to sleep. She saw on her caller-id that it was the gentleman from the county hearing. She answered the phone. The two of them spoke briefly about the zoning meeting, which had not gone the way they had wanted, and then began to talk about themselves and their lives. Before Faith knew it, they had been on the phone for almost three hours! She was very attracted to this gentleman. He sounded kind. Faith began to think about her list and about what she wanted. This gentleman might just change everything, but did she dare to hope?

During their conversation, Faith became aware that they had friends in common. Ben worked for a gentleman who was close friends with her father. He also went to church with a friend of Faith's from high school, a friend she loved like a sister. Faith was encouraged by Ben's statement of faith and to know that he wasn't just a Christian by word, but that he was actively involved in his church. Faith was also involved in her church, singing with the church's praise team. It was beginning to look as though this might be worth the wait and worth pursuing.

In a few days, Faith called her mutual friend, Erin Quinn, to get more information about Benjamin Kirby. When Faith asked Erin about him, Erin right away said, "Oh yeah, he is terrific. I should have thought about him for you before now. He is a terrific guy." Erin told Faith about how Ben had gone with her to a charity fundraiser as friend because she wanted to go but didn't want to go alone. She explained about Ben's most recent relationship and how the girl had been all wrong for him. She told Faith that, even though it was not a relationship that would make it to marriage, the breakup had still been difficult for Ben. Erin invited Faith to go with her to her Bible study where she could get to know Ben better. Faith was excited to go.

Faith enjoyed going to the Bible study. It was led by the parents of another girl she knew in high school. They were terrific people, and they made her feel welcome at the Bible study. Faith and Ben continued to talk on the phone here and there over the next few weeks. Then an event arose that Faith wanted to go to, but she was apprehensive because the guy from the prior relationship would be there with his new girlfriend. Faith wanted to go but did not want to be there alone. She called Erin to ask her what she thought if she, Erin, and Ben all went together. Erin thought it was a great idea. Faith thought that it might be too soon to be on a date with Ben, and she didn't want him to think she was being forward. Going as a group seemed less of a date and, perhaps, more appropriate at that time.

When the event rolled around, Faith also asked another friend to accompany them, Regan Adams. Regan had been a sorority sister of Faith's, and she had just moved back to Cary from Nashville, Tennessee, after getting divorced. The group met at the event. It was the opening of a smoothie shop for a mutual church friend of Faith's and Ben's. The friend had attended Ben's church but was now attending Faith's. When the group arrived, the party was well underway. Faith picked up Regan on her way after dropping Stewart at her parent's house. Faith filled Regan in on everything that had occurred thus far between Ben and herself. Regan was excited for Faith.

The party was fun, and this group of friends seemed to get along very well. They had smoothies and sat and talked with each other. Much to Faith's surprise, her ex and his new girlfriend had already come and gone before Faith and her friends had arrived. She felt relief and was able to relax and have fun. After about an hour, Ben suggested that they all go and get some dinner together. Everyone agreed. They met at a local steakhouse. Everyone ordered and continued to talk and have a great time. Ben was wonderful, and at the end of the meal, Ben reached over and picked up the check. Faith had just assumed everyone would pay for their own meal, but Ben insisted on picking up the check. Faith marveled at his kindness and generosity. Before everyone left, Ben pulled Faith aside and asked her if she wanted to go out together, alone. Faith turned bright red. Somehow, she muttered out the words, "Yes, I would." In her mind she had totally blown her answer, but Ben laughed and said, "Ok, I will call you and we will work it all out." Faith just smiled from ear to ear.

After their first official date, Faith and Ben were never apart except for work. They met for lunch each day and then a few nights during the week, they ate together. Faith knew that this relationship was special, and she wanted it to work out. She prayed every night about this budding relationship and how to work Stewart into the formula. She never wanted Stewart to "fall in love" with someone only to have it not work out. Liam had made no attempts to be a father to Stewart. Her father and Mr. Avery were his father figures. Even when Liam did come to town, he only spent a few hours with him and then bought him clothes that didn't fit and toys he shouldn't play with.

Liam remarried after just two years after their divorce. Faith discovered not long after their separation that he was living with a woman off base in California. She did not like it, but there was nothing she could say about it. He had called her many times begging her to come back, only to call her later and cuss her out for leaving and taking Stewart. The woman Liam married was from the Philippines. Her English was pretty good; she called Faith several times and told her to stay away from her husband, even once after Stewart had called to wish his father a happy birthday. It seemed as though Faith and Liam would never be able to move passed their failed marriage, even for Stewart's sake. Faith forgave Liam, but she still deeply desired recognition of the truth of their breakup and an apology. She knew she would never get either.

Faith decided to have Ben over for dinner one night and to have Stewart there so that they could meet. Faith cooked a nice dinner and then everyone sat at the table together. This wasn't the norm for Faith and Stewart who usually ate together in the living room, if he hadn't eaten already with her parents who often picked him up from school to spend time with him. Everything seemed to be going well until Faith had to scold Stewart for not eating what was on his plate and he snapped at her. Ben looked at Stewart and said firmly, "Look Stewart that is your mother and you do not speak to her that way. You need to eat the dinner your mother made for you." Both Stewart and Faith were taken aback, but in a good way. Faith was happy to see that Ben had no reservations about scolding Stewart, but in a respectful way. Of course, Stewart did not want to comply, but he did, and he apologized to his mother for his tone. After dinner, Stewart went to his room to play, and Ben and Faith watched television in her living room. It was a very special evening.

The twosome continued to see each other almost daily and Faith could tell that she was falling for Ben, but she was scared to say anything about it, or act as if she had feelings. One night when the two were together at Ben's house, they went into the living room after dinner to watch a movie on his big screen television. They were about thirty minutes into the movie when Ben reached over and pulled Faith towards him and kissed her. Faith melted, but she was still terrified. As time went by, Ben asked Faith to move over to the larger sofa to lie down together and watch the movie. She was hesitant, but she agreed. It seemed like just seconds went by when Ben looked at Faith leaning in to kiss her and said, "I am falling in love with you, Faith." That was all it took for Faith to allow her feelings out.

"I am falling for you, too, Ben." After that night, the relationship went fast forward. Ben invited Faith to meet his parents, Ellis and Kay Kirby. They lived just outside of Cary in the country. Faith was nervously excited. The dinner went fabulously. Everyone was kind and accepting of Faith. She wondered if her parents would be as accepting of Ben as his parents were of her despite the short time they had been dating.

Faith's parents invited Ben over for dinner a few weeks later. Faith's mother, Ellen, had been traveling with her job and trying to take care of her mother, Esther Larson. By this time, there had been some additional bad news in the Roberts family. Faith's dad, Lee, had been diagnosed with Alzheimer's disease. The Roberts family was all too familiar with Alzheimer's as it had taken the life of Faith's paternal grandmother, Mary Rose Roberts and two of her sisters. While the diagnosis was not a surprise, it was devastating to Faith because she had watched what her grandmother went through, and she desperately did not want that for the dad she loved so much. She did not want him to forget her or Stewart.

Lee Roberts was quickly transitioning into the middle of his Alzheimer's struggle. He did not communicate well and he could not remember anything on a short-term basis. Mr. Roberts smiled at Ben and let him know he approved in his own special way. Ellen was a much more difficult to win over than Lee. Ellen had high standards, and after everything Liam had her daughter through (though she had no idea just how awful it truly was), she did not want her daughter to suffer ever again. While she never said anything to Ben about her feelings, she let Faith know that she needed to be very careful and to make certain this relationship was going to be a positive and supportive one, especially for Stewart.

Within the next month, Mrs. Larson took a turn for the worse. She had only just recovered from having a brain aneurysm. She no longer spoke much because her speech had been affected. She was small and frail. Faith told her mother that she wanted to go see her grandmother and to take Ben with them. She wanted her grandmother to meet the man she wanted to marry. Ellen worked out the arrangements for all of them to go to Tennessee to visit her mother. She arranged a hotel for Ben, while the Roberts would stay at her mother's home.

The visit with Faith's grandmother was wonderful. Mrs. Larson tried to speak and interact with Ben and the rest of the family. Stewart loved his great-grandmother. He loved to crawl up on the sofa and sit next to her. He would pat her on the leg and tell her, "It's gonna be okay Nonnie." Ben,

Faith and Stewart went out into the yard in the evenings to catch lightning bugs. Stewart was excited to bring the bugs in the house in a jar to see if they would light up a room. The house was lonely without Mr. Larson and Faith's Aunt Elizabeth. Mrs. Larson still cried at unexpected times, but she was easily cheered at the sight of Stewart and his toys. For Faith, it felt like she finally had a new family, and she was happy.

After they returned to Cary, a few weeks passed before Ben set up a special dinner for Faith. They went out to a rather expensive restaurant in Cary and then returned to his home to watch a movie. Before he put the movie in the VCR, he told Faith that he wanted to talk to her. He took her hand and led her over to the loveseat and asked her to sit down. He then knelt in front of her, "Faith Rose Roberts, will you marry me?" Faith was surprised; she had not expected him to propose for many more months, but she was ecstatic.

"Yes, Ben, yes, I will marry you!" responded Faith. Ben opened the ring box and Faith was taken by the beauty of the simple one carat, round diamond in Tiffany mounting that Ben had picked out for her. Ben put it on her finger and kissed her.

"You will always know how much I love you when you look at this ring," said Ben. Then, the couple began to talk about details and forgot about the movie. Ben told Faith some things he wanted her to know before they got married, and so did Faith. They were honest and forthright with each other which made everything so much better. Faith felt that she could trust her heart with Ben…forever.

They decided to get married in August before Stewart started school. That way their honeymoon would not cause any disruption to his schedule. They would live in Faith's house and prepare Ben's to rent. They decided that they would pay the costs of the wedding since they each had already had a wedding that their parents helped to pay for. They would be married at Faith's church by her minister, and they would have the service on a Friday night so that they wouldn't have to compete for Saturdays with other, younger brides and grooms.

Ben and Faith decided to meet the next evening at her parents' home so that they could deliver the news to her parents. Ellen and Lee approved and were excited about having a new son-in-law. Then, they needed to tell Stewart. He was in another room playing when his mother came in to see him. Faith knelt beside Stewart, "Stew, I need to ask you something. Can you take a break for a minute?"

"Yes, Mommy. Is something wrong?" Stewart grimaced as he looked into his mother's face as if he was expecting bad news.

"Oh, there is nothing wrong, Stewart, but I do need to ask you if it would be okay if I got married to Ben? What do you think about that?" Faith took ahold of Stewart's hand.

Stewart was quiet for a few seconds. You could almost see the wheels turning in his head. "I think that would be alright, Momma. Will he live at our house?"

"Yes, Stewart, he would live with us in our house. Is that okay with you?"

"Yes, Mommie." Then Stewart went back to playing with his toys. Faith was relieved that Stewart did not have a temper tantrum, expressing any anger over Faith's decision to get married.

C H A P T E R 3 8

A Hopeful Future

Faith couldn't wait to share her news with everyone she loved. She called her brother David to tell him the news, and David was happy for his sister. "This time, David, I want you to be here for my big day. I don't care what anyone else thinks about it. You are my brother," exclaimed Faith.

"That's just great, Faith. I am happy for you and Stewart. We will all be there." By this time, David had married himself and had a son, Carter, who was about four years old." David had married a girl he had known during high school. He had left the military and returned home to raise his family. Faith was not keen on David's wife, however. She came from a seriously dysfunctional family and had a child out-of-wedlock who was now in foster care. David was doing everything he could to get the little girl back. Faith was worried that Chelsea would disappoint David and not live up to what he desired in a spouse. She never expressed her doubts to David, though. She just prayed that it would work out.

Faith told David that she would also be inviting their biological grandfather, Jonas, and his wife, Julia, as well as their aunt Anna Katherine and her husband, Calvin, and daughter Leah. She asked David if he was uncomfortable with her decision. David told Faith that, if she wanted them there, it was fine. "I will be okay with meeting them. I don't really care to have a relationship with them, though. They should have done more to help our mother and they didn't because they didn't give a crap about her. I am not okay with that," David told Faith.

"I totally understand. Whatever you choose to do, is fine with me. I would never force them on you, David. We have to do what we are comfortable with. They made their decision years ago not to have us in their lives, so now it is our turn to decide if we want them in ours," Faith said lovingly.

"Thank you. I know it was a lot of work on your part to find them, and I understand why you wanted to. Your experience was completely different from mine. I might feel differently if I had gone through the same things you did," David responded.

After finishing her conversation with David, Faith prepared to call Jonas. She felt sure that he and Julia would want to come to her big day, but she still felt some apprehension. They were building what Faith felt to be a good relationship, but there were still questions Faith had about her mother and why situations were handled the way that they were. She built up her courage and then picked up the phone.

"Hello, Jonas here," said the man on the other end of the phone.

"Hello, Jonas, it is me, Faith," she responded.

"Well, hello young lady. I am so glad you called. 'How are you, kiddo?" Faith could hear Jonas yell to Julia that she was on the phone.

"Oh, I am terrific, Jonas. I called to give you some great news," said Faith.

"Really? What kind of news?"

"I am getting married! I couldn't wait to tell you and Julia."

"Well, my goodness, sweetheart. How did this come about? We didn't know you had a serious boyfriend." Jonas sounded sincerely excited for his granddaughter.

"Well, it has sort of happened quickly. We met in February. I am so excited. He is such a good man. You will love him. We all do."

"Well, tell me about his fine, young man, Faith," Jonas inquired.

"His name is Benjamin "Ben" Kirby. He is four and half years older than I. He went to the same high school as I did but he graduated before I got there. He works as a sales rep for a local business. He is very kind, and he loves me and Stewart."

"That sounds wonderful. We couldn't be happier for you and Stewart. So, when will the wedding be?"

"It will be in August before Stewart goes back to school. I do hope you and Julia will come."

"Well now, we appreciate the invitation, but we would not want to intrude on your parents. This is a big day for them, too."

Faith could tell what Jonas was getting at. He felt that his and Julia's being there might be a problem for Faith's adoptive parents. Faith knew it would be no problem for her father; it might be an issue with her mother; however, Faith was not going to let her mother's insecurity over nothing keep her from inviting Jonas and the rest of her biological family. "It will be fine. I wouldn't invite you if I thought it was a problem. They will be happy to meet you, Julia, Aunt Anna Katherine and the rest."

"Well, okay then. Send us an invitation and we will be sure to be there!" Faith spoke a little more with Jonas and Julia before ending her conversation. She then called her Aunt Anna Katherine to invite her and her family. Anna Katherine, too, was excited for her niece and couldn't wait to get the invitation so that they could make plans. Her aunt also invited the new family to come visit after the wedding was over. Faith thought that would be a fine idea now that she had Ben to be a buffer.

Faith couldn't wait to tell Ben her news. Ben would be coming over after work to eat dinner and watch television. They spent every evening together since they had gotten engaged. Faith couldn't believe how incredibly happy she was. She thought to herself that she needed to bottle up some of her happiness for any bad time that might come along.

While Ben was there that evening, Faith told him her news and the couple sat down to talk about their wedding. They made a list of what needed to be done and who would do what. They looked at their savings and made a budget. Faith's mother insisted on planning and paying for the reception, which they planned to have at her parent's home. Faith didn't want any of the issues she had in her first wedding to happen in this one. Her parent's, however, she found, we receptive to the couple's plans. Her mother arranged for a guitarist to play during the reception. They would have the food catered and have tables set up inside and out for people to eat.

Faith picked out her flowers and her cake. It was a gorgeous multilayered cake with ivory icing and raspberry filling. They bought sparkling apple juice, rather than champagne, since neither were drinkers. Her mother's home would be decorated with magnolia and gardenias. They would put candles in the swimming pool, along with lighted torches around the patio. It would be beautiful.

CHAPTER 39

Wedding Day

The weekend of the wedding came quickly, but they were prepared. Out-of-town guests stayed at a local hotel that Faith's mother had reserved rooms. Faith and her bridesmaids, Regan and Kara, arrived at the church two hours prior to the service. The wedding photographer was to be there an hour before to take photographs of the parties and the service. The florist would be there an hour before to set up the candles and greenery and to deliver the parties flowers. Faith also invited her friend Sunny James' daughter, Maddie, to be her flower girl. Stewart would walk his mother down the aisle and give her away.

Ben's brother James and his best friend, Wallace Jones, were his groomsmen. They were meeting at Ben's house to get ready. Ben and Faith had purchased ties for the men to wear that day, and they were wearing black suits. Because the wedding was at five o'clock, they wanted it to seem more upscale; but, to keep costs down, they did not use tuxedoes and the girls wore black dresses of their own choosing. Faith selected a beautiful and elegant, ivory, linen dress with jacket to wear.

When the florist arrived, Faith became extremely upset. The florist brought the wrong type of flowers. Faith had asked for an ivory rose with deep red on the tips. The florist showed up with fuchsia-colored roses. Faith hated the color fuchsia! The fuchsia clashed with the deep red color of men's ties. She started to cry. Thankfully, Kara came to the rescue. "Don't worry. I have an idea, Faith. It will be fine, and no one will notice that the flowers weren't meant to be this way," Kara told Faith as she dried her eyes. The florist had also forgotten the baby's breath halo for her flower girl.

"Ok, Kara. This is just horrible. My photos are going to be horrible." Kara pulled all of the fuchsia roses out of the boutonnieres and out of the bridesmaids' bouquets. They still had delicate white flowers and greenery which were quite pretty. Faith's bouquet was white lilies and roses; no one was going to notice, except the bride.

Faith's mother and her friends, Jeanna and Sandra, decorated the church with the same greenery, magnolias, gardenias and candles that would be used at her home later for the reception. The church's chapel had five small windows along the side of one aisle where the flowers were placed. The florist decorated the rest with candelabras and ferns. It was small space, but it looked beautiful.

Faith's friend Charlotte Simmons sang during the ceremony. Faith chose two songs. One was a song from the Broadway play *"Jekyll And Hyde"* that she had always loved, and the other was a popular wedding song, *"The Prayer"* which Charlotte would sing with the minister of music from Faith's church. Faith could hear them practicing as she was getting ready in the bride's room, and she got chills down her back and tears welled up in her eyes.

It wasn't long before everyone was at the church, and it was time for the service. Unfortunately, this day was not a great day for Faith's father. He knew that something good was happening, but he did not know what and he did not recognize most of the people there. He was in a great mood, however. He walked up and down the aisles speaking to everyone who had come. His older sister had come with her daughter which made Faith's father happy.

Like most weddings, the service was over in a flash and the happy couple was on to their way reception. Everything at Faith's parents' home was beautiful. The evening felt magical with their guests milling around inside and outside of house. The acoustic guitarist just set the mood for the evening's reception. The couple was toasted, and the cake was cut. Ben and Faith could not be happier. When the reception ended, Faith hugged Stewart and told him to have fun with his grandparents while she and Ben were away for a few days on their honeymoon. Stewart kissed his mother and then ran upstairs to his room to play.

Ben and Faith went back to Faith's house to sleep until the next morning when they would head out for their honeymoon in the mountains. They planned to hike and visit the sites in the North Carolina mountains.

CHAPTER 40

A New Life

As much as Faith wanted her biological family to be in her life, she began to have some reservations. Jonas and Julia had been upfront and honest with Faith from the very beginning, and she appreciated that, even if the situation was terrible. Her aunt Anna Katherine was a different story. Faith's interaction and conversations with her aunt were beginning to make her question her aunt's sincerity. Over time, it seemed that Anna Katherine was attempting to derail Faith's relationship with her grandfather, albeit in a rather covert way. They would have two or three nice conversations; and then, out of nowhere, her aunt would drop an emotional bomb on Faith—information about her birth family that was unnecessary for Faith to know and that caused Faith additional emotional trauma.

In one such conversation, her aunt alleged that Faith might have another unknown sibling on her biological father's side. Apparently, it was a rumor she had heard while living in her grandparent's home. The information was senseless. Faith didn't care to know anything about her biological father, much less that he may have fathered some other illegitimate child, possibly by violence like her mother. And, if he did, the child would be so much older than Faith.

At other times Anna Katherine made comments that were hurtful. Once her aunt said to her in a phone conversation, "Have you ever stopped to realize that your grandfather is also your stepbrother?" Faith was flabbergasted by this comment. It was completely unnecessary and hurtful. Of course, Faith understood that, but it didn't mean she wanted to acknowledge it to anyone…ever! What did Anna Katherine gain by being cruel? It made Faith angry.

On another occasion, years into their relationship, Anna Katherine told Faith about a family secret. Faith, of course, always thought that she and David were secrets, but she could never have anticipated what Anna Katherine was going to tell her. As if Faith's own situation weren't bad enough, Anna Katherine had some sick need to share this with Faith. She was so angry and hurt by it that she didn't speak to Anna Katherine for almost a year, and she broke off the relationship completely after Jonas' death.

Anna Katherine told Faith that there had been a relationship between siblings in her father's family. She told Faith that no one had ever denied it. Faith hung up on her aunt. She could not unhear what she heard. It was despicable of Anna Katherine to lay this emotional baggage on her. Faith never needed to know this after knowing what her mother Susan had gone through. Were all of these people deviant sickos? She was going to need help with this. She did not want to believe what Anna Katherine said.

Because of this bombshell, Faith decided to reach out to her grandfather's sisters, Millicent and Laura. She wanted to find out why her aunt would tell her this secret and how they might suggest that she handle the situation. Since her first interaction with her grandfather and her aunt, Faith heard how nice his sister Laura was. Over and over, time and again, she was told about how loving and kind Laura was. On the other hand, her Aunt Millicent was a different story. In fact, the bombshell Anna Katherine dropped on Faith was about Jonas and Millicent. From what she had heard, Millicent was quite different from the rest of the family. Her grandfather did not seem to be fond of this sister. He called her wild and unruly. The situation was serious enough to Faith that she felt she needed input on how to go forward with her Aunt Anna Katherine. She couldn't repeat this story to her family because they would just tell her stop talking to her and her grandfather. She would not feel comfortable talking to him about it, so talking with his sisters seemed at the time to be her only choice.

She called Laura first. She expected to be greeted with warmness, but that was exactly what she did not get. When Laura answered the phone, she told Faith that she was glad to hear from her, but then she became hostile and belligerent. Laura questioned whether Faith was even her niece. She wanted proof of Faith's relationship to her "daddy" and brother. Faith was taken completely aback; Susan was her niece. Faith did not realize at first that the 'daddy" she was referring to was Paul and not Jacob. She was silent for a few moments trying to grasp what she had gotten herself into. This was not the loving and kind person she had been told about. This person was a monster. Faith gathered herself and came back at Laura with confidence and poise in the midst of Laura's vitriol.

"So, how do we even know that you are who you say you are? We don't know what Susan was up to back then," said Laura with a hate-filled tone. Yet another family member blaming the victim!

"What? How dare you?! Your brother has never asked me that. He accepted me with open arms," replied Faith.

"Well, you could be anybody. What proof do you have?" Laura continued this speech about the alleged behavior of Faith's biological mother Susan.

"I have a DNA test. Is that good enough for you?" retorted Faith in an equally hostile tone. Her blood was boiling.

"How could you have a DNA test? Don't you have to have DNA from the alleged parent? How could you get a DNA test? Daddy's been dead for years." Hearing her aunt call her stepfather "daddy" was offensive. Faith wondered if Laura had always called her stepfather "daddy", or if she was just being territorial. She was an adult when her mother married Paul Clarke, so she did not understand why Laura would call him "daddy".

"Haven't you ever heard of genealogy? I am a DNA match with one of his sisters, a niece, and a few cousins. And I match Anna Katherine. If you don't believe me, I will send you a copy of the results to prove it to you, but I don't owe you a damn thing. That bastard took advantage of a defenseless child, and you know it! She had an IQ of less than 70. You should know that as a teacher. Not-to-mention, she wasn't the only family member of yours that he raped. The other one just never told anyone after seeing how Susan was treated." There was silence on the other end of the phone for a few seconds.

"How do you know that? Was it Anna Katherine? She's never said anything to me, and we are very close," retorted Laura.

"No, it wasn't. I spoke to this person, and she told me in confidence. I will not tell you who it is, but I believe her. That man was a monster!" Faith hung up the phone. Faith was angier as she had been in years. She was seething. She went to her computer and typed a letter to Laura, telling her that she would never contact her again and that she would not answer if she attempted to call her. She printed a copy of her ancestral DNA test along with a copy of the DNA matches showing her Walker cousins. There was no doubt that Faith was who she said she was. Why would **anyone** choose to be in this set of circumstances? No one on earth would.

When Faith cooled down and decided to call her Aunt Millicent, she had no idea that her Aunt Laura had already called her sister. It did not occur to her because she didn't think that they were close. So, when Millie answered the phone in a hostile tone, she knew what had happened. Millicent began to scold Faith for her tone with her Aunt Laura. Faith explained to Millie that she only wanted to ask her about the conversation with Anna Katherine and that she had never expected Laura to confront her about who she was. It was uncalled for in Faith's opinion and she was not going to apologize for it. If they had doubts about her, they should have expressed those doubts to her grandfather and allowed him handle it. Millie agreed and she asked Faith about the reason for her call.

Faith went on to explain the conversation she had with her Aunt Anna Katherine. Millie was astonished that Anna Katherine told Faith the story. She agreed that it was unnecessary and hurtful; however, Millie also became defensive. She pooh-pooed the story as being nothing and said that those kinds of things happened "back then". Faith could not believe her ears. It was disgusting and reprehensible. How could she possibly justify such deviant behavior? But much to the surprise of Faith, that is exactly what she did.

After the conversation ended, Faith was more perplexed than ever about these women and her biological family as a whole. She prayed about it because she knew no other way to deal with the situation, but to ask God to help her. She also wrote a letter to her Aunt Millie, explaining that she would also not contact her again. She told her that she, as a Christian woman, could not condone such evil behavior, and that her acceptance of the situation was wicked; and she didn't care how Millie felt about it. Anna Katherine should never have told her, but Millie and Laura were despicable for their behavior and treatment of her. After much thought and prayer, Faith determined that she would never speak with her aunts again. She never regretted that decision. Faith never discussed the issue with Jonas. He was aging rapidly and was not healthy. She saw no reason to increase his already burdened heart.

CHAPTER 41

The Best Life

Ben and Faith built an amazing life together. They worked every day to make sure that their life together was a good one. They never had an argument like most couples do, especially like those Faith had with Liam. No one slammed doors or threw things. Neither of them ever cursed or insulted the other. They had an occasional "snippet" moment, most often out of frustration, but neither held anything against the other. They each had enormous love, respect, and trust in each other.

It wasn't all roses, though. Faith lost a baby a year after they were married. It was a defining moment. Faith wanted a sibling for Stewart; she had never intended for him to be an only child. After the miscarriage, though, she wasn't sure that she wanted to risk going through that again. Even though she wanted a child with Ben, she was scared. She felt like Ben felt the same way because he never spoke to her about the miscarriage. He held his emotions inside. However, in June of 2008, Faith found out that she was pregnant again. Faith was beside herself. She was terrified to tell Ben. They were looking for houses and she knew that would have to put that on hold.

Faith was so nervous about telling Ben that she went to her boss to share her news with him and ask his advice. Faith's father was now in a nursing home and could not help her. Her boss had become like a second father to her. He took out a fifty-dollar bill from his wallet and gave it to her saying, "Take him out to dinner. He can't act up in public. He will be thrilled after the shock wears off." So, she tried, but Ben called her bluff.

"Why would we be going out to dinner if we're trying to buy a house, Faith? We have talked about this. I thought we were on the same page."

"Well, we are but it might be the last time, and Mr. Chandler gave me a bonus of fifty dollars today."

"Faith, I can tell that there is more to this story. I can tell by how you are acting. What is going on?" When Ben crossed his arms, Faith knew the gig was up.

"Okay, hold on. Go sit down in the den, I need to get something from my purse."

"This is something I need to sit down for? Faith what is going on?" A look of fear came over Ben's face.

Faith walked over to the counter where her purse was, and she pulled out the pregnancy test. Tears welled up in her eyes. "I know that this isn't the best time and that we will have to stay here a little longer. This shouldn't have happened. It wasn't time. I'm sorry, Ben.'

Ben turned white as a ghost. He sat for a few moments staring at the test, speechless. "Would you say something, please?" Faith was distraught waiting for his response. Ben stood up and put his arms out towards Faith.

"Well, you are right about that. I guess we will go out to eat and talk about this. What happened the last time really hurt me, so this is going to be challenging, but we'll get through it. I love you." That was all Faith needed to hear.

About seventeen weeks passed and Faith had to go to a specialist in Raleigh to check the baby over for any unforeseen issues because she was over thirty-five. It was considered a high-risk pregnancy. They knew that, at this appointment, they could find out the gender of the baby and Stewart was stoked. He and his grandparents waited impatiently for Faith to call with the news.

When the call came, much to Stewart's dismay, the word was a baby girl. Faith was excited that her family would be complete, though she was terrified about having a daughter because of fear her daughter might be brutalized like she was. She knew it was an irrational fear, but after everything she had learned about Susan and what she had gone through herself, she knew it would take prayer to get her through it. But, over the months of her pregnancy, she managed to work through her fears and get excited about their little bundle of joy.

When Ben and Faith welcomed an 8 pound, 19 ½ inch little blessing a few months later, they named her Joanna, which means *"gift from God"*. Joanna was a blessing to everyone, even the Averys loved her. Liam's father doted on little Joanna whenever Faith would take her and Stewart to their home. Joanna would crawl up in his lap and watch golf with him for a few minutes before returning to her mother.

Joanna was a completely different child from her brother. Stewart was an easy to manage child, a rule follower for the most part. Joanna, on the other hand, was a risk taker. Both of Faith's children were highly intelligent, but Stewart struggled in school because of ADHD. Joanna loved school and learning. Faith was determined to help her daughter with her education in a way she had not been able to with Stewart. Ben's job made it possible for her to stay home and to homeschool Joanna. This built a close bond between mother and daughter. Faith was also extremely close to Stewart. They talked about anything and everything.

Faith was determined not to pass on what she saw as a family curse to her children. All of the deviant behaviors of her birth family, Faith believed, had been caused by a curse brought about by, in her opinion, by participation in Freemasonry or the KKK. She did research online to find out to break such a curse. She also spoke to Olivia Avery, Liam's mother, about the situation. Mrs. Avery was a Bible scholar and teacher. Olivia provided Faith with a specific prayer to break the curse. She told Faith that she understood her feelings because she had gone through a similar situation with a family curse. Faith took the information home, and when she was alone, she knelt and prayed the prayer to God.

Faith and Ben had high expectations for their children, but they allowed their children to be who they were and not who they wanted them to be. They encouraged them to succeed on their terms, and they did. Joanna grew into a beautiful young lady who worked hard in school. Stewart grew up and left home. He became successful in his career making both Faith and Ben proud. But their proudest accomplishment was that both of their children accepted Jesus and worked diligently on their personal walks with Christ.

Faith and Ben modeled for their children how to be a servant to others. Both children spent time serving in soup kitchens, packing food boxes at the were child slaves too, whatever the Company called us. I want to go fight.”

I nodded. “I’ve been thinking about that too. Helping them would give purpose to the ship, and to Pilot. I think he would like that.” I thought for a moment. “But I would like to travel a *little* bit first. Just a little bit. We already have to go back to Hub Chiba to get our winnings and drop off Zipper, and then...maybe head over to Imago 5? I’ve heard they have great waterfalls.”

“Cass,” said Joren with a grin. “We can go anywhere we want.”

“Yeah,” I said, returning his smile. “We can.”

Una walked up. “Hey guys, you *have* to hang out with me. I don’t know anyone here.

“Not having fun?” asked Joren.

“At a party full of dirty strangers?” replied Una. “No.”

Joren laughed. “Your loss, snob.”

She looked at him seriously. “The three of us are going to stick together from now on, right?”

“Us and Pilot,” confirmed Joren, nodding.

“Us and Pilot. What a crew.” Una gave a little smile.

“Sounds perfect to me,” I said, wrapping my arms around them both and pulling them into a group hug, grinning from ear-to-ear. “Let’s party!”

T HE E ND

food pantry, serving on mission trips, and doing other volunteer work in their community. Faith and Ben instilled in their children financial stewardship, not only by teaching them money management, but also by living a simpler type of lifestyle. If Faith had chosen to continue working, they could have a much higher standard of living, but choosing to stay home and making the sacrifice was much more important to them.

This is not to say that they didn't have the things other children had, because they always had the latest technology, but Faith and Ben had their children pitch in money on some of these things. When Stewart was ready for his first car, Faith knew she would not get any help from Liam, so Ben had a friend find a car for them. When it was time to purchase the car, Stewart had to pay half from his own bank account, which Faith had established for him when he was young. When he wrecked it two weeks later, he got a junker the next time!

As with most boys getting them to do chores or clean their rooms is difficult; Stewart was no different. Joanna was the complete opposite. She took after Ben. She became a great helper to Faith and, so, they gave her a weekly allowance for doing extra chores. It was a great money-making opportunity for her. Before they realized it, Joanna saved up almost a thousand dollars at the tender age of eight!

The most important legacy Faith gave to her children was herself. She shared her hurts, successes, and some secrets with them. After she found her birth family, Faith realized how wrong her thinking had been growing up. She realized that she had been self-centered by only thinking about her pain, her needs, and her fears. She came to understand that she had, in many ways, misjudged her adopted parents because she was so wrapped up in her own hurt. She realized just how blessed she was to *not* have been raised by Susan or anyone in her birth family. She realized, too, that what she had seen as a slight by her mother in telling everyone about Faith's adoption could have been pride in it, rather than shame.

All the time she spent in her head making up stories about where she had come from were so much better than the reality. Life might have been horrific if Susan had kept Faith and David. She would never have been able to support them on a seventh-grade education and mental illness. Most likely, Faith would have been the "grownup" in the house because she was intelligent and independent. Not-to-mention, they would probably have been removed from the home by DFACS anyway.

Faith found her strength in her faith in Jesus, and she passed this on to her children. When times were bad for Faith, she prayed for God's help to have a servant's heart. In all situations she trusted God to get her and her family through. Faith believed for so long that God had forgotten her, that she was punished for the sins of her birth, but through the circumstances of her life what she discovered was that we can find joy in our pain if we know and love the Lord Jesus Christ. She discovered that Jesus had always been with her; he had never abandoned her. She found an overwhelming sense that God wanted her to be born because He had a purpose. He had rescued her, not only from her birth family, but also from herself. Only a loving, caring God would do such a thing. He knew her before she was conceived, and He had plans for her life that only He could understand. He knew her name because she was His creation. God does not make mistakes; and He, and only He, can make all things new, even out of the ugliest of circumstances. She learned that all things come in God's time, and God's timing is perfect.

"Before I formed you in the womb, I knew you.
Before you were born, I sanctified you.
I ordained you a prophet to the nations."
Jeremiah 1:5 NKJV

To be continued...